ROYAL BRIDESMAIDS

By Stephanie Laurens

The Lady Risks All

The Black Cobra Quartet
The Untamed Bride
The Elusive Bride
The Brazen Bride
The Reckless Bride

The Bastion Club Novels
The Lady Chosen
A Gentleman's Honor
A Lady of His Own
A Fine Passion
To Distraction
Beyond Seduction
The Edge of Desire
Mastered By Love

Prequel
Captain Jack's Woman

By Gaelen Foley

My Scandalous Viscount
My Ruthless Prince
My Irresistible Earl
My Dangerous Duke
My Wicked Marquess

By Loretta Chase

An Original Anthology

ROYAL
BRIDESMAIDS

STEPHANIE LAURENS

GAELEN FOLEY

LORETTA CHASE

AVONIMPULSE
An Imprint of HarperCollinsPublishers

Excerpt from *The Lady Risks All* copyright © 2012 by Savdek Management Proprietary Ltd.

Excerpt from *My Scandalous Viscount* copyright © 2012 by Gaelen Foley.

Excerpt from *Scandal Wears Satin* copyright © 2012 by Loretta Chekani.

Excerpt from *Circle of Danger* copyright © 2012 Carla Swafford.

Excerpt from *Heat Rises* copyright © 2012 Alice Brilmayer.

Excerpt from *Somebody Like You* copyright © 2012 Candis Terry.

Excerpt from *A Most Naked Solution* copyright © 2012 Anna Clevenger.

A RETURN ENGAGEMENT. Copyright © 2012 by Savdek Management Proprietary Ltd.

THE IMPOSTER BRIDE. Copyright © 2012 by Gaelen Foley.

LORD LOVEDON'S DUEL. Copyright © 2012 by Loretta Chekani.

EPub Edition JULY 2012 ISBN: 9780062209795

Print Edition ISBN: 9780062227348

10 9 8 7 6 5 4

CONTENTS

A Return Engagement

Stephanie Laurens

"There she is!" Hereditary Prince Frederick of Lautenberg, heir apparent to the principality, beamed as he watched his princess-to-be emerge onto the deck of the royal barge as it angled to approach the dock.

Standing beside Frederick, Robert Knightley, second son of the Earl of Rockingham, smiled as Frances Daughtry, a sweet, slender, fair-haired English rose, raised a hesitant hand in response to the crowd's cheers. Frances would, in Robert's estimation, be the perfect Princess. Aside from her excellent pedigree and the inbred manners that went with that, her refined and elegant beauty, and her experience in the socially demanding arena of the ton, she was English, and as the British envoy to the Court of Lautenberg as well as the Prince's closest friend, confidant, and personal advisor, Robert definitely approved of that.

Installing Frances, the youngest daughter of the Duke of Pemberton, as the Hereditary Princess of Lautenberg was a coup with which the British government and Robert's masters in the Foreign Office were openly thrilled. And while Robert hadn't played Cupid—Frederick had met Frances in London during a short visit the previous year and had been instantly smitten—he nevertheless felt that in facilitating the budding romance and steering it to a successful conclusion he'd discharged his duties on all fronts in exemplary fashion.

Frances turned her head, apparently listening to someone behind her, then faced forward, walked to the railing, and smiled and waved more definitely.

Delighted, the crowd roared, waved, and cheered back. Huzzahs filled the air; a faint breeze whisked over the water, making the flags strung up all around snap and flutter. Frederick, Robert noted, could not have been more pleased. Good. Everything was progressing smoothly.

Returning his gaze to the deck of the barge, sent to ferry the princess-to-be from the mouth of the Rhine, he surveyed the others in the bridal party as they emerged on deck. They'd traveled from London by ship to the Rhine mouth, then transferred to the barge for the trip upriver to Koblenz, before turning southward on the Mosel. The Mosel formed the eastern border of Lautenberg, and the principality's capital, Kremunz, stood on its western shore.

Robert recognized the tall figure of the Duke of Pemberton, with his duchess, Valeria, in her signature gauzy draperies, on his arm. Beside them, directly behind Frances's right shoulder, stood . . .

The person to whom Frances had listened. Robert blinked and looked again, but the tall, willowy, dark-haired lady, a few inches taller than Frances, did not transmogrify into either of her shorter, fair-haired sisters. "What the devil . . . ?"

Frederick—beneath his delighted veneer the prospective groom was distinctly nervous—cast him a sharp glance. "What is it?"

Schooling his features, Robert shook his head dismissively. "Just someone in the party I hadn't realized would be coming." Someone he certainly hadn't expected.

Someone he hadn't expected to see, not up close, not to speak with, much less to organize and oversee a wedding with . . . As he scanned the remainder of the bridal party, that last became all too clear. Frances's other two sisters, Felicity and Esme, weren't there. For some godforsaken reason, Lady Cornelia Daughtry had stepped into the shoes he'd been told her other sisters would fill.

"See?" Lady Cornelia Daughtry, Nell to those close to her, murmured soothingly, reassuringly, just loudly enough for her sister to hear. "I told you they'd be delighted. Just listen to those cheers. And as for your Frederick, if he smiles any more widely his face will crack . . ."

Nell's gaze had traveled beyond Frederick; her eyes widened, her lungs seized.

At her sudden silence, Frances, still facing the cheering hordes, nervously murmured, "What is it?"

Thanking the stars Frances couldn't turn around and see her face, Nell continued to stare at the man standing beside Prince Frederick. "Nothing. Just keep smiling and waving and looking delighted. That's all you need to do."

Finally dragging in a decent breath, Nell looked sideways and caught their mother's eye. Lowering her voice even further, she whispered, "Were you expecting Robert Knightley to be here?"

Valeria, Duchess of Pemberton, blinked her large violet eyes. "Why, yes, dear, of course. Robert is Prince Frederick's closest friend and diplomatic right arm, as it were." Looking past Frances to where Robert stood on the docks with Frederick and the rest of the official welcoming party, Valeria smiled. "As the British envoy to Lautenberg, dear Robert is in charge of all the arrangements. Should we require any assistance, it is to him we should appeal."

With a wordless "ah," Nell turned back to the prospect before her. One she hadn't until that moment realized lay before her.

A long-ago would-be husband who, while he'd never actually come up to the mark, had effectively spoiled her for all others.

That was how she saw Robert Knightley.

He looked well. She could admit that. Could let her gaze sweep over his broad shoulders, down the long length of his leanly muscled frame, before returning to the chiseled, patrician planes of his face with some small degree of detachment.

At least while several feet of river and rather more of planking separated them.

How would she manage when they were closer? A lot closer? When she was forced to interact with him on a daily, even hourly basis in the frantic days before the wedding?

How would she fare when she and he—if he was as close to Frederick as it seemed—perforce walked down the aisle together?

Oh, God.

She didn't dare voice the words, and in the end her feelings didn't matter.

She was there and so was he, and she would simply have to manage.

An hour later, standing in the castle's drawing room with a cup of calming tea in her hand, Nell decided the most appropriate strategy was to take the bull by the horns.

Some angel had consented to watch over her on the docks; in the joy and rapture of Frederick formally greeting Frances, then welcoming their parents, she'd managed to avoid exchanging more than a polite nod with Robert. The entire party had then piled into open carriages for the trip up a long, winding, stone-paved road to the castle, a sizeable structure in pale gray stone sporting towers and turrets with conical roofs, crenellated battlements, and countless pennants flying regally in the breeze. Perched above the red roofs of the town and the sparkling blue ribbon of the river, in the bright summer sunshine the castle possessed a fairy-tale radiance. Although Nell had been in the same carriage as Robert, indeed, although they'd sat on the same bench seat, they'd both been facing back along the cavalcade; she hadn't had to meet his eye and had taken care not to.

Their progression through the huge gates of the castle had been accompanied by a sudden drop in the surrounding noise, but almost immediately the carriages had drawn up before the steps leading into the castle keep; the extended and clearly modernized building filled much of the space within the battlemented walls. Frederick had descended first, then had handed Frances down to enthusiastic applause from the assembled courtiers. Nell had quickly followed Frances, allowing a liveried footman to assist her to the flags.

As she'd followed Frances and Frederick up the stairs and into the great hall beyond the massive double doors, she'd been intensely aware of Robert walking alongside her, but there'd been so many others to smile at and exchange polite nods with she felt sure no one had noticed that she'd kept her gaze studiously from him.

Frederick had led Frances triumphantly into a magnificent formal drawing room, and had swept her sister up to a pair of ornate thrones. This part of the proceedings Nell and her mother had known about and had drilled Frances in thoroughly; her sister had made a very nice show of curtsying and greeting her future parents-in-law, Frederick's parents, the ageing Prince and Princess of Lautenberg. Both monarchs had been disposed to be delighted; standing behind Frances, Nell had seen her sister's tense shoulders ease.

Then Frederick had led Frances to one side, and Robert had stepped forward to introduce Nell. She had duly smiled, curtsied, risen, and had exchanged the regulation greetings and observations before stepping aside to allow her parents to come forward. She would have loved to have simply melted into the crowd, but she'd known her duty. She'd unobtrusively slipped into position behind Frances, ready to lend support when next it was needed.

But Frances had taken heart from the sincerely warm reception; as the tea service had commenced, Nell had watched her sister smile and chat with commendable spontaneity. Noting that her mother, too, was keeping a surreptitious eye on her soon-to-be-royal sibling, Nell accepted that, while she'd succeeded in avoiding Robert to that point, she couldn't avoid him for much longer.

Cup and saucer in hand, he'd retreated to stand by the wall a little way down the room. While he sipped, he constantly scanned the crowd, as any good organizer would. Balancing her own cup and saucer, she girded her loins and glided across to join him. Without meeting his eyes, she turned to stand beside him, to sip and survey the assembled courtiers, too.

He spoke first. "I had no idea you were coming."

"I had no idea you would be here."

He hesitated, then asked, "Would you have come if you'd known?"

She thought before truthfully stating, "I don't know."

From the corner of her eyes, she saw his lips twist, then he set his cup on his saucer and lightly shrugged. "It doesn't really matter, does it? Water under the bridge, so to speak."

She felt his gaze on her face, but didn't meet it, just nodded. "Indeed. My role here is to ensure that this wedding goes off without a hitch—at least from the bride's side."

He inclined his head. "And my role is the complementary one and my purpose the same, but . . . there is a wider consideration, and that not only for me, but for us both."

She frowned, glanced at him. "What wider consideration?"

Finally. Robert caught her dark violet eyes, several shades darker than her mother's, and felt the same jolt he had years ago—nine years ago to be precise. They'd seen each other over the intervening years, in passing in the ballrooms and drawing rooms of the ton, but not since they'd parted had they been this close, or looked so directly into each other's eyes.

And it was all still there—that indefinable connection, the spark of an attraction that was more than just physical, that welled from deep inside, then spread beneath their skins. Nothing had changed . . . or rather, if anything, the link had grown stronger, harder, more refined, more definite, the flash of connection more compelling.

She sensed it, too; of that he had not a single doubt. The slight hitch in her breathing, and her widening eyes, gave her away.

Those fabulous, rich pansy eyes searched his, then she blinked, and a frown started to form, drawing down her perfectly arched dark brows, setting a faint wrinkle in the unblemished expanse of her forehead; her straight nose, delicately curved lush lips, and decidedly determined feminine chin hadn't changed in the least.

What had he been saying? He denied the impulse to clear his throat. "This wedding has wider political and strategic implications for our country." He glanced briefly at the crowd in the room; no one was near enough to overhear. Although several courtiers had their eyes on Nell, eager to make her acquaintance, everyone knew he and she needed to consult about the details of the bride and groom's days, let alone the wedding, so were politely giving them some time. He returned his gaze to her. "Lautenberg is small, largely rural, and has no particular commercial significance, but strategically it's vital to our government's wider peacekeeping aims."

Her eyes on his, she nodded. "I see."

He was fairly certain she did; she was one of the most quick-witted females he'd ever encountered. "Indeed. So the government and our country have a vested interest in seeing this wedding goes off without a hitch. If you get so much as a whiff of anything not just going wrong, but not being perfectly right, let me know."

She studied him for a long moment, then inclined her head. "Very well."

He couldn't read her expression; he'd forgotten she had a particularly good, blank but alert, poker face.

Tipping her head, she continued to regard him for an instant more, then said, "I'll do that, and in return perhaps you will alert me should Frederick have any . . . concerns, or questions, of whatever sort."

He blinked.

She met his gaze for only a second more, then turned away. "As I said, do let me know."

He watched her glide into the crowd, saw several courtiers descend on her, surrounding her with smiles and offering introductions; he debated stepping in and assisting with the latter, but she was assured and experienced, and in such tame company needed no help in conquering them all.

"But what the devil did you mean, my long-ago love?" He might not be sure of much when it came to her, but from her manner, her tone, and not least her words, he was absolutely certain she knew of at least one potential source of trouble.

"I just don't know." Frances turned this way and that before the cheval glass, critically viewing her turquoise silk gown. "Oh, Nell—what do you think? Will I do?"

"You'll do, and that magnificently. Stop fretting. You know this panic's only to be expected, and that's why I'm here—to assure you it's all just nerves and will pass, and soon all will be well." Nell lifted a delicate necklace of aquamarines and diamonds, their parents' wedding gift to Frances, from its velvet bed. "Here—let me settle this."

She did, examining Frances's face in the mirror while she smoothed the fine links of the necklace; thus far, her sister was holding up reasonably well. "Now don't worry—I'll be beside or just behind you while we're in the drawing room, and Mama will be nearby, too. And as Robert will have overseen the seating for the dinner, I'll be placed opposite. Although I won't be able to converse directly, I will be there should you have any problems. And I will be listening, no matter that I won't appear to be."

Stepping back, she ran her eyes once more over Frances, then nodded. "Just remember—Frederick is head over ears in love with you, no matter what that silly little voice in your head whispers."

Turning, Frances met Nell's eyes, and grinned. "Thank you, sister mine." Stretching up, Frances touched her cheek to Nell's, found Nell's fingers with hers and squeezed, then drew back.

A deep *bong* resonated throughout the palace.

"That's it—the dinner gong." Frances whirled toward the door. "We should go."

"Indeed." Moving smoothly forward, Nell paused by the door. "But without any unseemly rush."

They glided, side by side, down the long corridors and down the ornate stairs. In her dark violet-purple silk gown, a perfect foil for Frances's paler beauty, Nell drew almost as many eyes as—and, indeed, many more openly admiring glances than—her younger sister. She was aware of the fact, but neither returned nor acknowledged any of those glances; her focus was on Frances, on being her sister's support.

The fabulously ornate drawing room—the Germanic states did so love their gilt and crystal—played host to an army of elegantly garbed courtiers, but everyone was disposed to be delighted and accommodating, and the hour Frances spent on Frederick's arm, being introduced to those who would shortly become her subjects, passed easily and without incident. Somewhat to Nell's surprise, while she'd seen Robert the instant she walked into the room—and he'd seen her—he kept his distance, leaving her able to concentrate on Frances without distraction.

For which she was grateful . . . except that not knowing where in the crush Robert actually was, knowing he was near, but not knowing in which direction, distracted her anyway.

It was almost a relief when he eventually appeared at Frederick's side to whisper in his friend's ear that dinner was about to be announced.

As a stentorian announcement that dinner was served rang out over the room, Nell steeled herself to take Robert's arm when he offered it—only to have a gentleman, one of the lords of the court, gallantly step in to offer his arm and lead her in. Uncertain of protocol and precedence in this court, she glanced at Robert; he'd been waiting to catch her glance and nodded.

Plastering on a smile, Nell inclined her head and accepted, settling her hand on the gentleman's sleeve and allowing him to lead her in her sister and Frederick's wake. Not exactly disappointed, but a trifle off-balance with the steeling of her nerves that was no longer required.

To her considerable relief, her prediction of the table placements proved to be sound; she was seated opposite Frances, with the attentive courtier beside her. At the very last, Robert took the seat on her other side, opposite Frederick, and the meal began.

One of Frederick's male cousins sat on Frances's other side, and for much of the meal, between the cousin's questions and Frederick's comments, Frances was absorbed enough to prevent any unease or uncertainty showing through. Nell, more than socially adept enough to maintain a conversation with her dinner partners while simultaneously monitoring Frances's every word, was wondering if, perhaps, the entire dinner would pass without any episode . . . when, as the dessert plates were being set out, she saw Frances press back in her chair, and start rather furtively glancing about . . .

Then Frances remembered her instructions, drew a deep breath, and looked across the table. Nell was waiting to catch her gaze, to smile and nod and, across the width of the table, project all she wished she could whisper in her sister's ear . . .

It worked. Well enough for Frances to breathe more calmly. After a moment, Frances gave a tiny nod, then Frederick spoke to her and she turned to him, and if her smile was a trifle wobbly, and significantly less strong than it had been earlier, yet still she smiled and went on.

After watching Frances for a moment more and detecting no further eruption of uncertainty, Nell inwardly sighed and shifted her attention to the courtier by her side.

From Nell's other side, Robert cast her a sharp glance, but her face was averted and he couldn't see her eyes, much less catch her gaze. But he'd seen . . . something. Whatever it was—whatever it was that had happened with Frances—it had made Nell tense. Tense as if about to spring forward to avert some incipient disaster.

Which did not bode well for a perfectly scripted wedding.

Robert glanced at her again. She was now animatedly engaged with the local lord; he could almost feel a wall between them—one she kept high.

What was it that had just happened? And what was going on?

He would, he suspected, get no chance to extract answers to those questions tonight, but answers he would have—and soon.

Robert did wonder if all he was detecting was caused by nothing more than the expected and excusable nerves, but Nell's continuing protectiveness, let alone her family's high social profile and the hours even the younger Frances would have spent in the most august of ton circles, all argued against that.

At the conclusion of the dinner, the entire company filed into the ballroom where the evening's soiree was to be held. The dinner guests were augmented by additional guests invited to stand in the ballroom and be introduced, each in their turn, to their Prince's soon-to-be bride.

Frederick, proud as any peacock, escorted Frances around the huge room. With her hand on Frederick's arm, Frances smiled, nodded, and acknowledged curtsies. She spoke easily, with natural charm; although her voice was lighter and lacked the warmth of Nell's contralto, Frances made a respectable showing.

But Nell, walking just behind Frances's right shoulder, was on tenterhooks the whole time. Even when he wasn't shoulder-to-shoulder with her in the press—a situation that raised tension of a different sort in them both—he sensed her focus, her unrelentingly fixed attention, the way she held herself in expectation of something going wrong . . . but what?

Nell knew better than to imagine that they would escape the soiree without any difficulty, not when Frances's uncertainty had already broken through once. Luckily, Frances managed to hold the whispers at bay through most of the event, and indeed, guests were starting to leave and the crowd about them was thinning before the problem resurfaced and Frances's confidence wavered, then fell.

With, finally, no one left to greet, Frederick turned to Frances and smiled. "Perhaps, now, we can stroll on our own and speak privately, liebchen."

And suddenly Frances was breathless. "Yes—no! That is . . ." Attempting to draw her fingers from Frederick's, wide—wild—eyed, Frances glanced around.

Nell stepped in, closer, using her body to physically block any move the slighter Frances might have made; heavens above, she could not bolt. Could not be allowed to, not here, not now, not ever. Sliding a supportive—anchoring—arm around her sister's waist, Nell spoke to Frederick. "Your

Highness, I regret to say my sister is dreadfully tired. What with the long journey and the subsequent full round of engagements, she's sorely in need of a good night's rest."

Frederick was instantly contrite. "Of course, dear Lady Cornelia." He looked at Frances, then gently, if awkwardly, patted her hand. "My dear, I am full of apologies—it has, indeed, been such an unrelentingly busy day for you. We should have been more considerate."

With Nell's arm tightening around her, Frances rallied. Lifting her head, she managed a wan smile. "No—it's I who am full of apologies, sir. But I fear my sister is correct—I am wilting and in dire need of rest, and would like, with your permission, to retire."

"Of course, my dear. Of course." Frederick raised Frances's fingers to his lips, then bowed gallantly and released her. "Sweet dreams, liebchen—we will meet again in the morning."

Frances curtsied, as did Nell, then Nell looped her arm in Frances's and together the sisters turned and left the now largely empty ballroom.

Standing beside Frederick, Robert watched them go—watched Nell's head tip toward Frances's. It was Nell who was speaking to Frances, while all Frances did was nod.

"Is anything amiss, do you think?"

Robert glanced up to see Frederick, puzzled, frowning slightly at the pair.

"Have we not done something we should, perhaps? Or have we been too demanding—"

"It's not that—nothing like that." Robert clapped him on the arm; Nell's earlier words—that Frederick might have concerns or questions—echoed in his head. "It's tiredness and, at most, just nerves. Don't worry."

Frederick's frown lightened, but didn't leave his eyes. "If you do learn that there is some problem, you will tell me, nein?"

"Of course. But trust me, there's nothing that's going to come between you and Frances and your appointment before the altar in six days' time." Of that, Robert was quite certain.

It was his job to make sure of it.

To Nell's relief, Frances woke the next morning with renewed enthusiasm and no hint of any lingering nerves. That, of course, wouldn't last, but Nell was ready to accept whatever boons fate granted her. Over breakfast, they learned that a tour of the town had been arranged for that morning; duly fortified, they met Frederick and Robert in the front hall, and left the palace in an open carriage with an escort of six mounted soldiers, more, Frederick assured Frances, for ceremonial show than out of any need for protection.

With Robert's presence on the bench seat beside her once more pressing on her senses and her mind, Nell determinedly distracted herself by looking around at the neat squares, the well-tended houses, and the cheery flowers in window boxes hanging over the cobbled streets, while simultaneously keeping an ear on the conversation between Frederick and Frances, who were sharing the forward-facing seat.

The weather remained gloriously fine, and Frances's mood continued in similar vein through the various organized halts. The first was at the Rathaus, the town hall, where they were welcomed by the mayor, bedecked in his robes and weighted down by gold chains, and a bevy of aldermen. Nell, hanging back in Frances's shadow, was pleased by how graciously her sister dealt with the gentlemen—but then, in her usual state, Frances was customarily serenely assured.

After partaking of refreshments and chatting amiably, they departed for the town marketplace. There they walked among the populace—a delightful detour that had Frances laughing, setting Frederick beaming at the silvery sound. From the market square, they walked along a route lined with the town's best shops, a diversion guaranteed to absorb Frances. She grew animated; there was so much to see and enjoy, and she openly shared her delight with Frederick.

So well were matters progressing that Nell started to wonder if, perhaps, the family failing had struck, but was now loosening its grip on her sister, even waning. She could only hope.

Robert had been striding along beside her, silent and far too observant for her liking. As ever, she was intensely aware of him physically filling the space next to her. For some irritating reason, her susceptibility to that awareness hadn't died; she'd fully expected it would have after nine years of starvation. Refocusing on the couple ahead of them, she asked, "What's next?"

"The cathedral. I thought it might be helpful for Frances to see the place before the wedding."

Nell wasn't sure how to respond. Yes, it might be helpful— but then again, it might not.

Robert's gaze hadn't left her face. "Is that all right? I know you went through the rehearsals in London, but walking into a large and overwhelmingly ornate space for the first time . . . I thought she might prefer it see it first."

Nell forced herself to nod. "It's a good idea." And it was. She just had to hope there would be no unintended consequences.

The street they were walking along led into the cathedral square. An imposing, richly ornate stone edifice with a tall spire topped with a cross, the cathedral towered over the town, but was in turn overlooked by the castle, visible atop the hill behind the church.

The prelate and his deacons were waiting at the top of the steps before the carved wooden doors. Frederick led Frances up and introduced her. The prelate, a white-haired ancient, exuded kindness as he patted Frances's hand.

Nell watched closely, surreptitiously sighing with relief when she detected no stiffening in Frances.

Robert dragged his attention from Nell long enough to greet the prelate and introduce her. She responded with her usual calm composure; she was one of those females who could simultaneously do several things at once and perform well on all fronts. She was tracking Frances like a terrier, alert to every little nuance of her sister's mood, but she exchanged greetings with the prelate and even made him smile without giving any hint at all that she was concerned about Frances.

But she was concerned. Increasingly, Robert sensed that. And increasingly, he was determined to get to the bottom of it.

Turning, the prelate invited their party to follow him inside. They all did, pausing in the dim foyer to listen as one of the deacons related the history of the church. Then the prelate made a sweeping gesture, inviting them to follow him down the aisle. Frederick, with Frances on his arm, set out in the prelate's wake.

Abruptly, Frances drew back. She made a small sound, then blindly turned away.

And Nell was there. She'd all but leapt forward to come up by Frances's side, catching her sister—trapping her sister?—with one arm around her waist. "Actually"—Nell spoke over Frances's head, which was turned away so no one there could see, to Frederick—"it's thought by many in our family to be . . . possibly unlucky to walk down the aisle with one's groom before the wedding." With a gesture, Nell waved at the other aisle that led down the side of the church. "Perhaps we could walk down the side aisles, and"—she beamed at the deacon who had delivered the history lecture—"we might hear more about the church's history as we go."

Despite having no idea what was going on, Robert stepped up in support. "That's an excellent idea." For the prelate and the deacons, he added, "We'll see more of the church that way."

There was a second's pause as everyone looked at Frederick.

"Ah, I see." Although he looked a trifle uncertain and worried, Frederick nodded. "A wedding superstition. This is understandable and must be accommodated."

Nell smiled encouragingly at Frederick. She eased her hold on Frances, who straightened; Nell determinedly wound her arm in Frances's and started strolling toward the ornate chapel to the side of the foyer. Frederick fell in beside Frances, ducking his head to see her face.

Walking behind the trio, Robert saw Nell's arm tighten, then Frances raised her head and said something to Frederick, who smiled and straightened, transparently relieved.

By the time they'd walked down the side aisle and reached the main altar, all was well again. Frances might be a trifle quieter than before, but she seemed completely composed and attentive. She complimented the prelate very prettily on the magnificence of the altar, then she, Nell, and the prelate discussed the relevant positioning to be used during the wedding service.

Robert glanced at Frederick and saw him nodding as he followed the conversation. His friend appeared reassured by Frances's increasing animation.

All Robert had were increasingly urgent questions, but it wasn't Frances he needed to interrogate.

But he got no chance to isolate Nell. Once they'd finished their tour of the cathedral it was time to return to the castle for a private and more relaxed family lunch. Following Nell, Frances, and Frederick into the family dining room, and finding both sets of parents and Frederick's uncles and aunts already present, Robert put aside any thought of pursuing his questions immediately; he would have to bide his time.

He thought his time had come when, after the meal was concluded, Frederick suggested a walk in the gardens and Frances, after a momentary hesitation during which she'd glanced at Nell, accepted.

Robert would have preferred to take Nell elsewhere, preferably somewhere he could sit her down and watch her face while he asked his questions and demanded answers, but as everyone clearly expected her to act as chaperon, he fell in with good grace by her side. With Frances on his arm, Frederick led the way out of the terrace doors, across the paved terrace, and down the steps to the parterre.

Pacing alongside Nell as she followed, Robert expected her to slow, to allow the betrothed, shortly-to-be-married couple to draw ahead and have some degree of privacy, affording him and her the same, but instead Nell remained ferociously focused on the pair, allowing them to get no more than ten feet ahead.

Given the questions he wished to ply her with, he needed greater privacy; he slowed his pace, expecting her to do the same, but she continued to forge on, leaving him behind.

Exasperated, he lengthened his stride and caught up with her. "Slow down—I want to speak with you."

"Not now." She glanced at him, briefly searched his eyes; he thought she might have sighed. "Later." She looked at the couple ahead. "Trust me—not now."

Trust her? About what? And why not now?

They turned down a walk shaded by sculpted shrubbery. Ahead of them, Frederick and Frances strolled on. Nell's focus on the couple was so blinkered, so compelling, Robert followed her gaze and looked, too . . . and saw the hesitancy that had crept into Frances's manner. There was no one thing that screamed uncertainty, but rather her whole stance, the way she held her head, no longer high and assured but lowered, as if she were trying to calm herself—and failing—set his inner alarms ringing.

Frances slowed. So did Frederick. Looking down at his bride-to-be, concern filled his face. "Liebchen?"

Robert all but heard the breath Frances gulped in, then she drew her hand from Frederick's sleeve and started to turn away.

Before Frances had accomplished a quarter-turn, Nell had sped up and was there. Sliding an arm about her sister's waist, she masked Frances's turn with a wave and the words, "Isn't that the most wonderful magnolia? It's just like the one we have at home, isn't it?" thus disguising Frances's movement as a wish to point out the large flowering tree to Frederick.

Frederick blinked, then raised his gaze to the tree. "I see." After a moment, he drew breath and looked down into Frances's face. He smiled gently. "It is good that you have something to remind you of your home. Does your tree flower as well?"

Frances tipped her head, then studied the tree anew. "I believe this tree is bigger—older. It has more branches, so more flowers, I think."

"We should look to see what else there is here that's reminiscent of home." Nell cast a glance at Robert, faintly wide eyes imploring his aid.

His diplomatic mask in place, he waved ahead. "If we go on a little further, there are some elders. As I recall you have lots of elders around your family's country house."

The rest of their walk transformed into a ramble, one filled with spotting familiar plants. Although led by Nell, with Robert in support, both Frederick and Frances were eventually drawn into the game, and in the end, the betrothed couple were once again at ease and laughing together.

Robert glanced at Nell as, at last, she fell back to stroll alongside him. He could almost feel her exhausted relief.

When, sensing his gaze, she glanced up at him, he caught her dark eyes and said just one word. "Later."

She sighed quite audibly, nodded, and faced forward.

Looking ahead, too, hands clasped behind his back, he continued to pace beside her.

"Four more *days!*" Nell sprawled in an armchair in the sitting room of the suite her parents had been given. "Neither I nor Frances will survive."

"Don't be melodramatic, dear—it's so unlike you." In the other armchair, Valeria settled a gauzy shawl about her shoulders. "Besides, it's hardly a matter of survival. Merely of managing, and you, darling, are very good at that."

"Flattery, Mama, will, in this instance, advance your cause not at all. I'm exhausted."

Valeria sighed. "So what stage has poor Frances reached?"

"I had to step in twice today and stop her from . . . Well, I suspect if I hadn't interfered, she would have fled the scene."

"Oh, dear." Valeria looked more worried than she had. "That is troubling."

"Yes. Especially as—as aforesaid—we still have four more days to 'manage.' " Nell sighed. "And there's more, which is really why I'm here. Robert knows—oh, not the reason, but after today he's not going to rest until he has an explanation, and I fear Frederick's . . . a little more than curious. Suspicious, in fact." She met her mother's eyes. "So what should I do?"

They were in the hiatus between coming inside and dressing for dinner; Valeria had changed her gown, but had yet to have her maid put up her fair hair, or don her jewels. Nell watched her mother frown as she digested the news.

"Where is poor Frances?" Valeria eventually asked.

"I left her lying down in her room. She's mortified, of course, but I hope I've convinced her that as yet we've concealed the attacks well enough to pass—well, at least to all others except Robert and Frederick."

"And the attacks themselves?"

Nell sighed. "They seem more acute than either she or I expected."

Valeria grimaced. "Well, then, given, as you keep pointing out, we have four more days before the wedding, I believe we have no option other than to confide in dear Robert, and also Frederick. Perhaps if you speak to Robert and explain, he can pass the information on to Frederick in the most appropriate way."

"Hmm. I gather Robert considers seeing this wedding to a successful conclusion as vital to furthering his career."

"Very likely. You know how competitive the Knightley boys are about their efforts for the crown in foreign climes. I gather that since the Corsican upstart's fall, the family has gone from strength to strength in the Foreign Office. I know your father was told very favorable things about Robert before we came."

Nell arched her brows. "He was always observant and clever."

"Indeed. So I counsel you to see him and explain as required—and I see no point in hiding anything from him. He can then decide how much to reveal, and how, to his friend."

"Very well—that will solve that issue. But do you know of any way to"—Nell gestured—"*ameliorate* these attacks? If they grow more frequent, we'll have the devil of a time concealing them."

Valeria compressed her lips as she thought, then she looked at Nell. "Distraction. If she's thinking and doing other things, she can't be panicking, so fill her day—from morn to night—as much as you possibly can. Have her engaged with something interesting every single hour—I gather that worked for Selena, my cousin's daughter."

Nell frowned. "What sort of things—"

"The same things you would find interesting and engaging—Frances and you are very much alike, after all. Felicity and Esme are similar, and you and Frances share many traits—I've often noted it."

Nell arched her brows, but then nodded. "Thinking of it, yes, I daresay you're right. So . . ."

"So once you've explained all to dear Robert, tell him what we believe we need to do to help Frances through these next days and ask for his help, and his advice." Valeria smiled. "I find it's always helpful to have a solution ready to hand when one explains a problem to a gentleman—and asking for his help is a sure way to bringing him around. Men love to be thought helpful, and if you can make him feel like a savior, so much the better."

Nell laughed and stood. "You're incorrigible, Mama."

"Of course." Valeria held up her face for Nell to kiss. "But I'm right nevertheless. You'll see."

"Very well—I'll engage to put your sage counsel to the test. I'll arrange to meet with Robert later tonight."

Nell didn't have to arrange to meet with Robert. After another near-disaster in the drawing room after dinner, which she barely managed to contain and adequately disguise, when everyone else retired, drifting out through the drawing room's double doors and up the main stairs, Robert was waiting just inside the doors. He didn't just catch her eye as, feeling harried and even more exhausted, having consigned an inwardly shaken Frances to Valeria's care, Nell brought up the rear of the crowd; as she drew level with him, Robert reached out and caught her arm.

It was the first time they'd touched in nine years. The jolt to her pulse was stunning.

He paused, as if feeling it, too, then gentled his grip. For a moment, his eyes searched hers, then his lips thinned. "I'd like a word, if I may. In private."

She nodded. "Where?"

Releasing her, he led her upstairs to his study. It was a masculine room, all dark brown leather and polished wood. Eschewing the cluttered desk, Nell made for the armchairs angled before the empty fireplace. Sinking into one, she watched as Robert closed the door, then came to stand before the hearth.

Robert looked down at her, and asked the question she clearly expected to be asked. "What's going on?"

She looked up at him for a moment, then stated, "Nothing that should impact the wedding itself. Rather . . . it's a situation we—you and I—need to manage, one that will end with the dawn four days hence."

He blinked, calculated. "On their wedding day?"

She nodded.

When she didn't say more, he arched a brow. "Nerves?"

Her lips twisted. "Of a sort. I'm thinking of how best to put it—to explain it so that you'll understand."

"Just tell me."

She sighed. "Very well—Frances has proved to be subject to the Vayne family failing. We didn't know if she would be, although the chances were good that she would, given no other female in the family has escaped the curse to date."

"Curse? What curse?"

She gestured. "You've seen it—the sudden inexplicable panics. That's the Vayne family failing in action. More than anything else, that's why I had to be here—because one of us who understands and can remain with her at all times needed to be here to . . . stop her. Shepherd her and steer her out of it. Stop her from bolting if that's how the failing struck."

Blinking, feeling very much like shaking his head in disbelief, Robert shifted and sank into the armchair facing her. "Vayne—that's your mother's family, isn't it?"

Nell nodded. "That's where the failing comes from."

"And this failing can take different forms?"

Again she nodded. "With different ladies. For instance, Mama actually bolted. The day before their wedding, she got in a gig and was driving herself out of London when Papa caught up with her. But she'd felt no panic until that day. Luckily, Papa wasn't the self-effacing sort—he raced straight after her, which, as it happens, was the right thing to do. Mama had no idea where she was going, or even why—she just panicked."

"So . . . if Frances bolts, Frederick has to go after her?"

"One of us will need to, but I'm hoping it won't come to that."

He felt . . . disorientated.

"Felicity, now, had three days of attacks to weather, but they were relatively mild. She just got in a flustered dither and made no sense, but that wasn't hard to gloss over. Esme, like Mama, only had one attack and that on the day before the wedding, but we were ready and no one believed her wedding gown had suddenly been torn and stained beyond redemption. Once she snapped out of it, Esme didn't have a clue why she'd thought that."

"This . . . ah, curse. It doesn't last into the wedding day?"

"It never has, and that's from experience of many weddings, my mother's sisters and their cousins and my cousins— all the females with Vayne blood. For some reason, once we get to the day itself, the curse vanishes."

"Never to return?"

"Never to return in any form."

Relief washed through him. "Having encouraged and facilitated this match, that's comforting to know."

"I daresay. With Frances, we didn't know if, or when, or even in what form the curse would strike. Sadly, it first manifested on the barge, six full days before the wedding. And you've seen what it's like—she draws back, pulls back. But— and this is the critically important part—her reactions have nothing to do with her feelings, or what she truly wants. She's horrified when she snaps out of it, but while the panic is on her, she's not actually thinking at all. Frances is very much in love with Frederick, and she very definitely wants to marry him—the panic attacks don't in any way reflect or alter her feelings."

"Hmm." He frowned. "So we could characterize these attacks as an extreme case of bridal nerves and nothing more."

Nell nodded. "We could." She smoothed one hand along the arm of the chair. "Mama and I suspect that, in the circumstances, and with four days still to go, we need to explain at least some of this to Frederick. He's already noticed, and he must be wondering."

"He is." Robert met her eyes as she glanced up. When she arched her brows, he hesitated, then nodded. "All right. I'll speak with him and make sure he understands. Which leads to my next question, which will also be Frederick's next question—how should he behave during these attacks?"

"Essentially as my father did. Frederick won't be able to ignore the attacks, but he absolutely mustn't react to them by drawing back himself. That only gives the attacks a sort of internal credence, and will most likely make things worse. He needs to stand firm and not let Frances physically pull away. If he accepts that the attack is happening, but that it's nonsensical and irrelevant and will be over soon, and simply smiles, nods, speaks soothingly, and goes on as if the attack hasn't happened, that's the surest way to snap Frances out of it, and all will be well."

Robert spent some moments digesting that, then nodded. "All right. As Frederick is deeply attached to Frances, I don't foresee any problem in enlisting his aid, especially as this is purely a case of temporary and understandable nervy panics." He saw Nell's lips twitch upward, and permitted himself a self-deprecating smile; he was, indeed, already framing the situation in diplomatic language. "Let's assume we—me, you, and Frederick—are all apprised and acting in concert. I assume we can count on your parents if need be?"

"Yes, but they will only be with us during the evening events."

"Indeed. So is there anything we can do to . . . avoid the attacks, or minimize their severity?"

"We—Mama and I—think distraction might work. If we can fill Frances's days with events that keep her actively engaged and entertained, we believe that will reduce the scope for an attack."

He nodded. "That has a certain logic. What events are most likely to engage her interest?"

"As Mama reminded me, Frances and I are much alike, so what would work for me . . ."

Frances and I are much alike. Robert's brain seized on the words, focused on them—and their implications. All of him stilled. The Vayne family failing had manifested in Frances as a pulling back, a drawing back from the man she loved, even though she loved him and wanted to marry him. Frances's attacks had started earlier, further ahead of the wedding, than her family had expected. And no Vayne lady had ever escaped the curse.

Nell was as much of a Vayne as Frances. And Nell and Frances were much alike in many ways . . .

While Nell sat in the chair and talked, listing various excursions and events she felt would provide suitable distraction, and some part of his mind listened and cataloged, and he nodded every now and then, most of his mind, certainly all of his attention, followed her earlier revelations to the inescapable conclusion . . .

A conclusion that rocked him. That shattered his perceptions of their past, and reformed them.

Leaving him with a new and novel perspective.

A much more accurate view of how things had been.

Dragging a breath into lungs suddenly tight, he refocused on Nell.

To discover her looking at him quizzically.

His mind caught up with her words; he nodded. "We can arrange most of that, and yes, I think we should." Rising, he crossed to the desk, found a sheet of paper and a pencil, picked up a ledger for her to use as a support, and returned to her. He handed her the items. "Let's make a list."

While she settled the ledger on the chair arm, smoothed out the paper and lifted the pencil, he sat, and ruthlessly forced his mind to the matter at hand. "Let's do it day by day, and crowd as much into each day as we can."

Eyes on her list, she nodded. "So—tomorrow."

"Well!" Nell let herself fall into the armchair in Robert's study. "That went better than I'd dared hope. One attack only, and that relatively minor—and I have to compliment you. Whatever you told Frederick, however you phrased it, must have been exactly right. He came up trumps, and you may pass on from me that he isn't doing himself any harm at all in Frances's eyes."

Smiling, Robert came to sit in the other armchair. "I'll let him know. He was quite nervous, although I know it didn't show. But he did, indeed, hold the line admirably."

He'd brought their list of events, now superimposed on the affianced couple's official schedule. It was presently mid afternoon, and he'd suggested they seize the half an hour between their last event—a viewing of the castle's stables and kennels—and a formal afternoon tea to be attended by all the young ladies of the court to review their upcoming arrangements. He perused the revised schedule. "After this tea—and if Frances is immersed and entertained, we can extend the event until half an hour before the dressing gong—then we have the formal drawing room and dinner with all the ambassadors." He glanced at Nell. "I'll do my best to keep the ambassadors and envoys circling, but several are pompous old windbags, so be prepared to step in and divert any who linger too long. A few—the Russian envoy, for one, and the French ambassador almost certainly—will attempt to monopolize our pair. While Frederick won't need to leave Frances's side, it would be best if between us, we—you and I, because your parents will be fully engaged themselves—try to ensure one of us is there to back Frederick up at any time."

He grimaced. "I have this persistent vision of one of the ambassadors deciding to buttonhole Frederick and draw him aside while I'm not by to stop it, effectively forcing Frederick to leave Frances standing there alone."

Nell frowned. "What about the wives? They'll be there, won't they?"

"Yes, but they don't generally come forward. At these sort

of events they usually gather like a flock of geese and sit and cackle at one end of the room."

"With a new and shiny princess-to-be in their midst?" Nell threw him a look. "Leave it to me—and Mama. We'll have them with their gloved hands on their husbands' arms, sticking like glue to get as much time as they can with Frances. As they'll be intent on her and Frederick in a personal sense, and not interested in anything political, I should think their presence will restrict their spouses' ability to turn the conversation to political affairs."

He widened his eyes. "I hadn't thought of that, but you might well be right." He nodded. "I'll leave the wives to you."

Raising the schedule, he studied the following events. "After dinner, there'll be dancing in the ballroom."

"That will be no problem at all—Frances loves to dance, and as I recall so does Frederick."

Robert nodded. "So with luck we'll weather tonight well enough, and then tomorrow we have the visit to the orphanage, and then the guilds' luncheon at the Rathaus, and after that we've slotted in visits to a weaving factory, then the silk merchants' warehouse, and last but not least, to the crown jewelers." He glanced up. "That's going to be quite a day."

Nell nodded happily. "Yes, it is, and the curse is going to have to fight for an opening. Excellent!" She rose and shook out her skirts.

Rising, too, Robert laid aside the list and just looked at her for a moment—a rare moment when she wasn't looking at him.

Then she looked up and met his eyes. Searched them,

then said, "It's time I fetched Frances and Mama for the tea."

He smiled. "Indeed." He waved her to the door. "I'll go downstairs and make sure all's in readiness."

He followed her out of the study and they parted, each to do their part in managing the Vayne family failing.

The following day, they maneuvered to sit alongside each other at the end of one table at the luncheon the town's guild masters hosted to toast the royal bride and groom.

When the speeches got under way, at the center of the high table Frances sat, apparently rapt, alongside Frederick, whose protective tendencies had only grown more marked with every passing hour, especially as Frances seemed to be increasingly leaning on him to help her through her panicky flutters. Which, Nell felt, was an unexpected boon.

Satisfied her sister was as well-guarded as she might be, when Robert drew a sheet of paper from his pocket, unfolded it, and smoothed it out, Nell readily consented to turn her attention to their plans for the afternoon.

Having realized that she had an excellent memory for names, Robert duly filled her in as to whom they would meet that afternoon at the weaving factory, the silk warehouse, and the jewelers. "I estimate we'll get back to the castle only just in time to change for dinner. It's a family dinner tonight—only Frederick's immediate family and yours."

"Good." Nell sat back and met Robert's eyes. Steady gray eyes, stubborn square chin. He was as she remembered him, but with depth, or was it new facets? No—more like previously hidden depths that were now more discernible. She smiled. "We've done very well so far. Especially this morning. The orphanage was fun—I think they can be certain that Frances will want to become their patron."

Relaxing in his chair, Robert smiled back, and wondered if she had any idea how revealing her interest in the children at the orphanage had been. Although Frances had certainly been interested, too, she had largely followed in Nell's shadow. In truth, it was Nell who truly commanded the innate graciousness associated with a duke's daughter; she had just the right touch, leaving those she dealt with feeling honored, without in any way making an issue of her status.

Nell's gaze had drifted back to the guild master currently at the podium, leaving him free to let his gaze rest on her, to let his mind dwell on what he'd finally understood about the unraveling of their romance long ago.

As his gaze traced her face, he felt the determination to make a bid, again, for the only lady he'd ever wanted as his own well and harden.

"There you are, my dears." Valeria drifted up, setting a languid hand on Nell's and Robert's shoulders. She smiled at Nell as Nell glanced up, then, as Nell returned her gaze to the speaker, Valeria met Robert's gaze. And nodded. "You're doing very well."

With a pat on his shoulder, Valeria drifted on.

Robert blinked, looked again at Nell, and wondered at the ambiguity he'd detected in her mother's words.

"One more day." Perched sidesaddle on a sweet black mare, Nell cantered alongside Robert, mounted on a raking gray.

She nodded ahead to where Frances and Frederick were bowling along in a gig, with Frederick teaching Frances to manage the ribbons. "Teaching Frances to drive was an inspired notion. With luck, that will keep her entirely engrossed on the drive out, and the drive home again. And what with the lunch at the hunting lodge, then the visit to the farm, while I hardly dare to suggest it, we might reach tonight—or to be more precise, tomorrow's dawn—without major incident."

"The dinners tonight are private and separate," Robert said. "Your family at one, and Frederick's at another. No real likelihood of any untoward occurrence there, so once we get back to the castle this afternoon—"

"Oh, no—I'm not counting my chickens until tonight, until Frances retreats into her bedchamber and closes the door."

Robert grinned. His gaze returned to Frances. They'd let the gig draw ahead. "She's only had three minor episodes since we started our campaign of distraction, and Frederick's managed all three by himself."

"He's been more sympathetic than I expected him to be." Nell's gaze, too, dwelled on Frederick's and Frances's heads. "I feel even more confident than I was before that they'll truly have a wonderful marriage."

Robert made no reply, not that she'd expected one. About them, the morning had waxed warm, but a breeze off the river kept temperatures pleasant. Birds trilled and swooped in the hedgerows they passed, and the rich scent of grain ripening in the sun teased their senses.

"There's a lookout on that ridge ahead. They can't reach it in the gig—but we can." Robert met her gaze as she glanced at him. "You said it yourself—Frances is unlikely to have any difficulty while she's concentrating so hard on learning to drive." Tipping his head toward the ridge, he smiled, unvoiced challenge in his eyes. "We can ride down the other side and rejoin the party, and the view from up there is said to be the best in Lautenberg."

She laughed. "All right. I can see you're searching for a reason to let your mount stretch his legs." She waved. "Lead on."

Robert drew aside, spoke briefly to the captain of the honor guard of six riders following their Prince, then he urged his gray away and down a narrow track; perched on her black, Nell followed.

Once off the road, they let their mounts stretch into an easy gallop. The track they were following led into a forest; they slowed as, now a narrower bridle path, the track climbed the ridge in a series of switchbacks.

Eventually, they reached the top of the ridge and Robert led the way over and into the wide clearing carved out on the side of the hill. Before them, lush green fields stretched to either side, to the distant blue line of the Mosel on their right, and all the way to the cloud-hazed mountains that marked the border with Luxembourg to the left.

He reined in and Nell halted her mare beside his gray. She looked out, eagerly scanning. Her cheeks were rosy, her lips lush and ripe, her large, dark-pansy eyes bright with eager interest. He considered the sight, then swung down from the saddle.

She looked at him questioningly as he came to lift her down.

"We can sit for a little while. The road will take them around and over a pass—it'll be some time before they reach the stretch below us."

Her lips formed an "oh" and she slid her boots free, then allowed him to close his hands about her waist and swing her down.

She lost her breath. He was watching, so saw it, but pretended he hadn't.

Releasing her, he waved to the view. "Come—I'll point out the sights."

She didn't attempt any verbal response, just nodded and walked beside him to the edge of the cliff.

He started at the Mosel, and she was quickly pointing to landmarks and asking about the smaller towns and villages they could see nestling in the landscape. When eventually he'd named or explained all that they could see, she sighed. "It's really very peaceful here—much less noisy and crowded and bustling than London, but oddly the countryside seems more . . . alive somehow." She glanced at him. "The country here is different from the countryside at home."

He nodded. "Here there's less large-estate farming and more of other crafts, like woodworking, and metal crafting, and jewelry making, cloth making, and animal husbandry of many more types. The villages are a lot closer—to walk from one to the next would take less than an hour—so it's easier for the villagers and townsfolk to barter and trade . . ." He grimaced lightly. "I suppose the main difference is that there are no major landowners other than the royal family, so most people in Lautenberg have at least their own small patch to raise grain, or chickens, or build a forge and sell their wares."

"They're all independent?"

"They pay taxes to the royal family, but those aren't onerous and go primarily to keeping the various necessary arms of the government operational." His lips twisted cynically. "As the British envoy, I'm not sure saying so isn't a form of treason, but I prefer the peace and tranquility, and, yes, the relative equality of this place."

He felt her gaze on his face. "Will you stay here, then? Even when you're no longer the envoy?"

He shrugged. "Perhaps." He looked at her. "It depends." He let a moment tick past, then asked, "What of you?" With a wave, he directed her gaze back to the vista spread before them. "If you could, would you live here, surrounded by this brand of peace and harmony, with Frances near . . . or would you rather the bustle of London, and the quieter space of a large estate in the English countryside?"

She gazed out, considering, then her lips lightly curved. "If I could . . . strangely enough, I can see myself here, which is not at all what I'd expected. Lautenberg is . . . human-sized in a way larger countries are not."

"Aptly put." He didn't give her time to dwell further on his question, but waved her to the horses. "We should start down. The gig should have cleared the pass by now—it'll be coming along the road below us shortly."

Nell filled her lungs one more time with the sweetly scented air, then exhaled, turned, and walked back to the mare. And steeled her nerves, her senses, against the rush of feeling as Robert's hands slid about her waist and gripped, and he lifted her—so effortlessly—to her saddle.

Her lungs seized again, but she'd expected that; she didn't

let it ruffle her but used the moment while he walked to his horse and mounted to settle her boots in the stirrups and arrange her riding skirt, then lifting her head—finding him looking directly at her—she smiled and nodded at him to lead the way down.

As she followed him slowly down what proved to be a steeper track on this side of the ridge, she had ample time to let her gaze travel over his well-shaped head, his shoulders, and the long length of his back. He cut a dashing figure atop the heavy gelding, and managed the powerful animal with negligent ease. After nine years with no real contact, it seemed strange to have fallen so easily into the same relaxed rapport they'd previously shared; he was the only man she'd ever felt so at ease with, so free to simply indulge and enjoy his company.

She'd always regretted the fact that he'd drawn back, that he hadn't made an offer for her hand, and, now she thought of it, she had to own to considerable surprise to find him still unwed. He was a Knightley; his family were diplomats, one and all, and, in general, diplomats were expected to marry, to have a helpmate in their duties.

She tried to imagine what his wife would be like, when he finally chose her. She imagined several young English ladies she knew, measured them against the role, yet none seemed at all suitable; none found favor in her eyes. Then again, she was only an old friend, and a long distant one at that; he might have changed significantly since they'd been close . . . only she didn't think he had.

He was older, yet so much about him seemed achingly familiar. She'd had to steel her heart against the temptation to dwell on all she'd missed, on all she'd not had to enjoy for the past nine years . . . she wished she knew why he'd never asked for her hand. Wished she knew what she'd done wrong, what she'd done to make him step back when she'd thought he was about to step closer, close enough to take her in his arms . . .

With an irritated shake of her head, she banished the useless, repetitive meanderings. She was here, now, with him, and at least for the next several hours, she could take pleasure in his company.

He drew rein as they reached the road; as she halted her mare alongside his gray, she could hear the rattle of the gig's wheels drawing nearer.

She turned to him. "Will you be dining with us tonight? Or are you expected to dine with Frederick?"

His lips twisted. "Frederick's family will expect me, I fear, but . . ." Robert met her eyes. "Why don't we meet in my study later—once you've seen Frances to her bedchamber and can report, absolutely, that our campaign has reached a successful conclusion?"

Nell grinned. "Yes. All right."

The gig rounded the nearby corner and the rattle of its wheels cut off any further conversation.

Not that Robert wished to say anything more; he was more than satisfied with what he'd achieved.

It was just after eleven o'clock when Nell finally made her way down the corridor to Robert's study door. A line of lamplight showed beneath the door; feeling more lighthearted, freer than she had for weeks and weeks, she tapped lightly, then opened the door and swept in.

Robert was seated at his desk; he'd been reading some papers. The lamp on one corner shed strong light over the desk, striking deep red glints from his dark brown hair. He'd looked up as she entered; smiling, he laid aside the papers and beckoned her nearer. Leaning back in his chair, he reached out and lifted a small bottle of champagne from a bucket of ice, along with two glasses.

"Here." He held out the glasses.

Rounding the desk, she leaned back against one corner and took both glasses, holding them while he eased the stopper from the bottle. It popped and he seized one glass, deftly catching the foaming bubbles that cascaded forth.

He glanced up at her as the froth slowed and he poured bubbly liquid into the glass. "I hope celebrations are in order. I take it Frances has retired and all is well?"

"Yes, she has, and yes." Accepting the filled glass, Nell handed him the other. "I can report that we are, indeed, home and hosed, and the wedding will proceed with no further hiccups or hitches."

"Thank heaven!" His own glass filled, Robert clinked the rim to hers, then raised his glass in a toast. "To the successful conclusion of our campaign."

"Hear, hear!" She lifted her glass in salute, then sipped. "Mmm, that's nice." She looked at the glass, at the bubbles rising within the liquid, then raised the glass again. "To Frances, another Vayne lady who has managed to reach her wedding day without major mishap."

Robert's lips curved, but lightly. His gray gaze remained steady on her face. "To Frances and her wedding."

They both sipped again.

"And," Robert returned, "we shouldn't forget Frederick, who stepped up to the mark in sterling fashion, and in doing so forged an even deeper bond with his soon-to-be bride."

"No, indeed." Nell leaned closer and clinked her glass to Robert's. "We definitely shouldn't forget Frederick."

Robert sipped and watched her swallow a healthy gulp of the champagne, then he reached out and slipped the glass from her fingers.

She blinked as he pushed back his chair, rose, and set both glasses aside. "I hadn't finished."

"I know, but I want you fully compos mentis for what comes next."

She spread her arms. "But my travails are all over."

Shifting to stand before her, he caught her hands and drew her upright. Frowning, she studied his face. "What comes next?"

"Something I've been wanting to do ever since I saw you step onto the deck of the royal barge." Releasing her hands, he raised his, framed her face and tipped it up, and kissed her.

Gently, at first, but then his lips firmed and . . . Nell couldn't catch her breath. Couldn't steady her suddenly reeling head. A sensation like fizz erupted deep inside her and she felt giddy, deliriously whirling—and none of that had anything to do with the champagne.

She responded, not hesitantly as she'd expected, but with a certainty born of some seed that had been planted long ago. Nine years ago.

Sliding her arms over his shoulders, she moved closer, her lips meeting his with equal ardor, with an equivalent wish to explore, to know . . .

The tip of his tongue cruised the seam of her lips, tempting, enticing. Inciting.

They'd kissed, all those years ago, when she'd been nineteen and he twenty-two, but those tentative kisses had been nothing like this.

This . . . was an invitation, simple and blatant and sure. She read that, understood that, instinctively and in every other way. For an instant, she teetered on the cusp, unsure, but then she looked inward—just one second of consideration—and she knew what her answer should be.

This was her one chance—her last chance. Tomorrow was the wedding, and the day after she would leave, and she'd always—always—wanted him.

As a woman wanted a man, she'd yearned for him.

So she parted her lips and invited him in, surrendered her mouth, and gloried as he took. As he claimed and made his that which always had been.

His hands drifted from her face and his arms closed around her and she closed the last inches between his body and hers.

And desire flared.

At some point he steered her through a door into his adjoining bedroom. To his bed.

Later still, they lay together on the white sheets in a tangle of naked limbs, heated skin, and pounding hearts.

Hands shaped, explored, sculpted, possessed.

And passion burned.

Murmured endearments, encouragements, and soft moans of delight were the only sounds she heard. She was deaf to all else, blind to the world—for her there was only him.

And for him, it seemed, there was only her. Devotion and reverence invested his touch; his focus was absolute and unwavering.

Sensation and feelings and an upsurge of emotion swept her up and carried her on.

Urged her on.

Until they came together in a rush of fire and glory. And the moment was all, and everything and more than she'd dreamed.

And the man in her arms was the man of her dreams—he always had been. Even as cataclysmic sensation stole her breath, stole her mind and overwhelmed her senses, she yet recognized that as indisputable fact.

This was life, this was joy.

This was pleasure unbounded.

Then ecstasy claimed them, wracked them, shattered them, and satiation rolled over them and she knew no more.

Nell woke to the gray light of pre-dawn. For a moment, she was disoriented—the room was similar to her own, but not . . . Then on a rush of remembered sensation, she recalled what had happened. The bed beside her was empty, yet the sheets were still warm.

Silence lay over the room.

Raising her head, she searched, and saw Robert standing before the window, staring out. He'd thrown on a robe.

The bed was in complete disarray; detaching the coverlet required little effort. Wrapping the warm folds about her, she walked quietly across and joined him.

He glanced at her as she halted beside him. Looking out at the glimmer of light just edging the eastern horizon, she murmured, "You seduced me. I'm not complaining—I'm glad you did—but now I can think again, I have to wonder why."

Turning her head, she met his gray eyes, the shade softer in the faint morning light.

He held her gaze. "Because I realized it's what I should have done nine years ago."

She frowned.

His tone hardened. "Well, maybe not that precisely, but . . . I want you with me, Nell—here, wherever I'm posted. I've always wanted you and only you. I haven't been a monk over the years we've been apart, but there's never been anyone else—only you." He held a glass of water; he raised it, sipped, then went on, his gaze moving gently over her face, "When you drew back, I tried to find someone else—someone who wanted me. But I could never find any woman to take your place. For me, it seemed only you would do."

She frowned more definitely, her gaze locked with his. "I didn't draw back—you did."

His lips curved, but ruefully. He shook his head. "Stop and think. Are you, or are you not, the oldest girl of your generation on the Vayne family tree?"

She didn't stop frowning. "I am."

"So in the same way you've been watching out for Frances, who was watching out for you? Who thought to watch your behavior? No one. At that time, nine years ago, the Vaynes didn't know whether your generation would be affected, did they? And you hadn't yet become betrothed. But, my darling Nell, you and I were always sympathetic, empathetic, toward each other. You *knew* I was going to ask for your hand . . . and you drew back."

Confusion overwhelmed her frown. "I did?" She honestly didn't think . . . but then Frances and her sisters and all the other Vayne females rarely had much comprehension of what they did while panicking . . . She refocused on his face. "Are you sure?"

She couldn't disguise the hope that colored her voice. Was that why he'd drawn back, because she had?

His nod was absolute. "Yes. You pulled back. And I didn't know anything about the Vayne family failing. I was twenty-two, and while now I would probably grow suspicious, press, and ask questions, back then . . ." He paused, holding her gaze. "I thought you didn't want me to propose, that you didn't want me as your husband, and that was why you drew back."

"No!" She searched his eyes and didn't doubt his veracity. "I *wanted* to marry you."

Anguish rang beneath her words. Robert captured one of her hands, drew his thumb soothingly over the back. "It doesn't matter, darling Nell, because that was long ago and this, here and now, is where we are." He held her dark gaze, the rich violet only just taking on color as the sun slowly rose. Raising her hand, he pressed a kiss to her knuckles, and spoke to those wonderful eyes. "I've never stopped loving you, and through these last days, as we worked side by side through our campaign, I came to hope that you still loved me."

Her answer came without a heartbeat's hesitation. "I've always loved you. Only you."

"And as I love you in the same, all-consuming fashion, then it's time, don't you think, that we married?" He drew a breath, and it was tight. "And that's the answer to your question—why I seduced you. Because, my darling Nell, you may draw back, fluster and bluster all you like, but this time, I'm not letting you go."

Nell stared at him, then a laugh bubbled up—a happy, joyous laugh—and she had to let it out.

He smiled in return.

Then before she gathered her wits, he went down on one knee and looked up at her, draped in his coverlet with one shoulder bare and her hair cascading in a tousled mane, and said, "Marry me, Nell, and make me the happiest of mortals."

She dropped onto her knees, too, pressing into arms that closed around her, steadying her and holding her, and smiled into his eyes. "My heart is yours, Robert Knightley. I'll marry you and gladly, and I trust that you'll hold me to this vow—to be your wife and stand by your side forevermore." Then she leaned in and kissed him.

And he kissed her back.

Minutes later, he rose, lifting her in his arms, and carried her back to the bed.

The wedding of Hereditary Prince Frederick of Lautenberg to Frances Daughtry, daughter of the Duke of Pemberton, went off without a hitch.

Until he'd seen the evidence with his own eyes, Robert had privately questioned the assumption that the Vayne curse would vanish with the day's dawn, but from the first—when he'd glimpsed her going into the private family breakfast— Frances had glowed, happiness and joy and delighted expectation rendering her nothing short of radiant.

Nell, gowned in deep violet satin of a shade that matched her eyes, followed Frances into the room, smiling and laughing at something Frances had said; she transfixed Robert's eyes and attention effortlessly. Even walking in Frances's train, to him, Nell was beyond compare.

Throughout the long day, he and she consulted frequently, working through an extensive list of items to be tweaked and last-minute matters to confirm.

As in any major diplomatic event, adjustments had to be made due to unforeseen happenings—like the elderly Grand Duchess of Bavaria, being unable to stand and so unable to see from her allotted perch in the gallery, having to be accommodated nearer the altar—but between them he and Nell rose to the challenge, and not a single disturbance marred the day.

Frederick and Frances made a perfect royal couple, the glow in their eyes and investing their expressions whenever they looked on each other clear for all to see. The populace of Lautenberg, many of whom had crowded into the streets of Kremunz, roared their approval.

The wedding breakfast passed off without incident, and then it was time for the newlyweds to depart on the royal barge on the first night of a romantic wedding cruise.

All those who could followed the royal couple and their attendant families to the docks, where the barge, suitably bedecked, bobbed on a gentle swell.

Half an hour of laughter, cheers, and a short thank-you speech from Frederick to his assembled countrymen, and the ropes were cast off and the barge eased into the river.

Robert watched the gap widen between the dock and the deck, and finally felt the pressure of the day slide from his shoulders.

Nell, standing beside him, sent one last wave toward her sister and her new husband, then linked her arm in Robert's and heaved a heartfelt sigh. "It's done."

"Indeed." Standing in front of Robert, Valeria turned and considered him and her daughter. "And what about you?"

As ever, her question was ambiguous, but, unruffled, Robert smiled and answered it as his future mama-in-law had intended. "As it happens, Your Grace, I'll be returning to England with your party." Raising his gaze, he included the duke, who had come to stand beside Valeria. "I intend to return to London, at least long enough to marry Nell."

The duke smiled. "Excellent!" He clasped Robert's hand and shook it heartily. "About time." The duke beamed at his daughter.

Valeria looked at Nell expectantly, as did Robert. She was staring at them all, apparently struck dumb. Valeria arched her fine brows. "If she'll have you, I suspect you meant to say."

"No, Your Grace." Meeting Nell's stunned eyes, Robert placed his hand over hers on his sleeve. "Regardless of what she says from now until then, I will meet her before the altar at St. George's. I have no intention of drawing back. Again. I love her, and I know she loves me, and"—raising her hand, he pressed a kiss to her fingers—"once I finally get my ring on her finger, I look forward to a long and happy life side by side."

Valeria looked from him to Nell, then smiled delightedly. "Amen."

July 7, 1826
The Deck of the Mary and Henry,
bound for the Rhine, crossing the English Channel

The wind blew fair and the schooner leapt through the waves. Clutching the rail a little short of the bow, Nell stood with Robert, a comforting shield at her back, and watched the coast of Holland take shape on the horizon.

They were returning to Lautenberg, to what would be their home for the foreseeable future, possibly for the rest of their lives. Robert's masters at the Foreign Office had been beyond delighted to learn of his proposed alliance with the Daughtrys; the reassurance of having a sister to support Frances in her role, and the benefits of having a noble lady of Nell's caliber to assist Robert in the delicate diplomacy predicted to be necessary to keep peace in the region, were considered unparalleled boons. As for Robert's family, they, too, were in alt; he was the last of his brothers to wed, and the family had all but given up hope—a hard thing in a family steeped in diplomatic ways.

Her hair whipped by the wind, the tang of sea spray unrelenting, Nell glanced down at the shiny gold band on her ring finger. The last two weeks had been frenetic, hectic, and filled to the brim, but perhaps because their recent brief engagement was effectively the second time for her, she'd fallen prey to no more than several short bouts of frantic dithering, and they'd been married yesterday in St. George's in a relatively small, family wedding; after Frances's recent extravaganza, that had suited them both.

And now, soon, they would reach the mouth of the Rhine, and transfer to the barge that would be waiting to ferry them along the river and then up the Mosel to Kremunz and its fairy-tale castle.

"A penny for your thoughts."

She smiled and leaned back, nestling her head against Robert's shoulder, crossing her arms over his as they circled her waist and held her securely. "I was just thinking . . . this is very much my dream come true, but I never thought beyond this point." She glanced up and caught his eye. "Beyond the wedding. And now we're here, on the threshold of beyond, and I feel . . . so *excited*, so enthusiastic about what lies ahead."

"About making a life together?"

She nodded. "That, and the challenges of managing whatever comes."

His chin against her head, he was silent for a moment, then he murmured, "Just as long as we're together, as long as I can hold you in my arms, I don't care what fate flings at us."

"Just as long as we're together, we can triumph over anything."

"And as we'll always and forever be together, the future, my love, is *finally* ours."

THE END

Keep reading for
an excerpt from
Stephanie Laurens's
next historical romance

THE LADY RISKS ALL

Available October 2012

PROLOGUE

Lord Julian Roscoe Neville Delbraith, second son of the Duke of Ridgware, was a wastrel. Indeed, profligate beyond belief, he gave the term new meaning. Tall, dark-haired, and dangerously handsome, he prowled the ton with the lazy grace of a well-bred panther whose appetites were perennially sated, as, indeed, he ensured they were. He was considered by the gentlemen to be a capital sort, one with whom many wished to claim acquaintance, while the ladies appreciated his ineffable elegance, his expertise on the dance floor, his ready charm, and his occasionally exercised rapier wit. His attire, naturally, was invariably exquisite, and his horses turned Corinthians green. Wine, women, and gaming, in reverse order, were his principal occupations, which surprised no one; the Delbraiths had a long and venerable history of spawning males with an addiction to wagering. It ran in the blood.

That said, Lucasta, Lord Julian's mother, acknowledged Savior of the Delbraiths in the recent generation, was credited with having been sufficiently strong in her handling of

Marcus, Julian's father, to have preserved the family fortunes. Marcus would have liked to have gambled his income away, but Lucasta had put her foot down and vetoed it. Adamantly. More, her firstborn son, George, was the first Delbraith in generations uncounted to have escaped the family curse.

Some felt that Lucasta's sterling efforts with Marcus and George had left her with insufficient reserves to effect a similar transformation with Julian, while others considered Julian's headstrong will beyond even his mother's ability to rein in, even had she been free to concentrate solely on him. In society's eyes, Julian was the epitome of the archetypal male Delbraith.

Yet to society and the family, Julian's enthusiastic embracing of the Delbraith curse mattered not at all. George was the heir.

Large, solid, quiet, and rather stuffily reserved, unlike his younger brother, George appeared to have no vices at all. While Julian could be counted on to be flippant, irreverent, and entertaining, George stood with his hands behind his back and said as little as he could. In short, George was boring, but that, too, wasn't a concern, because, after all, George was *safe*.

Consequently, when, on Marcus's death, George succeeded to the title, the family and society smiled. They continued to smile when George contracted an eminently suitable marriage with Caroline, daughter of the Earl of Kirkcombe, a sensible young lady well-regarded within the ton.

Caroline, following her mother-in-law's lead, considered George a paragon, at least with respect to his lack of susceptibility to the family curse. That she found him significantly less of a paragon in more private arenas she kept very much to herself; outwardly, she championed George at every turn, and society nodded approvingly. Unsurprisingly therefore, Caroline had no time for the rakishly attractive, outrageously dissolute Julian; her attitude made it clear that she regarded him as a potentially corrupting influence, one she wished to keep well distanced from her husband, herself, and the child she was soon carrying.

Not at all insensitive, Julian bowed to his sister-in-law's unspoken wishes; she, after all, was his brother's duchess. His visits to the family estate, Ridgware, in Staffordshire, previously quite frequent when he would dutifully call on his mother and then stay to play with his three much younger sisters, grew further apart, eventually dwindling to rare. The great house's staff, who saw far more than anyone supposed, counted that a real shame, but no one paid their opinion any heed.

Then Caroline's baby was born and proved to be a son. Christened Henry George Neville Delbraith, the boy bore all the physical hallmarks of a true Delbraith. Viewing said signs with due concern, Caroline swore that, come hell or high water, her son would never be touched by the Delbraith curse.

On the morning of the christening, Julian arrived at the church, sat with his mother and sisters, then under Caroline's baleful eye, feeling very much like the wicked witch of the fables, he passed his entirely innocuous christening gift to his mother to convey to his nephew, and immediately the service was concluded, shook his brother's hand, civilly wished his sister-in-law and the bundle held tightly—protectively—in her arms well, and drove himself back to London.

Subsequently, Julian only called on his mother and sisters when Caroline, and preferably baby Henry, too, were not—at least at that moment—under the same roof. If George was about, Julian would look in on him, but with such dissimilar characters and the weight of the title on George's shoulders, the brothers had never had all that much in common; a comment, a shared observation, and they parted, amicably, but distantly.

Meanwhile Julian filled his life with his customary round of gambling and dissipation; cards, dice, horse racing— anything racing—he was always willing to gauge the odds and sport his blunt accordingly. Dalliance, with Cyprians initially, but increasingly with bored matrons of his own class, filled whatever time he had to spare. His reputation as a wine connoisseur continued, but no one could recall ever seeing him in his cups. Then again, it was widely acknowledged that being three sheets to the wind while wagering large sums was never a winning proposition, and everyone knew Julian took his worship at the altar of his family's curse very seriously.

And the years rolled on.

Through those years, if any had requested enlightenment as to Lord Julian Delbraith's financial state from anyone in the ton, the answer would have been that Lord Julian was certain to be one step away from point-non-plus. From falling into the River Tick and very likely drowning. To all seasoned observers it was inconceivable that anyone could maintain such a profligate lifestyle, and wager so consistently and so extravagantly, without outrunning the constable. Gamblers always lost, if not immediately, then ultimately; everyone knew that.

Caroline, Duchess of Ridgware, certainly subscribed to that view. More, she believed her feckless brother-in-law was draining the family coffers, but whenever she attempted to raise the issue with her husband, George scowled and told her she was mistaken. When, driven by the need to protect her son's inheritance, she pressed, George's lips tightened and he coldly and categorically assured her that Julian received only the modest quarterly stipend due to him under their father's will and nothing more—that Julian had never requested further funds from the estate, not even from George personally. Caroline didn't believe it, but faced with her husband's uncharacteristic flash of temper she had to accept his word and retreat.

In actual fact, only two people knew the truth about Lord Julian's financial position—his gentlemen's gentleman, Rundle, and Jordan Draper, the son of the family's man of business. At Julian's request Jordan had assumed the handling of Julian's financial affairs, thus separating them from his brother's ducal holdings. Only those two knew that Julian was one of the Delbraiths who cropped up every third or so generation. He was one of the Delbraiths who won. He didn't win every bet, but over any period of time he always came out ahead. Not since he had, at the age of five, first discovered the joys of wagering had he ever ended a week a true loser; some weeks he only gained a farthing, but overall, he never, ever, lost money.

It fascinated Jordan Draper that no one had ever questioned why it was that a family as old as the Delbraiths, cursed with such a ruinous compulsion, had never run themselves or their estates into the ground. Through his association with

Julian, Jordan knew the answer. Grandfather, father, son—over the three generations, one male at least would have the winning touch. Of course, that no longer mattered as, thanks to Lucasta and her influence on Marcus and subsequently George, the family was no longer hostage to the curse. The curse had been defeated . . . but in administering Julian's accounts and investments, Jordan had to wonder if, all in all, the family truly was better off.

Consequently, Julian's life, along with his extravagant lifestyle, rolled on largely uneventfully. He was well aware of the ton's view of him; the knowledge reinforced his natural cynicism and made him inwardly smile.

Until late one night in 1811, a knock fell on the street door of his lodgings in Duke Street.

It was November, and the weather had turned bleak. Few of the ton were still in town, which explained why Julian was sitting by his fire, his feet propped on a stool and an open book in one hand. At the knock, he'd raised his head; hearing Rundle's footsteps pass the parlor on the way to the front door, he waited, vaguely wondering—

"My lord!" Rundle burst into the room without knocking, not his usual practice. "It's Higginbotham from Ridgware."

Looking past Rundle at the senior groom from his brother's estate, taking in the man's disheveled appearance and grave face, Julian straightened. "My mother?"

Higginbotham blinked, then shook his head. "No, m'lord. It's your brother."

"George?" Julian couldn't imagine why George would have sent Higginbotham racing to town to summon him, the wastrel younger brother. "What's he want?"

Higginbotham looked like he'd swallowed his tongue, but then he shook his head again. "His Grace don't want anything. He put a pistol to his head and pulled the trigger. He's dead. We think you'd better come."

Julian drove like the devil and reached Ridgware midmorning. Leaving his phaeton in the stable yard, he crossed to the house, entering via the side door. A pall had fallen over the mansion; the silence was oppressive. His footsteps echoed as he walked onto the tiles of the front hall. For a moment he stood silently, at a loss. Higginbotham had known nothing of what had driven George to such a rash and irreversible act. To an act so out of character.

To an act so *inexplicable*.

A sound down one corridor had Julian turning.

From the shadows, an older man in a fastidiously neat dark suit emerged. "Thank you for coming so promptly, my lord."

Lips tight, Julian nodded. "Draper." This was Draper senior, his brother's man of business, Jordan's father. The Draper offices were in Derby, much nearer than London. Julian searched Draper's face. "Do you have any idea why George . . . I still can't believe it . . . why he took his life?"

Sober and solemn, Draper nodded; he looked pale, worn down—significantly more aged than Julian remembered him. "Sadly, my lord, I do. That's why I was relieved the staff had taken it upon themselves to send for you. This is a bad business, and we'll need decisions made quickly if we're to protect the family."

"Protect . . . ?" Julian frowned. "I don't understand."

"I know." Draper waved down the corridor. "If you will come to the office, I'll endeavor to explain."

Julian hesitated. "My mother?"

"Prostrated by the shock, as is the duchess, but the doctor was here yesterday and both were sedated. I'm told they might wake in a few hours."

"My sisters? And Henry? Good God, the poor boy's the duke now."

"Indeed, but the staff have the young people well in hand, and I fear . . ." Draper broke off and rubbed his forehead. "I fear our discussion won't wait, my lord. In such a situation, time is of the essence."

Draper was a solid man, a steady, unruffleable, conscientious man, which was one reason Julian had chosen his son as his own man of affairs. Growing even more puzzled—more alarmed—Julian nodded. "Very well." He gestured. "Lead on."

Following Draper down the corridor, he asked, "When did it happen?"

"Yesterday morning, my lord. The staff heard the shot at eleven o'clock, I believe. They had to break down the library door, but of course there was nothing they could do."

Julian had had time to think during the long hours of the drive. "How many others know of George's death?"

"At the moment, my lord, I believe the knowledge is restricted to the indoor staff, the stable staff, and the family. And the doctor and myself, of course."

"So we have a chance of concealing the suicide." His first

thought was for his sisters, his mother, for Henry, and even for his sister-in-law; a suicide in the family, whatever the reason, cast a long social shadow.

Draper hesitated before saying, "Possibly." He didn't sound at all certain.

Julian followed Draper into the estate office.

Draper waved him to the chair behind the desk. "It will make it easier for me to show you the accounts."

"Accounts?" Lowering himself into the chair, Julian frowned. "Why do I need to see the accounts?"

Lifting a heavy ledger from a shelf, Draper turned and met his gaze. "I regret to inform you, my lord, that your brother wasn't, as was generally supposed, immune to the Delbraith curse."

"**H**ell's *bells!*" Julian speared the fingers of both hands through his hair and stared at the evidence of George's addiction. In the past half hour, Draper had laid ledger after ledger before him, driving home one very simple fact.

George had succeeded where all Delbraiths before him had failed. He'd run the estate into the ground, then had compounded the damage by mortgaging every last asset to the hilt.

Lowering his hands, Julian sat back. "All right." His mind was whirling, juggling figures and sums, chances and possibilities. He now understood why Draper had wanted him there. "Tot up the sum. All of it. And send for Jordan—tell him to bring all my current accounts."

"Yes, my lord." Draper hesitated, then admitted, "I took it upon myself to send for Jordan earlier—he should arrive within the hour."

Julian raised his gaze to the older man's face. "That was strangely presumptuous of you." He said it without heat, more as a question.

Draper met his gaze. "I apologize, my lord, but I've known you and your brother since you were infants. I knew the family could count on your help, and, as I've said, we—"

"Don't have time." Julian grimaced, then nodded curtly. "Very well." He pushed back his chair. "I'm going up to see my sisters. Send for me when Jordan arrives."

H₂ He found Millicent, Cassandra, and Edwina in the small upstairs parlor they used as their own. They'd been informed that George had died, but they had been told nothing else. However, having heard the shot and witnessed the resulting furor, they were more than capable of putting two and two together.

"He killed himself, didn't he?" Millicent, fourteen years old and bidding fair to becoming another Lucasta, sat sideways along the window seat, knees to her chest, and cut straight to the heart of the matter.

Having exchanged kisses and longer-and-tighter-than-usual hugs with all three, Julian sat on the cushion beyond Millicent's toes and hesitated, wondering what he could spare them, whether he should . . .

Cassie, eleven, snorted. "Just *tell* us—you know we'll get it out of the staff if you don't."

Julian sighed and complied, keeping an eye on Edwina, just ten, to make sure nothing he said was too much of a shock.

"But . . . why?" Millicent frowned. "It's a thoroughly horrible thing to do—he must have had a reason."

This was the tricky part. "I understand from Draper that George had begun gambling. It seems the curse had caught up with him, and rather than risk the estate and his family, George . . . well, he put a stop to it."

Julian hoped they would swallow the white lie.

All three frowned, considering, then Cassie humphed. "That sounds like George. So stuffy that he couldn't bear asking you for help." Cassie turned her gray eyes on Julian. "You've been living with the curse all your life and it's never hurt you—and you've never hurt the estate or the family, either."

He managed a weak smile. "Sadly, George wasn't me."

"No." Millie swung her legs down and briefly clasped his arm. "You're made of much sterner stuff. But what about the taint? Of suicide, I mean?"

"You don't need to worry about that. The doctor left a note saying that in the circumstances he would suggest we put it about that George died suddenly and unexpectedly of apoplexy."

The three thought for a moment, then Edwina said, "Well, then, I suppose what we need to do next is get some mourning clothes so we can see George off in proper style."

Millie grimaced. "True. He might have been an idiot, but he was our noble idiot and he sacrificed himself for us, so we should at least do him proud in the matter of his funeral."

From the corner of his eye, Julian spotted a gig, driven by Jordan Draper, come bowling up the drive.

"We should go and talk to Mama," Cassie said. "Discussing clothes might cheer her up, or at least take her mind off the manner of George's passing." She looked at Julian. "Have you seen her yet?"

"No. Not yet." He paused, then said, "Why don't you three go and distract her, and tell her I'm here, and that I'll be up to speak with her as soon as I can?" He rose along with the girls. "I have to go and sort things out with Draper, just to get everything squared away. Tell Mama I'll come up as soon as I've finished."

His sisters nodded and hugged him again, then they all quit the parlor. Parting from the girls in the corridor, Julian surreptitiously sighed with relief; that had gone better than he'd hoped.

He spent the next hours with the Drapers, father and son, then they were joined by Minchinbury, the family solicitor. The office was crowded with all four of them in it, but no one suggested they take their discussions into a less secure and well-shielded room.

Minchinbury confirmed that George's will named Julian as sole executor, and also joint guardian of three-year-old Henry. In regard to the latter, Julian merely nodded and set that problem aside for later; one hellish scenario at a time.

"There's no way around it," Jordan eventually concluded. "No matter how we structure payments, even if we liquidate every saleable unentailed asset and devote the entirety of the estate income to said payments, the outgoings still far exceed the duke's ability to pay."

While they'd been going over the horrendous figures, a plan had taken shape in Julian's mind. It was beyond outrageous, but outrageous was something he did well. Across the desk, he met Jordan's eyes. "Factor in my funds—all of them. Liquidate my assets, all of them, and add them in, too—reduce the capital owed. Leave me . . ." He considered, then said, "Ten thousand in cash. Assume an ongoing income through me of . . ." That took a little longer to calculate, but eventually he named a sum.

Draper and Minchinbury looked startled, but Jordan only grimaced, jotted down the figures, and started reworking the complex web of mortgage and loan repayments again.

While he did, Draper and Minchinbury traded looks . . . and slowly worked out Julian's direction. It was Minchinbury who, faintly shocked, finally looked at Julian. "My lord . . . what are you planning?"

Julian held up a finger and patiently waited while Jordan did his sums.

Eventually, Jordan blew out a breath. "We're close. Just a whisker in it." He looked at Julian. "You could pull it off."

Julian hadn't needed to explain to Jordan what he was thinking of doing; Jordan had worked for him for long enough to guess what he might, and could, do, but he was grateful for the younger man's unequivocal support. "You've included the running of this house and the estate in general, the usual payments to my mother, the girls, and the duchess, and left the girls' portions intact?"

"Well, the girls' portions are already long gone," Jordan

said, "but that will return them to their previous amounts by the time each of them reach sixteen. I've also included an escalating amount for Henry in the years to come, starting from his fifth birthday."

"Good man." Julian paused to gather his arguments, then transferred his gaze to Draper and Minchinbury. "What I'm proposing to do, gentlemen, is this."

He told them his plan, the whole of it; if he was to succeed in saving the Delbraiths—family, title, and estate—he needed them on his side. At first, they were shocked, then aghast as the full ramifications of what he was proposing came clear in their minds, but finally, like Jordan, they, too, accepted that, when it came to it, he had no other choice.

George had taken the easy way out and left Julian to rescue the Delbraiths.

His interview with his mother was difficult, not least because Lucasta was inclined to blame herself for George's disgrace.

Seated in an armchair angled before the wide window in her sitting room, a still handsome woman with graying hair pulled back from a grief-stricken face, she clenched a damp handkerchief in one fist. "I should have seen it! I can't *believe* I missed the signs."

Contrary to general assumptions, Julian got along well with his mother; they were much alike when it came to will. They'd long ago reached an accommodation; Lucasta didn't try to push him, and he didn't push back.

Standing gazing out over the rolling lawns to the trees of the home wood, he sighed. "Mama, if *I* didn't see anything, there wasn't anything to be seen. He was . . . excellent at hiding it."

"He deceived us. He *betrayed* us." After a moment, in a quieter voice, Lucasta asked, "For how long?"

Julian hesitated, but he knew better than to try to lie to her. Turning, he said, "According to Draper, since he started at Eton, but initially the amounts were small enough not to alert Papa or you. Only after he inherited did he start wagering larger sums."

Helplessly, Lucasta shook her head. "You never heard any whisper?"

"No." Which said a great deal about what establishments George had frequented. Any socially accepted hell, and Julian would have heard of it, so George had slid into the underworld to sate his addiction.

Slowly, Lucasta drew in a deep breath, then exhaled and raised her chin. "What's done is done. We'll do as Doctor Melrose suggested—George died of an apoplexy. We'll bury him with all due circumstance. And then"—she looked at Julian—"we'll pick up the pieces and rebuild." She paused, eyes narrowing on him. "So." She heaved a tight sigh. "Given George blew out his brains rather than face the consequences, tell me—how bad is it?"

He didn't try to soften the news—pointless where she was concerned. His mother had always been fierce in defense of her family; she would detect any prevarication and, terrier-like, drag the truth from him. So he drew up another armchair, sat and told her all, and when the shock, unsurprisingly, held her stunned and silent, he smoothly continued, "I've spoken with the Drapers, both of them, and with Minchinbury, and worked out a plan. It's desperate, but for us these are desperate times. They've agreed that it's our only possible way forward—we've canvassed every other course, and none will get us through this except what I propose."

She looked him in the eye. "I'm not going to like your plan, am I?"

"No, but it is the only plan we have." He proceeded to tell her the whole of it.

She heard him out in silence.

Then they argued.

That he'd expected; he held to his guns and eventually, bit by bit, inch by inch, she backed down.

Except, to his surprise, over one aspect, and on that she wouldn't budge, wouldn't shift, would not concede.

"I have lost one son—I will not lose you, too. *No!*" She held up a hand. "I appreciate that to be successful your plan makes open association impossible, *but*"—she fixed her eyes on his—"you will continue to visit this house, to visit me and your sisters. They are my daughters and are as capable of keeping your secrets as I am. You will *not* cut yourself off from us—and I assure you we will not let you go." Her eyes filled. "That, my dear, is something you cannot ask of us. If your plan is to succeed, you will need to factor that in."

He hadn't expected such a vehement reaction. Searching her face, knowing her adamantine will, he reconsidered, then nodded. "Very well. But my visits will be, for want of a better word, furtive."

"Secret." She nodded. "You know the staff will do anything for you, so that won't be a problem."

"The girls . . ." He grimaced. "I'll leave it to you to tell them—you'll know better than I how to put it, and I don't have time for the inevitable arguments and explanations. Jordan and I must leave for London as soon as possible. If we're to paper over the gaping holes George has left in the family's financial façade, we need to act immediately."

Lucasta's eyes searched his face, then she quietly asked, "And Caroline? I'll explain to her if you wish."

Lips thinning, he shook his head. "No—I'll speak with her. She's Henry's other guardian. She and I are going to have to find a way to work together, for Henry's sake if nothing else."

He rose.

Lucasta rose, too, gripped his arm, and stretched up to plant a kiss on his cheek. "Go, my dear. I know you must."

She released him and turned away, but not before he saw a tear slide down her cheek.

His interview with his sister-in-law set the seal on a long and horrendous day.

As he approached her suite, he saw Draper and Minchinbury emerge from Caroline's sitting room. They closed the door behind them and came along the gallery. When he and the pair met, they all halted.

Minchinbury spoke. "I've explained the terms of the will to the duchess. She understands that you are sole executor and also her son's co-guardian, and comprehends the rights that are yours by virtue of those facts."

Julian felt his lips twist. "And how did she take that news?"

Minchinbury grimaced. "Not well, but she had to be told. At least she now knows and understands the situation."

"We also informed her of the financial straits the late duke left behind." Draper's lips primmed. "I explained that, contrary to her long-held belief, you have never drained any undue resources from the estate, and that the current situation has arisen entirely through the late duke's depredations. We did not, of course, venture to explain your plan, although we did allude to the fact that you had one, and that, given the situation, we believe it is the only route by which the family, and indeed the dukedom, can be saved from financial devastation."

Julian looked from one to the other. "Let me see if I understand this correctly—you've left the duchess knowing that whatever I propose, she must agree if she wishes to save herself and her son from ruin?"

Both men thought, then both nodded. "We"—Minchinbury flicked a glance at Draper—"have been privy to the duchess's view of you, my lord, and considered it our duty to clarify matters for Her Grace so that your words should fall on more fertile soil."

Draper nodded. "Least we could do to assist you with your plan."

Julian inclined his head. "Thank you, gentlemen. I appreciate your assistance."

Both bowed and stepped back. Minchinbury said, "If you need any assistance subsequently, my lord, please know you have only to ask."

Julian nodded and continued along the corridor. Reaching Caroline's sitting room, he didn't pause to let himself think but tapped on the door. Hearing a muffled "Come," he turned the knob and entered.

Caroline was standing with her back to the window, her arms wrapped tightly about her. Inclining his head, Julian closed the door, then walked toward her. "My condolences. I would it were otherwise, but we have to talk." Halting a yard away, he met her blue eyes. "Minchinbury and Draper told me they'd explained the situation. Is there anything about it you don't understand?" He kept his tone even, uninflected and distantly polite.

Her face stripped of all masks, Caroline stared up at him; he could see the emotions, the questions, the rage, roiling behind her eyes. In the end, she rasped out one word, hoarse and ragged. "*Why?*"

Julian shook his head. "He couldn't help himself."

"But—" She broke off, then waved a hand and looked away. "I can't . . ." She hauled in a breath and, lifting her head, continued without looking at him. "I'm still finding it hard to . . . accept that, for all these years, while I've been imagining you the villain, it was him all along."

Julian frowned. "You suspected?"

"Not him." She laughed harshly. "Never him. But some of my jewelry—it's paste, not real. Even some of what used to be real is now paste." She glanced at Julian. "I thought he'd used the jewels to pay your debts, perhaps thinking that I would never notice the difference in the stones, and that in his mind that was better than drawing from the estate—" Her breath hitched and she swung away. "Oh, you needn't tell me—I can't believe how stupid I've been."

He didn't have time for hysterics, even of this sort. "Caroline—if I'm to avert financial catastrophe, I need to act quickly."

She cast him a bitter glance. "According to Minchinbury and Draper, I have no choice but to allow you to do whatever you wish, not if I want to continue to live here in comfort with Henry, or for my son to have any kind of future at all."

This was the downside of the older men's well-intentioned interference. "In that, they're correct, but what they didn't make clear was that for my plan to succeed, you, too, need to play a part. And for that, you need to know what the plan is."

Caroline considered him for a long moment, then settled on her feet facing him, arms tightly folded, and nodded. "All right. Tell me your plan."

She didn't sit, much less invite him to. So he stood and told her his plan.

When he'd finished, she stared all but openmouthed at him.

After a minute ticked by, he baldly asked, "Well? Will you do your part? Play the role you obviously have to play to carry the fiction off?"

She blinked, stared again. "I . . . don't understand."

His temper was getting the better of him. "It's a simple enough question. Will you—"

"No, not that. I . . ." She lowered her arms and drew a huge breath. She paused for a second, then, her gaze on his face, said, "You're proposing to sacrifice yourself. *Why?* That's what I don't understand—what I don't trust. If I accept this plan of yours and actively support it, I'll be placing myself, and even more my son and his future, in utterly insurmountable debt to you."

He thought, then nodded. "True."

She laughed, a broken, discordant sound, and turned away.

"Caroline." By main force, he kept his tone even, calm. "Are you really proposing to let your pride dictate your actions even now, and to reject my help?"

She glanced at him, met his eyes.

A distant, high-pitched shriek reached him—a sound of happiness, not despair. Glancing through the window, he saw his sisters and Henry come out of the wood. They'd been for a walk and were returning, Millie and Cassie swinging a delighted Henry between them. He was only three; the reality of his father's death hadn't yet touched him. Two footmen and a nursemaid followed behind, talking quietly while they watched over the foursome.

Julian looked at Caroline. He was much taller; she couldn't see what he could.

Although tempted to grasp her arm and haul her across, he beckoned to her and stepped closer to the window. "You want to know why I'm doing this?" When she joined him, he pointed at the group below. "That's why. None of the four down there—hell, none of the seven—have done anything to deserve the future they will have if I don't act to fix this. And there is only one way."

He watched her watching her son and let that sink in.

After a moment, she moistened her lips and more quietly asked, "No other way?"

He hesitated, then said, "The Delbraith curse got the family into this. It's only right that the Delbraith curse get us out of it again."

"But at what cost?"

"Regardless of the cost. And, ultimately, that's my decision to make, not yours."

She continued watching for a moment more, then her features firmed and she nodded. "All right. I agree. I'll do whatever I have to to . . . shore up the situation."

One hurdle down. He drew breath, metaphorically girded his loins, and approached the next, the even higher and more thorny one. "Speaking of the curse, I have one stipulation which is entirely nonnegotiable. In return for acting as I must to save the family—yourself and Henry included—you will ensure that Henry knows the truth about his father's death, that it's never hidden from him."

"*What?*" Caroline swung to face him. "You can't be serious! He's a baby—"

"Not now, obviously. I mean as soon as he's old enough to know—to ask. Because he will. I don't want you hiding the curse from him." He held her gaze. "I'm not doing what I'm about to do only to have you encourage him to think he's immune to the curse and so throw everything away the instant he reaches his majority." She opened her mouth. Julian pointed a finger at her nose and spoke first. "What's more, when I come to visit, as his guardian I'll expect to meet him, to talk with him. You can be present if you wish, but I will speak with him."

Caroline's face set. "No. I won't have you—"

"Caroline." The steel in his voice cut her off. He held her gaze and ruthlessly stated, "Neither you nor Mama saw the curse in George. Try to 'protect' Henry, and you'll make the same mistake Mama made with George. The curse will still bite, but he'll hide it. If he does, you won't see it. I will because I know what to look for—and I assure you that with Henry, I'll be watching." He searched her eyes. "Understand this— the curse is real. It's an inherited disease—if Henry gets help, the right help, it can be managed. Pretend it's not there and it will eat him alive, just as it did George."

"And what about you?" Caroline produced a credible sneer. "Is your addiction so well managed then?"

He was silent for a moment, then said, "As things stand, my addiction is what's going to stand between you and Henry and the poorhouse. Think about that before you dismiss my use of it. Also as things stand, I'm the only one living who has personal experience of the curse—who knows what Henry will face as he grows, who knows the tricks of dealing with the compulsion." He paused for a moment, his eyes locked with hers, then more quietly said, "I know this is hard for you to accept, but as matters stand, I am Henry's only hope for a future, both financially and personally."

Until he'd said the words, he hadn't realized how true they were—how much responsibility he was taking on.

Not that it mattered; in this he had no choice.

When Caroline said nothing, simply chewed her lower lip and looked shaken and lost, he stepped back and turned to the door. With his hand on the knob, he paused, then glanced back at her. "Don't risk your son, Caroline—if you want to keep him safe, you'll do exactly as I've said."

She swung to face the window and didn't reply.

Julian opened the door and left.

Half an hour later, having bid good-bye to his sisters and his small nephew, Julian tooled his phaeton down the long drive, then whipped up his horses and headed for London.

In the small hours of the morning, he drew rein outside the stables near his lodgings. Handing over the ribbons to a sleepy stable lad, Julian walked slowly out into the street.

Sinking his hands into his greatcoat pockets, through the quiet darkness, he strolled toward Duke Street, and finally allowed himself to think of what he was about to do, something he'd refused to dwell on during the long journey; the activity smacked too much of a dying man's last thoughts.

Reaching his lodgings, he climbed the steps, put his key to the lock, and opened the door.

Stepping inside, he shut the door.

And his life as Lord Julian Delbraith was, quite simply, no more.

The Treaty of the Kingdoms of Fire & Ice,
Or,

THE IMPOSTER BRIDE

Gaelen Foley

Prince Tor of Rydalburg threw down his sword, chest heaving, his face streaked with dried blood and black powder. The din of battle still rang in his ears. The smell of cannon fire clung to his sweat-drenched uniform, and his shoulder ached from wielding the weapon for countless hours. But he had fulfilled his task. Another war won.

"What are you waiting for? Call the attack!" cried King Hakon. "Don't just stand there. Finish them!"

"They are finished, Father. What more do you want me to do? I've already cut off their general's bloody leg. Trust me. I know this foe. They are defeated," he said wearily. "They just need a moment to let that fact sink in." He couldn't even remember the cause of this particular episode of the longstanding conflict between the neighboring kingdoms of Rydalburg and Saardova.

But his father was, predictably, unsatisfied. The older man, slightly shorter and much stouter than he, sent Tor a glare, then marched over to the artillery captain and pointed past the groaning southern army spread out across the plain below them. "Aim for the city," he instructed. "I want nothing left of their capital but rubble—"

"Belay that order," Tor clipped out sharply.

His father turned to him in shock. "What did you say?"

"There is no need for this. There are women and children in that city, Father."

"You lack the killer instinct of your ancestors, son. Let me show you how it's done."

"Sire, hear me out! Saving face is everything to the Saardovans. If we humiliate them with destruction of their city on top of defeat, they will opt for a proud but senseless death over surrender." Then he snorted. "They likely would've quit all this by now if it weren't for their stupid hothead, Prince Orsino."

"So?" His father scoffed. "Let them fight. We will pound them into dust. Now, give the order to the gun-crews."

"I will not, sir."

"How dare you defy me?" His father stepped closer, fixing him with a pugnacious glare despite the fact that he was half a foot shorter than Tor. "I gave you an order! I am your father and your King!"

"And I am your successor, and when you're dead, I would like there to be something left for me to rule. Besides," he added calmly, "why would I break a vase I'm about to own?"

"What?" Hakon furrowed his brow, turning as Tor moved past him to gaze out across the bloodied plain.

"Be happy, Sire," he murmured. "I'm about to double the size of our holdings."

"How do you intend to do that?"

"By marrying the Princess of Saardova." He beckoned for

the messenger, then put together a small contingent to ride out for a parley. "The price of my mercy."

All that had been three months ago, and now, here they were, on the morning the wedding caravan was to set out from the lush, exotic capital of sensual Saardova, a place full of mystery and whimsy, kissed by ocean breezes.

So he'd heard. His bride was expected to arrive by tonight. Tor wanted the marriage treaty sealed up by tomorrow. Not the most romantic way of looking at his pending nuptials, perhaps, but then, unseemly emotionalism was the domain of the Saardovans.

Sentimentality was promptly beaten out of young Rydalburg children before they reached puberty. They were a warrior people of Viking origin, long since settled in their little corner of the Alps. Disciplined, hard, matter-of-fact. This practical nature had allowed King Hakon to come around to Tor's plan once the old chieftain's rage had puttered out.

He still fumed a little now and then about it. "A mistress, yes, but I can't believe you're willing to marry some sleazy southern belly dancer."

"Now, Sire, that is no way to speak about my future wife. They say the Princess Giulietta is a great beauty."

And a great pain in the arse, Tor admitted to himself, but he did not say it aloud.

No need to bait his father.

Besides, he was not surprised in the least by what his spies had reported. All Saardovans were famously temperamental, as fiery as they liked their food. With her royal blood, Princess Giulietta had apparently got a larger-than-usual dose of lowland spice in her nature. She was rumored to be notoriously difficult, manageable only by her chief lady-in-waiting, Minerva de Messina, the daughter of the very general whose leg he had cut off in the heat of battle.

Tor winced slightly. No doubt he had made a sworn enemy of this young woman, who was universally respected in her city as a model of womanly dignity and virtue. Or at least, what passed for virtue among that race of seducers.

He had been weighing the possible cost in girlish tantrums that he might pay if he forbade Giulietta from bringing her best friend to Rydalburg, but then his spies had told him there was no need for concern.

Lady Minerva would not be accompanying the princess to her new home. Oddly enough, she had been accepted as the first female ever allowed to enroll in the University of Saardova. Tor shrugged off this bizarre notion.

All that mattered to him was that the lady scholar was staying behind. He did not need a sworn enemy in the palace undermining him with his new bride.

Rumor had it that Lady Minerva was the only one who could keep a rein on the rebellious princess, her junior by a couple of years, but no matter. Giulietta would quickly learn how to behave herself properly once she got here.

His sister, Princess Katarina, a maiden as pure as the winter snows, would help to make a lady of her. Tor himself was also prepared to be a good, calm influence on his spoiled Saardovan bride, for nothing ever really moved him.

His own nature was cool and controlled. Let her rail away; tears; yelling; it did not signify. She might come to hate him. In fact, from what he heard, she already did. But he did not particularly care.

What mattered was that the war was over. He had expanded his territory and ended the strain it put on his people. As for this marriage, why, it was only a tool of political expediency.

No doubt it was not what Giulietta's girlish heart and overemotional southern nature would have hoped for, but too bad. All that unseemly romantic rot was the purview of slimy Saardovans like her brother, Prince Orsino.

Falling in love? Rydalburg warriors like Tor scoffed at the notion.

It was as absurd as a female attending university.

"I know, daughter, this was not what you had envisioned for your life. But the House of Messina will always do its duty."

"Yes, Papa," Minerva quietly agreed.

Her father laid his hands tenderly on her shoulders and gazed down into her soulful brown eyes.

General Farouk de Messina, commander of Saardova's beaten army, had lost a leg to Rydalburg along with the battle. But the keenest loss of all was at hand. They both knew disaster was the likely result if she did not go with her flighty royal friend.

A rare tear glistened in the general's one good eye. (The other was covered by the eye patch.) "Defeat is bitter enough without also having to say farewell to my little girl," he said abruptly, lurching forward on his peg leg to embrace her.

Minerva hugged him back, squeezing her eyes shut

against her tears. "All will be well, Papa," she tried to comfort him, knowing how much he blamed himself for everything. "No one could have led our forces better against those barbarians. We were outnumbered, and besides, they had the high ground. Wave after wave of those terrible cavalry charges . . ." She shuddered. "What infantry could withstand them? But at least now our people will have peace."

"As long as Her Highness can bear to do her duty."

Pulling back, Minerva smiled fondly at the old, sunweathered soldier. "Don't worry, Papa. If I have to drag Giulietta up to the altar myself, I will not let anything disrupt your treaty with the Horse Danes. Not even the tantrums of the most spoiled princess in the Mediterranean," she added in a confidential whisper.

"Go. Before I refuse to part with you."

"I love you, Papa."

"And I you." With tears in his eyes, he kissed her on the forehead then released her and sent her on her way.

Minerva drew her silken scarlet veil across the lower half of her face and headed for the door.

She paused in the doorway, however, glancing back uncertainly. For a moment, facing the prospect of being an exile, forced to dwell in enemy territory far from home, she feared her heart might break.

"What is it?" her father asked. "Did you forget to pack something?"

"Oh, Papa," she whispered, fairly quivering with her hidden rage. "How am I to stomach being in the same room with the man who did this to you?" she burst out. "It's bad enough poor, silly Giulietta has to marry this barbarian, but after what he did to you—"

"Now, now," he chided, glancing down ruefully at the sturdy wooden peg below his left knee. "It was a fair blow, and neatly executed."

"Papa! What a dense, perfectly male thing to say. You could have died!"

He gave her a hard look. "Prince Tor had the chance to kill me when I was on the ground; he did not. Remember that."

She let out a disgruntled sigh.

"None of us likes the terms of his treaty, Minerva, but if King Hakon had had his way, trust me, it would have been much worse. Because of the prince, we finally have a chance at lasting peace. Provided Her Highness doesn't ruin it for the rest of us."

"I won't let her," Minerva grumbled. "That's the only reason I'm doing this."

"I know," he answered softly, pride shining in his leathery face. "Farewell, my dear. Now go."

Minerva tore her gaze away from him and obeyed him, going out to where the royal guards waited to escort her back to Giulietta and the palazzo.

As she climbed down into the waiting gondola, she looked her last upon the sunny villa and committed it to memory: the brightly colored tiles of the fountain lilting in the central courtyard; the shady grape arbor where she had spent endless hours studying her books; the mounds of bright bougainvillea burgeoning against the whitewashed walls; and the swaying palm trees peeking above the red-tiled roof.

As the royal guards poled her gondola through the lazy waters of the canal, she imprinted the sights of buildings and bridges on her mind, saying a particularly woeful farewell in her heart to the great University as they floated past. She was to have begun her classes in the autumn, but it seemed her country needed her to serve another role. She hung her head with a pang.

But if Papa was willing to give up a leg and an eye for Saardova, this was the least that she could do.

When her gondola drifted up to the restricted landing behind the royal palazzo, she found the entire wedding caravan gathered there. Everyone who would be traveling to Rydalburg had assembled. The camels were laden with luggage. The royal guards' Arabian horses pranced in place and tossed their long manes, as if the morning air made them eager to be under way. At least today they wouldn't be charging into a battle, she thought wryly.

Near the brightly adorned royal elephant she saw Giulietta surrounded by ambassadors and dignitaries, her royal mother weeping by her side.

Minerva braced herself to join the fray.

But then, a familiar face emerged from the crowd: Crown Prince Orsino, Giulietta's elder brother, abandoned the throng of well-wishers and came to hand Minerva up from her boat.

Black-haired and fiery-eyed, the Prince of Saardova was the object of countless ladies' dreams, but privately, Minerva found him a bit of a headache with his touchy pride, his moods—and his wandering hands.

Saardovan men were known for their passionate nature,

which was probably half the reason they went to war with their northern neighbors once a decade.

Certainly it was why they insisted on taking several wives—at least the nobles. They had, they claimed, needs too powerful for any one woman to satisfy.

To Minerva, this backward and degrading practice, this excuse for lewd selfishness, was the reason she had privately made up her mind not to marry. One wife, one husband was quite sufficient.

At least the Rydalburgers had that much right.

Perhaps it was just as well that she was moving away, she thought as Orsino steadied her on solid ground. She suspected that the prince had it in the back of his mind to propose to her one day, and if he did, she did not see how she could get out of it.

He flashed a white-toothed smile. "My lady Minerva." He kissed her hand before escorting her toward his sister. "It's not going to be the same around here with you girls gone," he said with a sigh. "Who will I get to tease?"

"Oh, I'm sure you will find someone," she said wryly.

He stopped and turned to her with the morning sunlight dancing in his black, tousled curls. "You will look after her, won't you? I know I've always been a beastly brother, but I do care about my little sister."

"Of course, Your Highness," she said fondly in spite of herself.

His gaze caressed her. "You put my mind at ease," he replied in his effortlessly beguiling tone. "We all feel better knowing the brat will have you with her. Voice of reason whispering in her ear."

"Are you sure you won't come to the wedding, Your Highness?" she asked, changing the subject. "It would mean so much to your sister—"

"No." He held up his hand and looked away with a blaze of anger registering in his midnight eyes. "I cannot. Do not ask it of me. If this alliance spares our people, then so be it. But you must excuse me if I cannot bear to stand by and watch my baby sister married off to my mortal enemy."

"I understand. Be well, Your Highness." She curtsied and took leave of the prince, rejoining her royal mistress.

The eighteen-year-old Giulietta finished her tearful good-byes to her parents and her brother, then she and Minerva and the other ladies-in-waiting climbed up the dainty little ladder into the howdah perched atop the royal elephant's back.

With that, the wedding caravan set out: camels, wagons, horses, all. Gaily festooned as they all were, Giulietta held back her tears as they rode through the streets of Saardova.

She waved gracefully and with great drama to her people. The citizens, half cheering, half weeping for her, threw flower petals in the air and thanked her for how she was about to sacrifice herself to the barbarian prince.

In the distance Minerva could see the cobalt waters of the Mediterranean, the white sails of colorful fishing boats and the mighty war vessels that had done her homeland no good whatsoever against an inland foe.

Ah, well.

They rode in silence for some time after they had cleared the city and set out across the plain that had been the battlefield. It was quiet now, but grave markers here and there studded the fields where the fallen from both sides had been buried.

The princess leaned on the edge of the howdah and gazed off into the distance. "It's so unfair. I'll never again stand out on my balcony and watch the sunset gild the waves and turn the gardens pink." She turned to Minerva, pouting as only a princess could pout. "Why would he not come to Saardova?"

She shrugged. "He can do whatever he wants. He won. We lost."

"And I am to be the virgin sacrifice to the barbarian for this treaty's sake?" she asked bitterly, gazing homeward again. "Doesn't anyone care what I want?"

"They say he is handsome."

"Big, blond, blue-eyed. Aren't they all? I can't even tell them apart. He doesn't have a soul. None of them do. None of them have any feelings!"

"Come now, dearest. Our views of them are probably as inaccurate as their beliefs about us. This is a chance for both sides to learn the truth about each other. You'll be starting a whole new chapter in Saardovan history."

"Pfft," she said.

Minerva laughed. The other ladies-in-waiting smiled uneasily, slowly getting over their fear as she made light of it.

"Try to think of it as an adventure," she said for all their sakes. "And don't forget, Your Highness, those mountains over which you will be queen are packed with jewels."

Giulietta sent her a sideways smile. "You always know just what to say to me."

Soon the road climbed from the fertile lowlands of Saardova toward the mountain kingdom of their enemies.

Great peaks loomed in the distance; around them, the colors changed from vibrant summer jewel tones to the dreamy watercolors seen in spring. Likewise, the temperature dropped by several degrees, and the ladies began to shiver in their delicate, flowing silks.

At the border, they were met by an elite contingent of Horse Danes, sent to escort them the rest of the way to Rydalburg. The Horse Dane cavalry officers wore smartly tailored indigo uniforms with gold epaulets and shiny gold buttons down their chests, red plumes on their gleaming helmets. They rode in perfect, precise formation—and Giulietta was right. None of their square, pale faces showed the slightest degree of emotion. They informed the wedding caravan that the journey was but three more hours.

Right on schedule (the northerners were always prompt, she'd heard), the caravan approached the walled castle-town of Rydalburg.

The ladies stared in openmouthed amazement at the white castle with its tall, fairy-tale spires.

The prince's home was nothing like the sumptuous palazzos of the lowlands, full of striped-marble columns and ogee-windows.

Its soaring lines and steep angles took Minerva's breath away, the turrets like the tips of lances thrusting at the pale Alpine sky.

They were received right away upon their arrival. The Saardovan ambassador hurried ahead of the princess and her retinue to announce Her Royal Highness to Their Majesties.

Arrayed across the dais at the far end of the great hall, waiting for them, stood the royal family of Rydalburg. King

Hakon and Queen Ingmar greeted them. Princess Katarina curtsied.

Giulietta curtsied back. The two princesses looked about the same age, but were opposites in appearance. Not much could be seen of her behind her veil, but Minerva knew Giulietta's complexion was tanned, her brown hair filled with golden streaks from the sun; her dark, thick eyebrows expressed every shade of emotion she felt.

Princess Katarina's emotions were concealed behind a serene smile on her lips and the perfect curtain wall behind her pale blue eyes. Minerva sensed the steel in her and knew at once this girl was a great deal stronger than her delicate appearance would suggest. Katarina had the porcelain complexion of all the northern ladies; her silvery-blond hair was pulled back in a sleek bun like her mother's. Both women wore high-necked, long-sleeved gowns of somber, dark-toned velvet. Minerva was rather awed by their air of dignity.

But as hard as she was trying not to look him, inevitably, her gaze wandered over to the fourth member of the royal family present: the Crown Prince, Tor of Rydalburg.

Her heart beat a trifle faster as she tried to assess him with a purely scientific eye. The broad-shouldered specimen stood well over six feet tall, towering over mere mortals like some rugged mountain rock formation. What on earth were they feeding these northern brutes to make them grow so strong and tall?

He had long golden hair that flowed back from his hard, square face like a lion's mane. His eyes were an interesting shade of stormy blue, but much too serious, of course. His nose was too big, his jawline too hard.

But his lips, well, she supposed she could find no flaw with his lips. They were nicely sculpted enough to cause an alarming stir in her spicy Saardovan blood.

Minerva tamped down the ridiculous reaction with an inward hiss at herself.

For one thing, he was about to marry her best friend. For another, he had cut off her father's leg.

And for a third, he had ruined her plans for an education, thanks to the bullying demands in his treaty.

She'd never trust him. She'd never like him. And she'd certainly never admit to finding him attractive. She was glad it was Giulietta marrying him, not her.

Yet, to be sure, there was nothing like him in Saardova.

Unless you counted the heroic marble nudes that graced the statuary niches in the piazzas and fountains back home.

His formidable physique was clearly made for warfare. But she refused to take any notice of his physical perfection. Under that polished gleam and impeccably tailored dark blue uniform coat, the man was still a Viking-bred barbarian.

Poor Giulietta.

Her Highness seemed nonplused. Giulietta offered her betrothed a begrudging curtsy; Minerva and the rest of ladies-in-waiting followed suit.

They kept their heads down and stayed silent. All the girls remained veiled, of course.

"Your Highness, I bid you welcome to our home," Prince Tor announced in clipped tones formal enough to match his ramrod, military posture. "Thank you for agreeing to our treaty. I look forward to familiarizing you with your new people and your new home once the marriage has been settled."

What poetry! Minerva mentally scoffed. *Well done. You really know how to sweep a lady off her feet. Did you practice that little speech for long? Or did your advisers write it for you?*

"My thanks for your mercy on our people," Giulietta replied, just as STET the ambassador had instructed, except that her tone bristled with haughtiness.

Tor's eyebrow lifted.

Minerva caught the glint of cynical amusement in his eyes when he looked at his spoiled bride-to-be.

He smiled at Giulietta with cool, knowing indulgence.

It was then Minerva realized rather uneasily that this warlord was a man of serious intelligence and exquisite self-control. She remembered her father's warning. *Prince Tor had the chance to kill me when I was on the ground; he did not. Remember that.* Maybe Papa was right.

Tor could have smashed Saardova into ruins but had chosen not to—and yet, here was the princess whose city and clan he had spared, treating him like some muddy farmhand.

Here was a man, she got the feeling, who was not going to be blinded by Giulietta's beauty once he saw just how beautiful she *was* beneath that veil.

Minerva glanced over at her friend, suddenly wondering if this was the perfect man for Giulietta, after all. One look at that hard face made it clear he was not going to put up with any nonsense. *The royal brat may have just met her match.* And from the look of things, she didn't like it.

"Well, that wasn't as awful as I'd expected," Tor said that night to his closest friend and fellow soldier, Rolf, after the first meeting with his exotic bride and her people in the great hall. "I'd say it all went smoothly enough."

"Yes, but what does she look like under that veil?" Rolf retorted as he poured them both a draught of vodka. "Wouldn't show her face, I hear. That can't be a good sign."

Tor smirked at him. "That's just their custom. An unmarried young lady of high birth does not appear unveiled to any male outside her own family."

"Wonder why!"

"Apparently, it's to avoid tempting the lusts of Saardovan men."

"Ah, they wouldn't be able to control themselves?" Rolf drawled in amusement.

"Apparently not."

"Well, I hope that's all it is and that your bride doesn't look like a monkey under those seductive, shimmering veils."

He clinked glasses with him ruefully. "I'll find out soon enough."

That night in the opulent apartments assigned to the princess and her ladies, everyone was tired from the long day's journey. Fatigue had done nothing to dispose Giulietta to embrace her fate. If anything, it had only made it worse. "I hate it here. He's terrifying."

"You did not think him beautiful?" one of the other ladies whispered.

Giulietta fixed her with a quelling stare. She dropped her gaze and mumbled an apology.

Minerva did her best to soothe her fretful mistress, sitting down beside her a little apart from the others and offering a sisterly hug. "It's going to be all right," she assured the younger girl. "He will give you strong, healthy children. At least there can be no question of that."

She scoffed with a look of disgust. "I don't want that beast to touch me. Who does he think he is?"

Minerva strove for patience, she knew better than to try to speak to her of duty. "You'll get used to him before long. I'm sure he has a good side. You just have to find it. Be patient. One day at a time."

Giulietta frowned.

"Try to smile, dearest," she cajoled her. "Tomorrow is your wedding day!"

Giulietta shrugged Minerva's hand off her shoulder and rose. "I'm going to bed."

Everyone curtsied as the Princess Royal retired.

The ladies exchanged a look that silently agreed her attitude had not made things any easier. Then the Saardovan maids saw to their final duties and wearily bedded down for the night.

Exhausted as she was, Minerva could not fall asleep for the longest time thinking of all the details of the wedding tomorrow. Something she had seen tonight in Giulietta's eyes worried her, a glitter of anger, a flash of hard resolve, almost as if the princess had something up her sleeve.

No doubt, Giulietta had noticed that her future husband was not the sort of man she would twist around her little finger. But the very strength that Minerva had seen in Prince

Tor gave her a cautious, newfound hope that someone else might eventually take over her long-held responsibility as Giulietta's minder—namely, him.

This just might work, after all, she mused. Who could say? A bit of structured Rydalburg discipline might be good for the brat. If Giulietta got settled into her new life more quickly than expected, then maybe *she* could return home to her father's villa and take up her classes in the autumn, just as she had planned.

At last, she drifted off to sleep, but her dreams were uneasy that night, haunted by a pair of stern blue eyes . . . and sculpted, but unsmiling lips.

"Wake up, wake up! Lady Minerva!"

Someone was shaking her. Someone who was sobbing.

"Oh, please, hurry, Minerva, we need you!"

"What?" Drawn from the depths of sleep and still groggy, Minerva opened her eyes and sat up in bed, still blinking in confusion.

Chaotic noises from the other room registered. Though barely awake, she jumped to her feet and hurried out into the sitting room, where she found the maids and the other ladies-in-waiting running about in a state of hysteria and crying.

"What's wrong? What's going on?" she exclaimed.

"She's gone! She's gone!"

"*What?*"

"We cannot find the princess! Giulietta's missing!"

Minerva looked at them in horror. She clapped a hand over her mouth and felt her stomach plunge all the way to her feet. But there was no time for panic. And there was no one else here to take charge. She lowered her hand from her mouth, but she felt slightly dizzy at this news, and was still not entirely awake. "Are you sure?"

"See for yourself! Her room is empty!"

She marched across the sitting room and flung herself into the doorway to the opulent bedchamber the bride had been assigned.

Empty. She gasped at the confirmation. Yet for a moment longer, she could do naught but stare in disbelief at the empty bed where Her Highness was supposed to be waking up to her wedding day. As if a part of her hoped her friend might magically reappear and this was all a bad dream.

It wasn't. The evidence was real. There was barely a dent in the pillow, nor a wrinkle on the coverlet. The splendid white wedding gown hung waiting on a metal maiden-form— abandoned.

Meanwhile, the maidservants ran about the gilded apartment, wailing in a panic. "Gone, gone! She is gone! The Horse Danes will blame us! We're all going to die!"

"No, we're not." Minerva clutched her chest, leaned in the doorway, and struggled to think what to do. But she had an awful feeling they were right. "Has anyone seen her since last evening? Did anyone hear anything during the night?"

"No, nothing, my lady!"

"Who could have done this?" one of the others sobbed. "Cursed Rydalburgers! What sort of fiend would steal away our poor princess before her wedding? To wreck the treaty?"

"Don't be daft. The little henwit ran away," Minerva growled. Shaking off her daze at last, she marched over to the door that joined the apartment to the rest of the castle. She was in such a state that she almost forgot to veil her face before stepping out into the marble corridor to speak to the Saardovan royal guards stationed there.

In low tones, Minerva explained the situation to their captain, Diego, a loyal soldier who had long served under her father. Diego turned ashen when he heard the news. There was no time for the hundred stunned questions that flashed in his dark eyes—nor had she any answers.

"We must not let the Horse Danes know there is anything amiss. Just find her and bring her back. You have three hours before the wedding."

"Do you think you can buy us some time?"

"Possibly," she answered. "While you ride out to search the town, I'll dispatch the maids to look for her inside the castle, though I fear she's long gone by now."

"What will you do, my lady?"

"I am going to stay here to head off the prince if the need arises. Maybe she'll come back of her own free will. But if she doesn't"—she swallowed hard—"this marriage will happen one way or the other, Diego," she said grimly. "I am not letting her plunge our people back into war. I promised my father I'd see this treaty through. And the House of Messina always does its duty," she added rather bitterly.

Diego gave her an uneasy nod. "Yes, my lady." Then he pivoted to his men and clipped out a command to follow, leaving only two behind to guard the door. Appearances, after all, had to be upheld.

The proud, cold Horse Danes would not countenance this insult if they found out the royal bride had fled.

Some thanks for their show of mercy—which, from the barbarians, was unprecedented, truth be told. Minerva knew her people should be grateful, but of course, Giulietta had never been grateful a day in her life.

As the soldiers marched off behind Diego, she retreated into the apartment and brushed back her veil, turning to the maids. They had calmed down a bit now that she had taken control. She gave them their instructions; they donned their veils and padded out silently into the castle to search for their missing royal pain in the bottom. Minerva, left alone in the apartment, shivered in the morning's chill so common to this alien land.

She pulled her silk wrap more tightly round her shoulders. Then she sat down by the window, as if she might be able to see her sunny homeland if she stared hard enough, but it was too far away.

By the gods, how could Giulietta do this? Never mind the practical facts of how she had managed to slip out in the night! Did the pampered beauty think she could actually survive out there without her servants and her guards?

Waited on hand and foot since the day she was born, she barely knew how to pour herself a glass of water.

And where did the little ninny imagine she might go? In spite of her fury, Minerva was worried to death about the royal brat out there on her own. *Spoiled, craven coward.* Still, she couldn't help feeling that this was, to some degree, her own fault. How could she have missed it?

After so many years as her lady-in-waiting, Minerva thought she knew all the princess's tricks by now. But even she had never anticipated that Giulietta might do anything this selfish. *Oh, Papa, why did I ever agree to come here?*

A pang of homesickness moved through her.

The first hour dissolved away into nothing, and still no word from Diego. The maids returned after the second hour. No sign of her in the castle. What were they to do?

Dry-mouthed, Minerva watched the clock hands inch down inexorably to the half-hour mark, and then, at last, she stood. Her face ashen, she glanced at the other ladies.

"Will you help me dress?" she forced out, her usually firm voice little more than a whisper. "The treaty must be saved at all costs."

They nodded in dread-filled resolve.

Filing into the other chamber, they took the royal wedding gown and veil down off the pegs where they were hanging. While one girl sorted out the veil and another set the gauzy white masterpiece of a gown on the bed, Minerva began to undress, her hands shaking.

She could not believe she was going to do this, but she had no choice. Before the mirror, the women worked together to carry out the deception, while somewhere in the palace, Prince Tor waited for his bride.

The day unfolded as a kind of dream. A carriage drawn by six white horses with plumes on their heads brought her to the cathedral. The bells clamored; a rain of confetti and flower petals filled the air; and a deafening thunder of cheers rose from a joyous populace. All across Rydalburg, and even down in Saardova, the ordinary people celebrated the peace of this wedding alliance.

As the carriage halted in front of the cathedral, Minerva

couldn't believe the honor Giulietta had chosen to forfeit in doing this service for her people.

As half a dozen dashing uniformed officers from the prince's own regiment assisted her and her ladies down from the carriage, Minerva turned back and blew the crowd a kiss. The cheers grew even louder.

She smiled in spite of the fear of what might happen to her when all this came unraveled, but bracing herself, she headed into the cathedral with her frightened bridesmaids in tow. She herself was to have been the maid of honor, not the bride, of course, but she played her part with dignity despite the *slight* change of plans.

She held on tightly to her composure and glided forward, determined to set the example for the other girls. Hidden behind their pink veils, the other bridesmaids' faces were pale with dread. All were wondering if she'd really get away with this, and what on earth had happened to the real princess.

There was no time for self-doubt as dignitaries from all the surrounding lands bowed to the imposter bride.

Minerva nodded back with what she hoped looked like regal self-possession. Meanwhile, the entire aristocracy of Rydalburg filled the pews. Lords and ladies craned their necks to get a look at her when she came to stand at the back of the cathedral.

Her heart thudded like it might break right out of her chest; she clutched her bouquet and refused to fidget, waiting for her cue.

Holding very still, she fixed her gaze on the tall, powerfully built warrior standing at the front of the church. The pale sunlight streaming through the rose window illumined his long, blond hair and danced on the gold epaulets on his wide shoulders.

Silently, she gulped. Of course she was terrified at the prospect of deceiving such a man. The stern, magnificent barbarian could kill her with one blow if he ever had a mind to.

But this was also a moment of strictest honesty. For she could not say she was not attracted to him.

In blind faith, she had no choice but to keep putting one foot in front of the other as she set out on her long march down the aisle, refusing to look back.

Prince Tor stared at her as she joined him in front of the Bishop of Rydalburg. Then the ordeal of marrying him began in earnest.

Somehow she found the presence of mind to force out the appropriate answers as the Bishop asked each question in turn. Did she pledge herself to this man in loyalty until death? She braced herself with a last mental curse for Giulietta, and bravely gave her word: "I do."

Rings were exchanged; the Bishop joined their hands in matrimony and spoke his final blessing. Then Prince Tor turned to her and with the Bishop's smiling nod of permission, took hold of the lower edges of her veil.

Minerva trembled deep in her very core as the towering blond warrior captured the lacy edges of her veil and lifted it over her head, letting it waft gracefully down her back.

He stared at her for a second, his gaze traveling over her face with a look of fascination. She watched him anxiously, unsure if he was pleased with her or not—or if he had instantly seen through her deception.

What if his spies had somehow found out what the real

princess looked like? She could not read him.

But then he offered her a courteous smile of reassurance. He laid his white-gloved hands on her shoulders and leaned down to kiss her.

She shut her eyes abruptly as he pressed his lips to hers amid thundering applause.

It was the first time any man besides her own blood kin had ever seen her face, let alone touched her, claimed her lips. *Oh, my.*

It was then she knew she was truly in over her head. The thunderous cheering was so loud as he went on kissing her that she marveled the reverberations did not break the stained glass windows. His kiss lasted another few seconds: deliberate but restrained; chaste, polite, as cool as a mountain evening.

How the lusty Prince Orsino would have laughed at him for this studied, schoolboy peck.

But Minerva understood. It was a kiss Tor only gave from duty. Her heart sank a bit. When he ended the kiss and straightened up again—glorious specimen—she was suddenly inspired with a strategy for how she might survive this.

In all likelihood, it was only a matter of time before her charade was uncovered. Impersonating royalty usually spelled death. But there was one way she might be able to mitigate the prince's coming wrath.

That kiss made her wonder if Tor was used to the half-frigid nature of Rydalburg women. So she had heard. Perhaps the famous sensuality of the Saardovans would be her salvation. If she could enthrall her northern prince as a man, bind him to her with pleasure and seduction the likes of which he'd never had, then even the great barbarian might find himself unable to punish her to the full extent of the law for her deception. He might just spare her life.

While these thoughts churned in her head and the prospect of it began to heat her blood, Tor took her hand, turning her to face their audience.

She reached habitually for the covering of her veil, but he stopped her with a gentle touch. "No, my wife, do not hide your beauty from my people," he instructed. "That is not our custom. Besides, once a Saardovan lady is married, she is allowed to show her face. Is it not so?"

She stared at him in surprise, shocked by the big brute's gentlemanly tone and his obvious familiarity with Saardovan ways. In truth, she was even more distracted by the strangeness of having this stranger tell her what to do.

But she nodded warily. "You are correct, my Prince. It was merely habit. I meant no offense."

"None taken." With a guarded smile, he caught her hand between his own and lifted it to his lips, bestowing a quick kiss. "I daresay it is time for our old habits to change—for all of us." His pointed look informed her he was speaking of their people's tradition of warfare.

To show him she wholeheartedly agreed that it ended now, she clasped his big, strong hand more firmly. Tor gave her a subtle nod, reaffirming their newly forged union. Then he led her down the endless aisle of the cathedral.

At the wedding feast that followed, Minerva had no choice but to accept the lavish praise of the people as her due. She nodded her thanks with what she hoped resembled regal self-possession, and soon forgot all about Princess Giulietta.

There were toasts and songs and speeches, and in all, the only person who seemed suspicious was Queen Ingmar, the mother of the groom. The Queen gave Minerva a piercing stare that worried her greatly. But if Her Majesty had an inkling of the switch that had been made, she did not utter a word about it.

Perhaps, as a mother, she, too, wanted an end to the killing above all else.

Then came the entertainments. First, in the cleared, empty center of the vast banquet hall was a performance of the elite Horse Danes. The cavalry officers in shiny plumed helmets streamed out in formation on their white prancing stallions. The horses seemed to dance to the clipped, measured music, enchanting the crowd with the equine version of a ballet.

They wove through an array of symmetrical formations with stunning precision. Minerva watched in wonder. It was like nothing she had ever seen. The riders made the horses leap in midair and then freeze, balanced on their hind legs while another row swirled by. Others marched to and fro, lifting their front hooves high with every stride while their necks flexed handsomely. Four of the horses spun, while others crisscrossed the open space with mischievous jumps, kicking out their back legs.

At the end of their performance, the riders lined up before the wedding table and finished with a bow, the horses bending down on their front legs. Charmed, Minerva applauded enthusiastically. Her ladies followed suit. And then it was the Rydalburgers' turn to be treated to a performance typical of the lowland culture.

The lights were dimmed to add theatrical flair; colored lanterns were quickly raised around the edges of the stage. As the Saardovan musicians set the mood with a pizzicato on their strings, down from the ceiling were lowered two trapezes and half a dozen long streamers of strong, colorful silk.

On these silken streamers the male acrobats descended, naked from the waist up, their arms, chests, and backs glittered with pearl dust. They were the finest aerial acrobatic dancers in Saardova. They swung on the silks, flipped and flew and leaped from place to place. Minerva enjoyed their marvelous stunts, thumbing their noses at gravity.

Most Saardovan youngsters played on the giant ribbons called silks at some point in their childhood. Doting Saardovan parents hung them from trellises and trees for their young acrobats to swing on, but it took years of dedicated practice to do the daring feats these artists displayed.

Even Minerva winced now and then, watching them, certain one of them would fall and break his neck. The Rydalburgers barely seemed to know what to make of the performance. The crowd gasped each time the acrobats seemed they would surely collide in midair. Then the performers raised the stakes with their favorite stunt: juggling fire.

"They're mad," Tor said with a low laugh as the men tossed burning torches through the air.

Princess Katarina was staring at the half-naked male bodies, wide-eyed.

When the acrobats were finished, the carnival clown

skipped out to delight the serious Rydalburg children with his spoofs and illusions. He beckoned a small boy onto the stage to help him find out what was in his brightly painted box. The boy dutifully assisted, then shook his head at the clown. "There's nothing in there, sir."

The clown frowned with exaggerated sorrow and showed the audience the boy was quite correct. The box was empty.

All of a sudden, the illusion was unleashed as half a dozen white doves came fluttering out of it.

Minerva smiled—the symbol of peace. She glanced at Tor and saw that he recognized the meaning of the trick. Everyone applauded, and as the clown retreated with a bow, King Hakon rose and lifted his gold goblet for a toast. "To my son. Tor, you have opened a new chapter in our people's history. Hear, hear!"

Minerva lifted her glass to her new husband, as well. He smiled modestly and nodded at everyone in appreciation. Minerva gazed at him a moment longer than she probably should; he glanced over and met her stare, and they both seemed to forget what they were about. A thrilling spark of wordless speculation passed between them at the prospect of the night ahead.

Once darkness had descended, fireworks were set off from the highest mountaintop so that the people for many miles around could enjoy their brilliance. As the bright, wondrous colors illuminated the night sky, countless hearts must have thanked the gods that for once, the booming noises across the land weren't cannon fire.

Minerva caught a sudden glimpse of a weary, dusty Captain Diego in the crowd. At a time like this, she was grateful he did not risk coming to speak to her privately about their delicate situation. But he shook his head discreetly to signify they still hadn't found the runaway princess.

She nodded back at him in subtle thanks for this grim news. It seemed like she would have to go through with the wedding night, after all. Give her virginity to the man who had cut off her father's leg. *Oh, help.*

It wasn't much longer after that that Tor captured her hand in the velvet darkness of the night and looked into her eyes. Sparing her maiden modesty from public laughter, he drew her away alone with him while the rest of the world remained dazzled by the fireworks.

Heart pounding, she offered no resistance. *Enthrall him with pleasure?* She scoffed at herself. This was her first time. She barely even knew what she was doing.

He took her to his chamber and softly closed the door. "I hope you will be comfortable in your new home, my lady."

"Oh—I'm sure I will."

"I'll try not to make this too unpleasant on you."

"P-pardon?"

"I am a-a large man," he said awkwardly. Her eyes widened as she realized what he was talking about. "I will try to do it quickly to minimize any discomfort you might feel."

She stared at him, frozen.

"Bloody hell, I'm already botching this, aren't I?"

Words escaped her.

"It's just I know you're a virgin, and I'm sure you already think me a barbarian, so I just wanted to try to assure you before all this begins that Rydalburg men put their wives up on a pedestal." He faltered and stared at her imploringly, and Minerva was shocked, utterly shocked by the honesty, even the vulnerability, in his eyes. "I come from a warrior people, you know that. But you must also know I will always treat you with the utmost respect."

She studied him in awe. Why, his earnest struggle to find the words to comfort her and allay her fears were more potent on her than the charm of ten suave, cocky Prince Orsinos.

"I won't bother you too much—if you are at all concerned about your, um . . . duties." He nodded discreetly toward the bed.

"Thank you, my lord." Minerva lowered her head, blushing scarlet and trying not to laugh. He was adorable. She had not expected this for a second. "Thank you for that kind reassurance." She could not resist glancing up at him from beneath her lashes, still holding back a laugh. "You need not be embarrassed, sir. I will comply with your wishes."

"Embarrassed? I'm not embarrassed!" The quick denial sounded even more awkward and chagrined, especially as his cheeks flushed.

She tilted her head and looked at him. *No. It can't be.* Surely he wasn't a virgin, too.

"I'm trying to be as considerate as possible, that's all," he insisted. "Because let's put our cards on the table—I know you didn't want this for your life. You don't even know me."

"I'd like to," she answered softly after a heartbeat, and to her own surprise, she meant it. She offered him a tentative smile, more intrigued by him than ever. "Maybe you're not an unfeeling barbarian, after all, my lord."

He relaxed at the gentle barb. "And maybe you're not a lazy, temperamental hedonist," he whispered with a rueful smile.

"Sometimes," she admitted.

Amusement mingled with a gathering smolder in his eyes as he leaned down to kiss her. His hands grasped her hips.

She reached up to embrace him, threading her fingers at his nape, but as his kiss deepened, she realized she had been mistaken. He was no innocent. He was just being extra careful with her because she was his bride.

It was supposed to be Giulietta, her conscience tweaked her. A part of her felt like she had stolen her friend's man. But it was Giulietta's choice to run away. Besides, if the princess were here right now in her place, she'd probably be crying. To hell with Giulietta, she thought, pulling the great barbarian closer.

Tor began undressing her, and she could not hold herself back from touching him, in turn. She ran her fingers down his cheek, caressed his thick, silky hair, then kneaded his magnificent shoulders while he unlaced the ribbons on her gown. She unfastened his coat and felt his hands tremble as he peeled away her bodice.

Soon they were both naked in the candlelight. Minerva traced the intricate ink designs that adorned the right side of his chest and curled up over his shoulder to spiral around his massive biceps. She had heard that the north men tattooed their bodies with runes and braided Celtic knots, but she had never seen one before. It fascinated her.

"What does it mean?" she murmured.

"It's complicated . . . and I don't feel like talking." He lowered his head to kiss her nipples one by one. She quivered with pleasure, sucking in her breath.

He lifted his head again and looked into her eyes, very much a barbarian, but perhaps a barbarian was exactly what she needed at the moment. She took his mouth violently in an all-consuming kiss. It was useless. Her Saardovan nature took over. She could not get enough of him. His smooth skin blazed to the touch as she caressed him everywhere, his sculpted abdomen, his broad back, his neck. She even dared to graze her fingertips along the tremendous part of him he had warned her about.

Tor gave her a very wicked smile. In turn, he feasted on her neck and earlobe while his fingers stroked between her legs. Minerva was soon panting, bucking with surrender as he pleasured her. His hands were all over her, but his blue eyes were wild and savage as he pressed her onto her back with an unyielding touch and covered her with his body. Minerva's heart thundered like the echo of the fireworks as she spread her legs and gave herself to him.

And when he took her, thrusting in deeply, she cried out just a little, half in pleasure as with pain.

They both paused. There was no turning back now. He kissed her cheek with unexpected sweetness. A moment later, he was back in motion, taking what was his, claiming the spoils of his victory in battle. His blond hair hung around her face as he rocked her; her long, black tresses were strewn across his pillow. Her tanned, olive skin was darker than his as she splayed her hand against his muscled chest and raked him with her nails. He winced with bliss at her rough affections. Then he gripped her buttocks in his hands and simply ravished her, until both of them were motionless, panting.

They lay in spent silence afterwards, their chests heaving. They looked at each other in amazement. Tor looked slightly incredulous—and thoroughly sated. At least for now. "You know," he panted at length, "this might work out even better than I'd hoped."

She laughed in spite of her distant dread of what might happen if and when her charade was uncovered. But at least her plan was working. She closed her eyes and hugged him. *Might as well enjoy it while it lasts.*

The next day, Captain Diego managed to slip a note to Minerva with the latest information. *"We have a lead. A witness saw a girl of her description trying to blend in among the Gypsies."*

The Gypsies! Minerva thought. *So that's how she slipped out of town.*

"Apparently they came into the town to make some money playing music and such in the public celebration after the wedding. They left last night. It shouldn't be long now. They can't have gone far. What do you want me to do with her when we find her?"

She wrote back instructing him to take her back to Saardova, maintaining secrecy. *"Bring her to my father. He'll know what to do."*

She entrusted one of the other ladies with her note and sent it back to him, then went on playing her part.

Guilt gnawed endlessly at her, but unsure where all of this

was leading, she had no choice. What was done was done, and she was certainly not about to let the truth come out when the castle remained full of her husband's highborn wedding guests.

It was bad enough that she had deceived him. If he also had to worry about saving face in front of his friends and kinsmen, the consequences for *her* would only be worse.

While Diego went off trying to find the band of Gypsies, Minerva proceeded with her charade in the castle.

She was dimly aware that her feelings for Tor were growing apace with every hour that passed, especially when they made love each night and sometimes even during the day. Every time their bodies joined, it brought their hearts closer. She feared she was falling hopelessly in love with him, this man she had been so determined to hate. But she felt helpless to stop it. There was so much more to him than she had ever expected. He was nothing like the cold, mindless killing machine she had believed him to be before she had actually met him. How could she have known? He was kind; he was loyal; he was incredibly patient, especially with his father, who was none of these things. What would he say if he knew how she was deceiving him? It went beyond a problem of politics now.

Her love would surely hate her if he knew the truth, that she had made a fool of him. He would banish her from his life—and that would break her heart.

She tried not to think about it, staying focused on advancing her course, now that she had committed to it. Maybe she could simply become the Giulietta everybody thought she was. He introduced her by that name to his friends, of course. They were all sitting around in the afternoon doing nothing in particular. She gathered from their jests that this was not normal Rydalburg behavior.

"You Saardovans are having an influence on us," his officer friends from his regiment teased her.

"What, teaching you how to relax?" she drawled.

"Don't look at me! I'm a shy virgin!" Rolf mimicked a high-pitched feminine voice, drawing his handkerchief across his face like a veil.

Tor punched him; he went flying off his chair in a gale of laughter. His companions began regaling her with stories about her new husband, like the time Tor had rescued a peasant who had fallen through the ice on a frozen river crossing.

At length, another rogue named Ivar tricked her into tasting a swallow of some strong traditional Rydalburg whiskey.

She coughed at the fiery stuff, and in return, dared the hearty northern braggart to try eating a Saardovan hot pepper.

He actually did it, though his face turned crimson and tears ran from his eyes. Ivar stomped his feet in protest at the pain he had subjected himself to while the others laughed heartily and mocked him.

"Right. Give me one of those," Tor commanded the servant who had brought out the peppers.

"You're going to regret it," she warned, but he looked at her with a playful challenge sparkling in his eyes, then he popped the whole thing into his mouth.

Minerva shook her head as the rest of his men (save Ivar)

followed their prince, subjecting themselves to the same punishment. She ate one of the pepper slices casually, then another, tossing it into the air and catching it in her mouth, while the great warriors writhed in pain and begged for water.

The next day, Tor escorted her out to the royal stables, where the revered Lippizan horses lived in splendor.

They watched the babies skipping around the meadow with their dams. Leaning on the fence, she was intrigued to see that the foals were actually born black and then turned white as they matured. Tor explained the steps they went through in their training to be able to do such tricks on command by the time they were full grown.

But on that sun-warmed spring afternoon, he gave her a certain look, and the next thing she knew, the newlyweds were in the hayloft.

Another day passed. She had the opportunity to take a stroll with her new sister-in-law, Princess Katarina. Minerva soon realized that Kat, as her brother called her, was as cautious and circumspect a princess as Giulietta was emotional and dramatic.

"You've certainly brightened things up around here," she said shyly as the two walked arm in arm in the garden..

"Have I?"

"You have! Now everyone is cheerful. Even Mama."

"Really?" She had been taking care to give Queen Ingmar a wide berth, for she had the uneasy feeling that Tor's mother completely saw through her.

Kat nodded. "It was always so gloomy around here before you came and married my brother. Maybe because of the war. I'm just glad it's over."

"I am, too."

"Are you very homesick?" Kat asked sweetly.

"A little," she admitted.

"Well, if there's anything I can do to make you feel more at home here, just say the word."

"How dear you are!" Minerva exclaimed, giving her a half-hug, an arm around her shoulders. Such affection seemed surprising to the princess, but she smiled, blushing a little. Minerva quite adored the demure creature.

"My brother seems quite smitten with you," Kat remarked as they strolled on.

"I have to admit the feeling is mutual."

"I'm so happy to hear that! He is a wonderful big brother. But I hear you have a brother, too. It must have hurt your feelings that he wouldn't come to your wedding."

It took Minerva an extra split second to realize Kat was talking about Orsino. "Oh, yes, well, defeat was hard enough for him to bear. Watching me marry Tor would have been more than he could swallow. It's better he stayed home, believe me. He's a bit of a hothead. He probably would have started causing trouble. He always does."

Kat looked askance at her. "Is he really as handsome as everybody says?"

"He certainly thinks so!" Minerva replied, and both girls laughed. "Come, tell me something about your brother that I don't know."

"Hmm . . . Did you know he has a green thumb?"

"Really?"

"Come this way, I'll show you."

Kat hurried her back to the castle and led the way to a conservatory that opened up off one of the wings of the palace that she had not yet visited.

"Why, it's just like being back in Saardova!" she breathed as she stepped through the white metal-framed door into the warm, humid air beneath the fanciful glass dome.

"Tor calls this winter garden," Kat explained. "He gives Mother and me roses in the dead of January."

Minerva was amazed. There were little orange and lemon trees in pots. Surely he had imported them from her homeland. There were mounds of pink flowers hanging from pots, an indoor grape arbor, and a fountain where oversized goldfish swam lazily. Containers sprouted neatly labeled medicinal herbs. She knew them well, considering she had once planned to study to become a doctor.

Shaking her head, she was so stunned by this discovery that she barely heard Kat prattling away. "Of course, Father makes fun of my brother constantly about his garden, but Tor says when he's king he'll never let our people starve. Or our horses. Come and see his experimental food crops." Kat beckoned her over to a long, rectangular section by the wall where an assortment of vegetables grew. Behind them stood a row of different grasses and grains.

If there was any doubt left, Minerva took one look at this project and knew she had fallen in love with the man.

"He's tried grafting different species of food plants so the corn will be more hardy and the turnips and such can better resist disease. You see, unlike Saardova, much of Rydalburg has rocky and difficult soil. Our climate can be very unforgiv-ing. Tor says a couple of harsh winters in a row is all it would take to push our people to the brink of starvation. Then our warriors would be too weak to fight so we could gain better territory."

Minerva turned to her in shock. "Is that the real reason our two countries have so often gone to war? My people dread the thought of running out of fresh water, like you have in all these mountain streams, while yours live in fear of insuf-ficient food?"

Kat considered this. "I think you may be right. Look at this." Then his obviously devoted sister turned away, gazing at his handiwork. "It's a wonder, isn't it?"

And so is he, she thought, nodding.

"I owe you an apology, Giulietta," Tor said, quite out of the blue, as they sat on the balcony that evening sharing a bottle of wine. The stars were popping out one by one as the light faded from the sky. Night birds began to warble.

Minerva looked at her husband curiously. "How's that?"

"I fear I've done you a disservice by even listening to the whispers from your kingdom," he admitted with a rueful half smile. "You are nothing like my spies said you'd be."

"Really?" she asked in a guarded tone. *I can imagine.* "What did they say?"

He studied the mountain view for a moment, debating on whether or not to tell her. Then he shrugged. "I hate to pass along idle gossip, but in this case, I'll make an exception. Because somehow, a lot of people back in Saardova seem to have the wrong impression about you."

"Do tell."

"I'm afraid they call you selfish and spoiled. Temperamental. Prone to tantrums."

"Me?" she forced out, laughing.

He nodded. "I admit, I was a little worried. I heard the only person who can keep you in check is Messina's daughter, your lady-in-waiting."

"Oh, that's an exaggeration." She scoffed, but was having trouble looking him in the eyes.

"Of course," he conceded. "Idle talk, as I said. Still, I'd like to meet this friend of yours sometime."

Minerva went even more on guard. "Why?"

"I believe she and I have a mutual acquaintance—besides your lovely self," he added, toasting her with his glass.

"Who?" she asked, fairly holding her breath to hear his answer.

"The old scholar, Montevecchio. I hear he's now the dean of the University of Saardova. He must be what, ninety by now? I imagine he's the one behind your friend being accepted as the first female student. He has peculiar views."

He was right, but she was astonished. "How on earth do you know Montevecchio or his peculiar views?" she exclaimed.

"Everyone knows Montevecchio," he teased.

"Tor!" She stretched out her leg to poke him with her toe. "Tell me, you ruffian!"

"He was once my tutor."

Minerva stared at him in shock. "You had a Saardovan tutor?"

She had heard that the old sage had gone traveling all around Europe ages ago.

"He showed up here when I was just a lad. Said he had come to study our ways."

"I can't believe he came here! Your father—"

"Thought he was a spy, yes." Tor shook his head. "He had the world-famous scholar thrown into the dungeon and tortured every day . . . until Father realized his mistake. Hakon's treatment of the great philosopher was a huge embarrassment to Rydalburg. So Father sought to make it up to him, gave him a plum post here for a while."

"I knew nothing of this!"

"He probably avoided talking about it back in Saardova for fear of fanning the flames of war. Thankfully, the old man found it in his heart to forgive my father for his brutality. My mother made sure our author friend was treated from that point on as an honored guest. Montevecchio was given his own quarters in the keep for his private study. I loved going to visit him up in the tower room . . . see all his books, hear his ruminations. He had a perspective on things unlike anyone else I knew."

Minerva gazed at him, marveling.

"He stayed with us two years. And just between you and me, my darling, I've always suspected that I was the real reason Montevecchio came to Rydalburg. He knew exactly what he was doing."

"What do you mean?"

"As I said, I was just a child, but he knew one day I would

be king. He wanted to teach me about your people. To show me that you were . . . good." He paused, lost in his thoughts. "I don't think I ever would've entertained the notion of a treaty uniting our lands if it were not for old Montevecchio."

"Then I owe him greatly," she whispered, leaning closer to kiss him.

Tor pulled her onto his lap. "We both do." He caressed her hair as he pressed his lips to hers. "Would you mind if I ask you an awkward question, Princess?"

She leaned back to peer dubiously into his eyes. "No. What's the question?"

He furrowed his brow, casting about for the words. "Was there—someone else who had your heart before you came here and were forced to marry me?"

"Why, no! No one! Why would you ask such a thing?"

He looked relieved but still uncertain as he slid his arms around her waist. "Because of the distance you put between us."

"I do?"

He nodded. "I can certainly feel it. Not to brag, but distance is not the usual reaction I get from females. Come, you can tell me. I won't be angry. Is there . . . something about me you don't like?"

"Nothing at all!" she exclaimed. "Tor, you're the most wonderful man in the world! Please don't feel that way. I don't understand why you would say that."

"Sorry, I'm botching this. What I'm trying to say is that you can be yourself with me, Giulietta."

She looked away with a wince.

"I don't demand the sort of obedience Saardovan men

expect. I want to know you," he said earnestly. "That is all I meant. Don't be upset by my question, please." He captured her chin and turned her face back to meet her fretful gaze. "You fascinate me. I've never known anyone like you. But I can feel you holding back. You don't have to, with me. Surely you know by now that I would never hurt you."

Minerva looked at him in distress. It was everything a girl could wish for a man to say to her. Only, in her case, it was all wrong.

He thought he was saying them to Giulietta. Wretched with tangled longing and guilt, she said not a word but wrapped her arms around him and laid her head on his shoulder.

He embraced her tenderly, running his hands up and down her back. She squeezed her eyes shut, wretched with the knowledge of how she was deceiving him.

She couldn't believe that the so-called barbarian warlord was perceptive enough to notice how she had been holding herself back emotionally. Her poor prince thought she was keeping him at bay because she held some sort of Saardovan grudge against him. The man had no idea she was a fraud. How she loathed herself for this—and loathed Giulietta! She hadn't seen Diego in three days.

He was off hunting for the real princess among the Gypsies. In the meanwhile, Tor seemed very determined to win her heart, unaware that he was wooing an imposter.

When he lowered his head slowly and caressed her lips with his own, it was more temptation than she could stand. She took his chiseled face between her hands and kissed him in aching desire. A beautiful sunset unfurled across the sky, but they did not stay out on the balcony long to admire it.

She took him by the hand and drew him wordlessly into their chamber.

There they proceeded to show each other that somehow, indeed, this had quickly developed into much more than a political match. And as he peeled her gown off her shoulders, Minerva half hoped the real Giulietta might never be found.

"Oh, sister! I have a surprise for you!" Princess Katarina's voice echoed from the corridor beyond the morning room where she and Tor were having breakfast.

Minerva looked over with a curious smile as the blond princess poked her head in the doorway. "Surprise! Your brother's come!"

Prince Orsino stepped into view.

She froze as he flashed a rueful smile. "Lady Minerva. Good to see you again. So where is she?" He glanced around the morning room in question.

Minerva's mind was a blank as both Tor and Kat looked at her in confusion.

"Minerva?" Tor echoed with a decidedly ominous note in his voice.

"He is joking!" she exclaimed, sounding rather shrill as she shot up from her chair. "Of course I'm not Minerva! He's always teasing. You are so silly, brother!" She hurried over to greet Orsino with a sisterly hug.

He furrowed his brow, but smiled as he hugged her back. "Now who's joking? Where's Giulietta?"

Tor suddenly swept to his feet and threw down his breakfast napkin with a curse. "I knew it!"

"What?" Kat murmured.

"Please—I can explain—"

"What's happened? Where is my sister?" Orsino demanded.

"Oh, Hades," she whispered, backing away from him, and backing away from Tor as he stalked toward her, his eyes ablaze.

"What is going on here? You are not the Princess Giulietta?"

"Of course she's not," Orsino retorted.

"I wasn't talking to you," Tor growled.

Minerva gulped. "I can explain."

"Who are you?" her husband demanded.

"Don't yell at her, Tor!"

"Stay out of this, Kat."

Orsino took a step toward him. "What have you done with my sister? Has something happened to Giulietta?"

"Don't try me, Saardovan!" Tor thundered without warning, then he turned back to the cowering Minerva. "Explain yourself," he said icily.

"It's true," she forced out, lowering her head. "I am Lady Minerva de Messina. The general's daughter."

He stared at her incredulously. "Why?"

"Please! I didn't want to deceive you!" she cried, lifting her gaze to meet his imploringly. "The real princess fled the night before the wedding! I promised my father I'd see the treaty through."

"*Fled?*" Tor echoed in fury.

"What do you mean, she fled? Where is she?" Orsino exclaimed.

"I don't know! Her guards have been out looking for her since the morning of the wedding. I dispatched them as soon as we realized she was gone."

"So you thought you'd take her place?" Tor asked in outrage. "How dare you lie to me? You'd make a fool of me in front of both our nations?"

"I was trying to save the treaty!"

He turned away. "Get her out of my sight. Guards! Throw this imposter in the tower. Saardovan treachery! I should have known! Maybe Father was right about you people."

"Tor, please!" she cried as they dragged her away.

"Unhand her!" Orsino ordered. "You have no right to do that to a lady!"

"I have every right," Tor said icily. "The little liar is my wife."

Minerva's heart pounded. The big, blond Rydalburg warriors' hold on her arms was implacable. Try as she might, she could not fight free. As they left the palace proper, she could still hear Tor and Orsino roaring at each other.

All of her pleading with his men had no effect. They were completely expressionless as they half dragged, half carried her up the stone steps of the tower. Before she could collect her thoughts, they deposited her in a room in the highest tower of Rydalburg Castle.

She heard them lock the door. She pounded on it. "Let me out of here!" They ignored her. As it sank in that the stony-hearted guards would not be moved, she turned away, feeling ill. She began to pace the austere stone garret, distraught over hurting Tor. She thought she had made the right decision for the treaty's sake, but now she wondered if she had only made things worse.

And where was Giulietta? Producing the real princess seemed the only hope of fixing this disaster. All she knew from Diego's last message was that the Gypsies were moving north. How hard could it be to find them? He should have been back by now!

An hour later, she heard voices in the stone stairwell outside her garret cell.

"Visitor!" the guard called roughly as he unlocked the door. *Tor? Orsino?* Or might it be Diego, bringing news that he had found the princess?

But when the door opened, Kat stepped in, looking shaken. She lifted her chin, waiting for the guards to close the door behind her.

Minerva's eyes filled with tears of remorse as soon as they were alone. "I'm so sorry—"

"There's no time," she whispered. "I'm not supposed to be here. I insisted the guards grant me a couple of minutes to make sure you're all right." Kat stepped over to the cot with a businesslike air and hitched up one side of her dark velvet skirt, producing one of the aerial silks like those used by the acrobats. "I hope you know how to use this thing. I got it from one of your ladies-in-waiting. I thought of stealing a rope for you, but then they'd know it was I who helped you escape."

"Oh, Kat," she murmured as her sister-in-law handed over the giant ribbon.

"You have to get out of here and find the real Giulietta, or they're going to kill each other. Tor and Prince Orsino."

"What?" she breathed.

"You saw them arguing," Kat said in a hushed, hurried tone. "Well, it escalated after you left, and now they say they're going to settle any future conflicts tonight, not with a marriage between our houses, but by single combat. They're planning a duel to the death!"

Minerva stared at her in horror. "When?"

"Tonight, sunset. There's no time to waste. You have to find the princess and bring her back, Minerva. It's the only thing that will satisfy Orsino—and our only hope of stopping this madness."

She was still reeling at the news while Kat marched over to the mullioned window and opened it, assessing the height of it with a slight wince. "You'll have to climb down. I think if you lower yourself to that roof, and then down to that lower gable, you can reach the ground from there. I left a horse waiting for you at the bottom of the wall."

"You're brilliant." She hugged her. "Thank you for your help. I'm so sorry for putting you through all this."

"You did it for the treaty. I understand. Besides, I know my brother loves you, and that you love him. I can see it in you both. Whether you planned it or not, you've fallen in love. But I must warn you, Tor does not forgive easily. You have to make this work. If you fail, one of our princes will end up dead, and sure as clockwork, the war will start again by morning." Kat gave her a sudden, sisterly embrace that was quite out of character for any Rydalburg noblewoman.

But the guard knocked again on the door to let her know her time was up.

"Be careful," Kat whispered.

Minerva quickly hid the silk streamer under the cot. Then the blond princess smoothed her hair and glided out as demurely as she had come in.

When the guard had locked the door again, Minerva glanced over at the window and swallowed hard. She had not swung on an aerial in years, and never from such a height. Never for such stakes.

She dragged the bed, the heaviest piece of furniture in the room, as quietly as possible over to the window. Jamming it against the wall so it could not slip, she then threaded the ribbon beneath one leg of the bed and tied the loose ends into a knot, which she fixed right at her waist.

Climbing up onto the windowsill, she felt the high mountain breeze on her cheeks as she peered down at the earth below in a cold sweat. *Here goes nothing.*

Checking her knot one more time, she inched backwards out the window, then pushed off and began walking down the wall, the ribbon cupping her bottom and her back, not unlike the seat of a child's swing. She gripped both sides of the silk streamer and refused to look down as she lowered herself bit by bit.

She prayed no one noticed her. She refused to look down, but if she had glanced earthward, she would have seen there was no one around to see her. It was a nerve-racking ordeal. Her biceps felt shaky by the time she reached the first roof landing.

When her feet stood on its solid surface, she untied the knot at her waist and pulled one end of the silk ribbon free from where it had been looped around the bed above.

It came spilling down from the window above in a tumble of bright fabric. She quickly caught it and repeated the process, this time using an iron gargoyle as her anchor. The second descent was shorter, and before she knew it, she landed breathlessly on the ground. She untied her knot again and pulled the streamer after her, balling it up as she ran to find the horse Kat had promised.

She found the waiting animal tied to a tree just inside the woods across from where she had landed. "Brilliant girl," she murmured, finding the water canteen and spyglass that Katarina had tucked in the saddlebag. Minerva vaulted up onto the horse's back and urged it into motion, heading for the rocky country to the north. She had to find those Gypsies and get Giulietta back to Rydalburg Castle by sunset tonight.

For the next three hours, she urged her horse on through woods, up hills, down valleys, and when she came to a river, she followed it. The royal henwit would at least have the sense to stay close to a water source.

Then Minerva began seeing signs of human life in the lonely landscape. A burnt-out campfire. Bits of garbage on the ground. Cantering up over the rise, she spotted the colorful caravan below. Gypsies!

She lifted the spyglass to her, searching their whimsical camp for Giulietta. Somehow the wandering bands of free-spirited Romany folk had managed to stay neutral in all those rashes of conflict between Rydalburg and Saardova. That was not to say that they were necessarily trustworthy. But the Gypsies hadn't gone terribly far from the castle, she thought. Why had Diego not reported finding them?

Puzzled, she rode on toward the camp, though she still had not spotted the runaway princess. Giulietta might be in one of the wagons or even wearing a disguise, she thought. It was hard to tell from this distance. She needed a closer look. She urged her tiring horse into a canter and hastened to catch up with them. After all, the sun was now directly overhead: high noon.

The Gypsies eyed her warily as she rode into their camp and asked to see their leader.

"Who are you and what do you want?" A dashing, dark-eyed fellow swaggered forward, a veritable Gypsy prince.

He was dressed in a dark brocade vest over a loose white shirt, with black trousers and boots. His long, raven hair was messily braided in a queue, tied with a red ribbon. Which Minerva instantly recognized as belonging to Giulietta. *Well, well.*

"I am looking for a lady who I have reason to believe has recently been traveling with you, sir."

"Ah, she wants the troublemaker."

They all started laughing.

"At least you're prettier than the last bunch who came looking for her."

Minerva considered the ribbon in his hair and understood. "She got you to lie to them for her, didn't she?"

"Forgive me if I am not an upstanding citizen. I don't like being told what to do. Not by soldiers to whom I owe no allegiance . . . and not by a fair-faced brat, either."

"I understand, believe me. I'm here to take her off your hands."

He lifted his chin. "And you are?"

"Her best friend. Please, it's very important. Do you have her or not?"

"Who is she?" he evaded. "She certainly seems to think she's someone of consequence."

"You might say that. Suffice to say she's a runaway who

left disaster in her wake. It's time for her to go back and face the music, or there will be far-reaching consequences for us all. Please tell me she is safe!"

"More or less. She isn't here," he finally admitted.

Minerva gasped. "Did something happen? Was she hurt?"

"Just her pride," he drawled. Then he gestured toward the hills. "I ordered her out of my camp about an hour ago. We left her by herself back by the caves to the west."

"By herself?"

He scowled. "I couldn't take her tantrums and demands anymore! But of course, I don't wish any harm to befall the chit. She does seem fairly helpless. You'd better go and find her."

"Thank you."

The flamboyant but slightly ragtag leader gave her a bow.

Minerva wheeled her horse around and rode off for rugged higher ground, where caves honeycombed the mountain. Blazes, there were too many of these caves to search. She'd never find her. She debated on whether to try calling for her, because if the princess saw her coming, she might decide to hide. Cantering her horse past more caves, peering into each one, she suddenly heard a familiar voice call to her.

"Minerva!"

She reined in and glanced back over her shoulder. Relief washed through her—and a degree of amusement.

There was the glamorous Giulietta—bedraggled, her silk finery smudged with dirt, her famously beautiful eyes full of misery. Minerva noted the princess had also done away with her veil. As Minerva began riding toward her, Giulietta burst into tears.

"Oh, thank the gods you've come! I've been so wretched—and I'm starving! Please tell me you've brought me something to eat."

"Is that all you have to say for yourself?" Minerva jumped off the horse. "That you're hungry?"

"Well, I am," she said with a pout and a wide-eyed blink, having learned absolutely nothing from her ordeal, it seemed.

Minerva's hands fisted by her sides. "Do you have any idea what you have done?"

"I couldn't go through with it! I'm sorry! But he's too much of a brute!"

"No, he's not! You didn't even give him a chance! You don't know him."

"And you do?"

Minerva glared at her. "I married him for you. No, not for you," she corrected herself. "For our country."

"What?"

"I tried to save the situation, but now everything's gone to the devil and you're the only one who can fix it. You have to come back, Giulietta, you have to. And if you don't agree, by the gods, I will tie you up and drag you from the back of the horse!" she thundered, reaching for the silk streamer to make good on her threat.

"Minerva, you've gone mad!"

"Yes, I have! And who could blame me? As if you're not enough of a pain in the neck, your brother went and ruined everything! Now he and my husband are going to duel to the death unless you come back and take responsibility for your actions! You have no idea the trouble you've left in your wake."

Giulietta frowned. No doubt, she didn't want to hear this,

but Minerva's tone conveyed the seriousness of the situation.

"Please, Giulietta. If ever there was a time to act like a true princess, that time is now. You have a duty to your people."

She winced, eyeing Minerva uncertainly. "What would you have me do?"

"Go back and apologize. Let your brother see that the Rydalburgers have not treacherously murdered you, because that's what he's accusing. Then fall to your knees before Prince Tor and beg him to let you carry out the terms of the treaty even now, and pray your beauty has the usual effect."

"What about you?"

Minerva was silent for a moment. "I am probably going to prison."

Giulietta trembled visibly and looked like she might faint. "I've caused all this?"

"Yes."

"Minerva, I never meant for any of this to happen—"

"You never do. There's no time. Come now and make it right."

She pressed her lips together and nodded. "Very well. There is nothing else for me out here, anyway." She cast a wistful glance back in the direction of the Gypsy prince's camp. Then she got up on the horse behind Minerva, and both girls rode back to Rydalburg Castle with all due haste.

They arrived at the castle minutes before sunset. The girls jumped down from the exhausted horse and raced to the field where the duel was to take place.

Giulietta was a mess, running bareheaded through the

crowd of courtiers and military men who had gathered to watch the grim proceedings. The mood in the crowd seemed to drive home to the frivolous princess just how serious the situation was that she had precipitated with her childish disappearance.

Each prince's entourage had gathered around him. They stood making their final preparations on the two opposite ends of the green, north and south, so the sunset in the west would not be in the eyes of either contender.

"Orsino!" Giulietta shouted.

He stopped, looked over, and then yelled her name in answer when he saw her racing through the crowd.

"Don't do this!" She did not stop to talk to him, but went barreling toward the other prince—at least until the guards surrounding him caught her. Two of them grabbed her by the arms.

"What do you want, girl?"

"Please! I need to see Prince Tor!"

"Who are you?" they demanded.

"Let her pass!" Minerva ordered as she came striding up behind her royal friend.

The guards hesitated. They had become accustomed to taking orders from her over the past few days, but of course, the last anyone had heard, she had been locked in the tower.

Tor turned at the sound of her voice and saw both women. His eyes narrowed.

"Please, Tor, hear us out. For Montevecchio's sake," Minerva begged him.

He glowered at her, but dismissed the guards with a nod. "Let them through," he growled.

As soon as the guards released her arms, Giulietta did exactly as Minerva had advised and rushed toward him, dropping to her knees. "Great Prince! Please forgive me! I have failed you, and shamed my people. I am not worthy of you, but if you can find mercy in your heart for a foolish girl's cowardice, I am the real Giulietta and I will uphold the treaty."

The sight of his sister bowing down to the enemy enraged Orsino, who came storming toward them, but Minerva held him back.

"Stop it. For once in your life, think with something other than your ego. Keep your mouth shut!"

"How dare you?"

"Because I know I'm right! You see?" she gestured toward his sister. "Alive and safe, as promised. You owe His Highness an apology for your false accusations."

He glanced back to where Giulietta was still pleading with Tor, kneeling, tears running down her face. "What is she doing?" Orsino demanded.

"She's asking him to let us fix the wrong that has been done him. It's the only way."

Orsino eyed her mistrustfully. "What if he doesn't accept it? If a woman did that to me, I'd spit on her."

"Well, he isn't you," Minerva whispered rather bitterly. "Besides, I signed Giulietta's name on the marriage license. She could make the claim she's already his legal wife. It just depends on how well the lawyers argue."

Giulietta must have finished her speech, for she had hung her head and awaited her sentence.

Tor glanced past her to where Minerva stood with Orsino. He dropped his weapon begrudgingly on the ground, but shook his head. "Very well. But you're mad if you think I'll ever have anything to do with Saardovan women again."

That was the moment that little Kat stepped into their midst and put them all to shame.

"I will uphold the treaty," she spoke out.

Everyone looked at her.

"I will marry the Prince Orsino, if he will have me—on the condition that he take no other wife but me."

The whole crowd gasped and Orsino's eyes widened.

Minerva gazed at the northern princess in anguished affection.

"Don't be silly, you can't do that, Katarina," Tor clipped out.

"Yes, I can." She looked at Orsino expectantly.

He seemed amazed.

"Orsino," Minerva said through gritted teeth.

He gave her a slight frown askance.

"You'll never do better than her," she said to him under her breath. "Believe me."

"Funny, before all this, on my way to Rydalburg, I was thinking of marrying you."

Minerva shook her head. "I'm in love with Tor."

"Poor creature. So that's why you don't want me to fight him."

"Well?" Kat demanded, her cheeks coloring as he left her waiting for his answer.

Orsino went to her and bowed with the courtly grace he was famous for. "Your Highness, it would be an honor. I humbly accept, and agree to your condition."

Katarina smiled in relief, but the only one who did not

look at all pleased was Tor. Minerva turned to him, aching with the knowledge of how she had hurt him.

Giulietta stood and backed away as she walked over to him slowly. Everyone watched as Minerva approached the man she thought of as her husband, even though she realized the marriage was not legal.

"If you have something to say to me, say it and be gone," he ground out.

Minerva searched his storm-blue eyes imploringly. "I'm sorry. I never meant to hurt you. I only did it for the good of my people and yours. But I understand as prince you are responsible for fulfilling the law." With that, fully expecting to be placed under arrest, she held out her wrists to be shackled.

He glanced down at her hands and then glared at her; he shook his head to signal the guards that she was not to be touched.

But he turned away, refusing to make eye contact with her again. "I want you gone from here, and don't come back."

Minerva flinched, tears rushing into her eyes. But it was too late now. She should have told him the truth before it came to this, she realized too far after the fact.

To avoiding causing any more of a scene, she bowed to him with what remained of her dignity and withdrew. She knew she should be grateful she was allowed to leave with her freedom. Yet her heart was broken to know she would never see him again, and every inch of her body ached with shame as the people she had deceived watched her pass.

She glanced at Katarina sorrowfully as she went by.

The princess touched her hand with a regretful gaze as she passed.

Back in the palace, Minerva fought back tears as she got her things together and bade the royal maids, her coconspirators, farewell.

She assured them Tor would not take revenge on them. However angry he might be, she knew by now the "barbarian" would not harm defenseless women. Then she evacuated her temporary post in favor of its rightful owner.

Tor wanted nothing to do with Giulietta at the moment, but they were already married on paper. Besides, Minerva had seen the power of her friend's charms work on countless males before. Just like that Gypsy prince. Even cold, stony Tor would eventually succumb.

It was only a matter of time.

Three months later, Minerva sat at her desk with her books opened in front. Instead of studying, however, she was gazing wistfully out the window toward the distant mountains, thinking of all that had happened, and the love that she had let slip through her fingers . . .

Upon her return to Saardova, she had cried on her father's shoulder, and then resumed her old life, except for her service as lady-in-waiting. She wasn't needed anymore. Giulietta hadn't come back. So Minerva had started her classes at the university as planned.

She sighed and picked up her pen once more, determined to finish the lesson for this week's class. After all, this was what she had wanted for her life.

A lot had happened in the weeks that had passed. Everyone's lives had changed drastically. Orsino and Katarina were married and madly in love. Giulietta was spending some time in a northern convent, learning contemplation and the service of the poor—particularly the Gypsies.

King Hakon had died of a heart attack in the middle of a feasting. Queen Ingmar was rumored to have entered into a torrid affair with Captain Diego within a fortnight of her difficult husband's funeral.

Tor had become king. Minerva had practically memorized the newspaper article describing his coronation. Things had not worked out between him and Giulietta. The marriage on paper between them had been annulled.

For her part, Minerva was debating on how or even whether to tell His Majesty that she was carrying his child.

Just then, a light knock sounded on her bedroom door.

"Yes?"

She looked over as Papa opened the door and poked his head into her room. "You have a visitor."

She frowned, annoyed that he had climbed the stairs again on his peg leg rather than sending up the maid to give her the message. "I have to study, Papa. Tell them I'm not at home."

"Minerva," he said quietly, "this is someone you're going to want to see."

She furrowed her brow as he pushed the door the rest of the way open; she gasped and jumped to her feet as the King of Rydalburg stepped into view.

Tor's towering stature nearly filled the doorframe.

She stared at him, wide-eyed, her mouth agape. She looked from him to her father, realizing how bizarre this moment was, all things considered. Her father gave her a bolstering look. "I'll leave you two alone."

"Thank you, General," Tor said in his stiff, formal way as he stepped into her room.

Minerva stared at him in amazement as her sire withdrew and pulled the door shut. "What are you doing here?"

"Hmm. I've been wondering that myself." He looked around the room, anywhere but at her. "Please, sit down."

She eased back down into her chair beside her writing table while he stood, fidgeting, in the center of her room.

"Lovely place, Saardova," he remarked. "Glad I didn't destroy it."

"I didn't know you were coming," she forced out.

"Yes. It was, ah, spontaneous on my part. I'm not . . . usually spontaneous, am I?"

She gazed at him in helpless adoration. "I'm sorry about your father."

He nodded with a guarded glance at her. "Thank you."

He hesitated. "Well, I'm just going to say it! What you did was madness. The way you lied to me." He shot her an anguished look, then dropped his gaze. "When Giulietta ran away, you should've just come to me and told me what had happened—but I know now you couldn't. You thought I was an ogre."

"Not an ogre."

"You didn't trust me. And yet you put yourself in my hands. You dared to deceive me . . . for the sake of our people. That means something different to me now than it did when I was just a prince." He held her in a tempestuous stare, as though he had been infected with Saardovan passion. Yet still he struggled for self-control. "You have some nerve, girl. And by nerve, I mean courage. The treaty was more important to you than your own safety." He shook his head, at a loss. "If that is not royal behavior, I don't know what is."

She swallowed hard and lowered her gaze. She could not keep looking into those big, blue eyes of his or she knew she would cry. "Well, you would be the expert on such matters. You are King."

"And I've never been more alone," he said softly.

She looked up again in spite of herself, captured by the heart-tugging admission of vulnerability from the warlord.

His gaze changed, softened. "I came to tell you what you did was madness. But if you hadn't done it, then I never would've got the chance to be your husband."

Her eyes widened as he took a step toward her and then went down on one knee. She drew in her breath as he pulled a diamond ring out of his pocket.

He offered it to her. "Minerva . . . my love, whatever your name is, I want you back. Please be my wife and queen."

Minerva looked at him in wonder, then burst into tears and threw her arms around him, kissing his face and whispering "yes" over and over again.

Keep reading for
an excerpt from
Gaelen Foley's
next historical romance

MY SCANDALOUS VISCOUNT

Available October 2012

CHAPTER ONE

Some people in this world (fools) were happy minding their own business.

Miss Carissa Portland wasn't one of them.

Seated between her cousins, the formidable Denbury Daughters, with their governess, Miss Trent, snoring softly on the end, she trailed her dainty opera glass slowly over the capacity audience of about a thousand souls in attendance that Saturday night at Covent Garden Theatre.

To be sure, the little dramas, comedies, and farces playing out among the Quality present were far more intriguing than anything happening on the stage.

Besides, knowing everybody else's secrets in the ton seemed the safest way to guard her own.

Perusing the three gilded tiers of private boxes, she scanned along at a leisurely pace, while the lenses of other ladies' opera glasses winked right back at her.

Fluent in fan language, as well, she watched for those coy signals a lady could discreetly send her lover.

Hmm, over there. Lady S——, sitting with her husband,

had just flicked her fan in an arc to Colonel W——, who
had come with the fellow officers from his regiment. The
uniformed coxcomb smiled slyly in receipt of the invitation.
Carissa narrowed her eyes. *Typical tomcat male. She'd better
be careful with him.* Drifting on, she picked out the subjects
of other various rumors here and there: the jeweled countess
said to be dallying with her footman; the political lord who
had just sired twins on the mistress he swore he didn't have.

From opposite ends of the theatre, two branches of a
feuding family glared at each other, while on the mezzanine,
a notorious fortune hunter blew a subtle kiss to the heiress
of some encroaching toadstool who apparently owned coal
factories.

Tut, tut, poor man, she thought when her casual spying
happened across the sad figure of a cuckolded husband who
had just filed a crim-con case against his wife's seducer.

Well, the demireps preening in their box and putting
their wares on display in low-cut gowns seemed more than
happy to comfort him.

Hmmph, thought Carissa.

All of a sudden, her idle scan of the audience slammed to
a halt on a particular box, second tier, stage left.

A gasp escaped her. *He's here!*

At once, her foolish heart began to pound. *Oh, my.*

Encircled in the lens of her dainty spyglass, there he sat,
lounging in his chair, his muscled arms folded across his
chest . . .

Staring right back at her.

A wicked smile slowly crept across his face, and just to

confirm that, oh, yes, he saw her ogling him, the handsome hellion sent her a cheeky little salute.

She let out an almost feline hiss and dropped her lorgnette onto her lap as though she had been burned.

She vowed not to touch it again—at which the audience let out another wave of rumbling laughter.

Oh, bother. She shifted in vexation in her seat and looked around uneasily. Of course, they weren't laughing *at* her, though she probably deserved it.

Devil take him, that rogue's glance made her feel like one of the demireps.

To her own dismay, Carissa Portland had secretly become fascinated by a libertine.

Again.

Where this weakness in her came from, this shameful susceptibility to a well-made man, she quite despaired to guess. Perhaps it was her auburn hair to blame.

Redheads were notorious for their more passionate nature. Probably hogwash, she admitted, but it sounded as good an excuse to her as any.

What *his* excuse was, well, he didn't bother making one. A golden demigod striding the earth like a wayward son of Aphrodite didn't have to. Charming, quick-witted, unbelievably handsome, with a smile that could have melted ice floes across the Nordic Sea.

Sebastian Walker, Viscount Beauchamp, could have got away with murder if he fancied. He was the Earl of Lockwood's heir, known to the ton as Beau.

They had been introduced some weeks ago by mutual

acquaintances: Her closest friends, Daphne and Kate, were married to his fellow Inferno Club members, Lord Rotherstone and the Duke of Warrington. So they moved in the same circles, and, of course, she'd heard his reputation. He had lived up to it in spades with her not long ago. The scandalous beast had actually kissed her.

In public!

She had made the mistake of stopping him when he was in a hurry on his way somewhere. She had been leery about confronting him, but she had needed a simple answer to a very serious question: *Where the dash has everybody gone?*

Both Daphne and Kate had been missing from Town for weeks without explanation. This was totally unlike them.

Because of Lord Beauchamp's friendship with their husbands, she was sure he must know something. The aforementioned husbands had also disappeared, supposedly on some hunting trip to the Alps.

But Carissa was starting to doubt everything she thought she knew about her friends. Everyone in their set had been acting so mysteriously before they had vanished. It was all very upsetting. She had no firm information (maddening!), but clearly, something was afoot. She did not understand why she had been excluded.

The truth was, frankly, it hurt.

Thankfully, she had received a letter from Daphne at last, confirming she was safe, but her friend's verbiage seemed deliberately vague. And so, with relief had come even greater annoyance.

Why on earth were they keeping her in the dark? Didn't they trust her!

In an effort to get answers, she had cornered Beauchamp in a safe (so she thought) public place. But when she had delayed him too long with her, as he put it, "nagging," the gorgeous brute had simply snatched her up in his arms and put a stop to her questions with a lusty kiss.

As if she were some wanton trollop on the corner!

If it had not been raining . . . if he had not shielded them from public view with his umbrella . . . she was sure the scandal would have been so calamitous, she'd have hanged herself by now, or (more fashionably) drowned herself in the Serpentine.

Well, the blackguard clearly did not understand the first rules of decent behavior. Though he certainly knew how to give a woman one hell of a kiss.

She put him and the whole discomfiting episode out of her mind with a will, redirecting her attention toward the stage. The evening's program had begun with a concert of Vivaldi's exuberant "Spring," followed by a mediocre tragedy called *The Grecian Daughter.*

The comic afterpiece, *The Fortune of War,* was the one everyone had been waiting for. It was the latest bit of hilarity by the popular Mr. Kenney, a notable wit of the day and founding member of the gentleman's club, Boodle's.

Though the play lacked Mr. Kenney's beloved recurring character, the rascally Jeremy Diddler, the crowd seemed to be enjoying it.

Waves of laughter washed over the audience as the characters bantered back and forth across the stage. Carissa did her best to pay attention, but from the corner of her eye, she was acutely aware of Lord Beauchamp.

When the curtain whisked closed briefly for the stage-hands to change the scenery, she could not resist another cautious peek in his direction.

Her curiosity instantly perked up as she spied one of the orange-sellers stepping into his box to deliver a message to the viscount. Carissa saw him take the little note and read it while the orange-girl waited for her coin.

Well, Carissa had no choice. Her innately nosy nature compelled her. She snatched her opera glass from her lap and lifted it to her eye just in time to see the smoldering look that gathered on his chiseled face. Lord Beauchamp glanced across the theatre with a suave nod, acknowledging the sender: Carissa zoomed her opera glass in that direction, too, trying to follow his gaze.

To no avail.

Whoever had sent him the note was lost amid the crowd.

Indeed, it could have been any of Society's highborn harlots wanting to take her turn with him tonight. Scowling, she searched the tiers across from him. Honestly, she did not know if she was more vexed at Beauchamp for having all the morals of a blood stallion, or at herself, for being jealous at how free he was with his meaningless affections.

She swung her opera glass back to the viscount to see what he'd do next. Beau turned to the orange-girl and asked for something; she handed him a pencil.

While he scrawled his reply, Carissa memorized what the orange-seller looked like: a tall, weary lump of a peasant girl. Then the libertine handed her his note along with a coin and sent her off to deliver his answer.

As the orange-girl disappeared through the small door of

his private box, questions gnawed Carissa. Who was he involved with these days? Of course, she knew there were many women around him as a rule, but was there any one in particular?

And why do you care? her better sense inquired.

I don't know. Do I need a reason?

Yes, it answered.

She shrugged, refusing to admit to anything. *I just want to know because—because I want to know!*

Suddenly, she was seized with a wicked inspiration.

Why, she could either sit here festering on it, burning with curiosity about which feckless female meant to hurl herself into his clutches tonight, or *do* something. And go find out.

After all, as a lady of information, she had long since discovered that orange-girls . . . could be bribed.

Right.

Instantly rising from her chair, she excused herself with a whisper. Miss Trent awoke with a disoriented jolt, while the Denbury Daughters rolled their eyes. Which was the spoiled beauties' response to most things, actually.

"What are you doing?" Lady Joss, age nineteen, complained at her.

"I have to go to the ladies' lounge."

"Can't you just hold it?"

"No."

"That's disgusting," Lady Min, age seventeen, opined.

"Sorry." Dismissing her cousins' perpetual irritation with her, she slipped out of the Denbury box and closed the little door behind her.

At once, Carissa swept off down the third-floor hallway, her slippered feet pattering busily in the quiet.

She had to find and intercept that orange-seller.

She knew she should not care who Beauchamp would be bedding tonight, but everything in her had to get a look at that note. Seeing it with her own eyes, she reasoned, would surely help remind her that gorgeous rakehells like Lord Beauchamp were nothing but trouble. They chased after pleasure and did not care who got hurt.

She should know.

On the other hand, in all fairness, she supposed, she had to admit there sometimes seemed to be more to him than just charm and charisma. And broad shoulders. Lovely muscles. Mesmerizing eyes the color of seafoam that danced when he laughed, which was often, a rugged jawline, and extremely kissable lips . . .

She shook herself back to the task at hand, hurrying on. Indeed, physical appeal aside, he had actually done a few interesting things in his life.

Using her usual methods, she had managed to ferret out a number of odd tidbits about him, including some highly colorful exploits in his past.

Of course, his origins came from a lineage as excellent as her own. His mother, Lady Lockwood, had been a great beauty of her day, indeed, still was, now in her fifties. His father, the Earl of Lockwood, was said to be a brusque curmudgeon who did not often come to Town but preferred the "huntin', shootin'" life of a country lord.

She did not know where Beau had spent his childhood, but as a young man, he had gone to Oxford, studied Greek and Latin, and excelled in his classes without having to try— so she'd heard. Too smart for his own good, according to her sources, he had been easily bored and had occupied himself with carousing and all manner of wild adventures. And even from his youth, there had been women.

An indecent number of women.

But apparently, the lusty young aristocrat had his heroic moments, too. On one occasion, at age twenty-one, according to the rumor mill, he had been heading home in the wee hours after a long night's revelries, when he had come across a lodging house on fire.

Whether the whiskey he'd been drinking all night had made him foolishly brave, or if he was always like that, she could not say. But he had rushed into the burning building and rescued everyone inside before the fire company could even get there.

He'd saved some twenty people's lives.

Not long after that, his father, the earl, had made him a Member of Parliament for one of the pocket boroughs he controlled. He had thrust the post upon his son so he might gain experience to help prepare him for one day taking his seat in the House of Lords.

Little had the earl expected the young MP to stand up and outrage the leaders of both parties with his fiery idealism, his blistering reproaches, and his regrettable refusal to compromise.

It was nice to know he had not always been a cynic, she supposed, and that he had a sense of civic duty despite his many romantic peccadilloes. By the time he had resigned his post a year later in angry disgust and returned to his rakehell ways, he had made enough political enemies to last a lifetime.

These, in turn, got their revenge on the bold young viscount in due time, when word got out that he had fought a duel against some hotheaded rival for the favors of one of Society's highborn wantons.

Beauchamp, universally acknowledged as a crack shot, had not deigned to kill the man who had challenged him but had wounded him. As a result, his opponent had to have his leg amputated below the knee, and unfortunately, he had turned out to be the nephew of a Cabinet minister.

Of course, there were rules on the books against dueling, but as a courtesy to the upper class, who lived and died by honor, these laws were almost never enforced.

Unless one had enemies in high places.

The bureaucrats had come down on Beauchamp like a hammer, claiming they must make an example of him to teach other young Englishmen that they could not simply go around shooting each other.

It was all Lord Lockwood could do to keep his merry scapegrace son out of Newgate. Instead, after a very large fine and damages paid to the now-one-legged hothead, the handsome young duelist had been sent off, unsurprisingly, to travel. Sow his wild oats abroad, as it were. He was given some post loosely attached to the war effort, she'd heard, but on his father's insistence, was generally kept out of harm's way, well behind the lines.

It was rather hard to imagine that one staying out of trouble, she mused, but somehow the war had ended, and here he was, back again, unscathed.

Rumor had it he had now returned home for good.

Of course, he was scarcely back in England three months before he was in trouble again.

She wasn't sure yet what the hell-raiser had done this time, but she had first caught wind of his latest scrape while snooping in her uncle's study.

She knew that her guardian, Lord Denbury, and his cronies in the House of Lords kept each other informed about the goings-on in their various committees. One of these parliamentary briefs sent to her uncle had revealed that Viscount Beauchamp was under investigation by a secret panel from the Home Office.

No details were given beyond that.

It was altogether perplexing—and just another piece of proof that, behind that sunny smile, he was one beautiful, bad seed.

Hurrying down the empty stairwell, she pressed on to the mezzanine level, glancing here and there, hunting for that particular, weary-looking orange-girl.

Muffled dialogue from the stage and swells of laughter from the audience poured through the walls from the play in progress. Mr. Kenney was obviously killing them with his famous sense of humor.

Carissa had no time for mere entertainment, however, bustling down the mezzanine corridor, all business.

"Can I help you, Miss?" one of the uniformed attendants whispered as she passed.

She shook her head, gave what she hoped looked like an innocent smile, and hurried on.

It would not do for anyone to discover this secret method of hers for gaining information. Glancing into her reticule to make sure she had a few coins for the bribe, she whisked along the curve of the mezzanine hallway where it hugged the back contour of the closed auditorium.

As she came around the bend, she finally saw the orange-girl she was after, but she ducked into the nearest curtained alcove with a gasp. Someone had beaten her to it!

Ever so cautiously, Carissa peeked around the edge of the alcove. *Blast it, who's that? He stole my plan.*

Then a chill came over her as she studied the man talking to the orange-girl.

He was beautiful, black-haired, and windblown, as if he'd just come back from his travels; and from his muscled body to his dark scowl, he looked decidedly mean.

Her mouth went dry as she watched him bribe the orange-girl for a look at the note some lady, perhaps *his* lady, had exchanged with Beauchamp. Carissa's heart pounded. *Oh, Beauchamp, I hope you didn't sign your name.*

They never did, on those clandestine notes.

Surely he was too smart and experienced for that. But if he *had* made that mistake, she feared the rakehell might be headed for another duel. It looked as though she might not be the only one feeling jealous tonight.

Huddling behind the curtain of the alcove, she watched in trepidation as the handsome, black-haired man read the note and scoffed.

A snort of cynical laughter escaped him. He shook his head with a bitter smile, then tautly asked the orange-girl for another piece of paper, which she gave him. He crumpled the original note in his fist and stuffed it into his breast pocket.

Then he wrote back another message of his own.

With a dark look, he handed his note to the orange-girl, laying a finger over his lips, as if warning her to secrecy.

He slipped a paper bill into her hand and sent her on

her way. Still unaware of Carissa, the stranger watched the orange-girl hurry off, his arms akimbo, his feet planted wide. Then, with a cold smile, as though satisfied his trap was laid, he pivoted on his heel and stalked out of the theatre.

Carissa eased out of her hiding place a moment later, dread tingling through her body. *Oh, Beauchamp, you're being set up.* She scarcely dared imagine what might happen to him if he went to meet his *femme du jour*, whoever she might be. He could be killed!

Once more, Carissa was in motion, hurrying after the orange-girl to stop her from delivering that note, which was naught but a piece of treachery. Beauchamp might be a bad, decadent libertine, but she was not about to let anyone murder him!

Rushing after the orange-seller into the quiet side hallway that backed the row of private theatre boxes, she skidded to a halt.

Too late!

The lump had just stepped through one of the narrow doors, halfway down the row. *Oh, no. What do I do now?*

Heart pounding, she glanced around uneasily.

Merely standing there, unchaperoned, in a part of the theatre where she did not belong was something of a gamble.

Having missed the orange-girl, the thought of venturing into Beauchamp's box to try to warn him—to risk being seen there by the other snoops in the audience—made her blood run cold. She could not afford in any way to become an object of gossip herself.

She already had too much to hide.

With that, she realized the intelligent thing to do was to

abandon this mad quest immediately, go fleeing back to her seat, and pretend she had seen nothing.

But a man's life could be at stake.

And although he was entirely exasperating, the world would be a darker, duller place without him. Come to think of it, perhaps she could turn this little twist of fate to her advantage . . .

Oooh, she mused. *An exchange of information. Yes!*

If he'll tell me where Daphne and Kate went and what the deuce is going on, then I will tell him what I saw. That's fair, is it not? If he refuses, then maybe the rogue deserves what he gets.

Unsure what to do, she crept toward the door to his box, then stopped. He was probably reading the false note even now, getting drawn into the trap.

She stood there, torn and hesitating, as another little problem with all this occurred to her. If she tried to warn him what she'd seen, he'd realize she had been snooping into his personal affairs.

He'd notice she was jealous, and then, oh, then he'd laugh his head off and taunt her like a schoolboy—and then, never mind the jealous husband, she would murder him herself, wring the rascal's neck.

At that moment, before she had quite made up her mind what to do, the little door to his theatre box opened and the orange-girl scampered out.

Right behind her, the rogue himself emerged, tall and princely, en route to his assignation.

He stopped the second he saw her and, at once, his eyebrows arched high.

Carissa stood frozen, staring at him, tongue-tied.

She knew she was caught; he flashed a wolfish smile that made her want to shriek with mortified fury and run away. But she held her ground with a gulp while the orange-girl rushed off, leaving them alone in the dim, quiet hallway.

Close enough to touch.

"Well, my dear Miss Portland," he purred, trailing his gaze over her in thoroughly male appreciation. "What a very pleasant surprise. Was there something you, ah, . . . wanted?"

LORD LOVEDON'S DUEL

Loretta Chase

"We'd best do it now," Chloe Sharp told her older sister. "Say goodbye and bawl, so that we don't make a spectacle of ourselves, or set Mama off."

"Y-yes. Oh, Chloe, I'll miss you so!" Althea fell weeping on Chloe's neck, heedless of the wrinkles and stains she made on two of London's costliest dresses.

Bride and bridesmaid stood in a dimly lit passage that ran between the picture gallery, which extended the west wing's full length, and the smaller of the two drawing rooms. The larger, the Gold Drawing Room, occupied the center of the first floor of the Duke of Marchmont's Jacobean mansion. There hundreds of wedding guests were celebrating Althea's marriage to Prince Louis of Massbeck-Holveg. From the passage, though, the merriment was practically inaudible.

This was the last time Chloe would see her sister for a long time. Her heart was breaking. Still, she made herself draw away.

"That's enough," she said. "We don't want the Beau Monde to see us with tear-streaked faces and crushed bows and creases. Come out into the gallery, where we'll have some light, and I can put you back to rights."

She started to open the door to the gallery, but paused

as a wave of masculine laughter spilled toward them. Althea stopped, too, and caught hold of Chloe's arm. They both giggled the way they used to do when they were children, hiding to spy on grown-ups.

"But everybody knows he was obliged to give up the girl he loved," somebody said. Mr. Crawford? Chloe had met so many aristocrats today that their names and faces were a hopeless muddle in her brain.

"Which girl was that?" another man said.

"A sweetheart Prince Louis left behind in Massbeck-Holveg," Crawford said. "Lovers torn asunder, you know, by Fate."

Althea inhaled sharply, her grip on Chloe's arm tightening.

"Love, gentlemen, is a luxury His Highness cannot afford," said a deep, drawling voice. "Three royal castles in his speck of a country, and all of them falling to pieces. He doesn't need love: He needs new chimneys."

Though Chloe had never heard that voice before today, she knew who it belonged to: James Bransby, the Earl of Lovedon.

A leader of fashion, one of Prince Louis's dearest English friends, a favorite of the King and Queen, and famously whimsical, he was London's most elusive bachelor.

The men went off again, into whoops this time, as though it was the wittiest thing they'd ever heard.

"Come away," Chloe whispered to her sister. "There's a doorway to another room—"

"He's hardly the first of the King's cousins to come to England for a rich wife," Lovedon continued. "For them, this sort of thing is merely a business transaction. Naturally he'll put aside any personal disappointments with Teutonic fortitude, like the staunch patriot he is."

While he spoke, Chloe was aware of Althea's breath coming faster and faster. She gave a small, choked cry, and let go of Chloe's arm.

Though she wanted to push Lord Lovedon out of a window, Chloe had to tend to her sister first. She pulled Althea toward another doorway, an open one leading to one of the back staircases. Althea was sobbing again, this time in deep, painful gulps.

Chloe half-dragged her to the door on the other side of the landing, through the recently abandoned dining room, and into a pretty sitting room. Its lone window overlooked the splendid gardens that spread out for miles, it seemed, from the north front of the house. Thanks to the afternoon's onslaught of rain, a grey haze shrouded the glorious vista Chloe had glimpsed this morning.

She grasped Althea by the upper arms and gently shook her. "Those men are *drunk*," she said. She was none too sober herself, she realized, as a wave of dizziness nearly toppled her. Firmly ignoring it, she went on bracingly, "I was amazed to see how much champagne Lord Lovedon could pour down his throat and still stand upright. But you know what aristocrats are like: heads of oak, and hearts even harder."

"It—it wasn't a secret. Prince Louis told me he was poor—but he s-said he l-loved me."

"Which he does, as everyone can see—except Lord Lovedon and his dimwitted followers. But you can't expect them to recognize a love match when they see one. Defective vision, you know, thanks to centuries of inbreeding—and the pox, too, probably. And don't forget the gallons of champagne they've swilled, or the fact that they do nothing but gossip because they lack the mental capacity to carry on an intelligent conversation. My love, you can't possibly take them seriously."

"But what if it's true?" Althea said. "Only think of Prince Louis pining for the girl he loves, while having to pretend to care for me."

"If there was such a girl, he forgot her the instant he clapped eyes on you," Chloe said. "I was there, recollect, on the day His Highness came into Maison Noirot with Lord Longmore."

Mama had patronized the French dressmakers practically from the day they opened their shop. Chloe and Althea had been waiting in the showroom for her when Prince Louis and the Earl of Longmore entered.

"Once His Highness got his first look at you, he couldn't see or think about anything else," Chloe said. "He certainly didn't know then that you were rich."

"H-he could have g-guessed, I wasn't p-poor," Althea said, "considering it's the most expensive dressmaking shop in L-London."

Chloe dismissed this with a wave. "The point is, he fell over head and ears in love with you, and everybody knows it except this pack of drunken degenerates. How can you let a lot of strutting ignoramus blockheads make you wretched on your wedding day?"

She went on in this way while she swiftly set about repairing the outward damage. Combining relentless mockery and mimicry of Lord Lovedon & Company with more practical remedies—the careful application of a handkerchief, read-justment of hairpins, and smoothing of wrinkles—she soon restored Althea to the state of glowing happiness she'd en-joyed only a short time earlier. By the time Althea returned to her prince—who lit up, by the way, at the sight of her—she was giggling.

Bride and bridegroom disappeared into the mob of well-wishers.

Chloe looked about her. All was in hand.

Except for one small detail.

She took a glass of champagne from a tray a passing foot-man presented to her, swallowed the contents, set the empty glass down on the nearest horizontal surface, then started back the way she'd come.

This time when Chloe opened the door to the picture gal-lery, the male laughter sounded farther away.

As she entered, she saw them gathered at the great bay window overlooking the north front.

He was easy enough to spot.

The Earl of Lovedon was tall and dark, yes, but not hand-some. His features were too harsh and angular for classical beauty . . . although from the neck down he was all too clas-sical, like a Greek statue. That chiseled profile and athletic physique had claimed her attention all too often this day. The view had left her much too warm and breathing too fast.

His big shoulders propping up a corner of the window embrasure, the usual faint, superior smile curving his cyni-cal mouth, he stood with arms folded, one long leg crossed in front of the other. The casual stance displayed the highest level of tailor's art: His fine wool coat skimmed the contours of his broad shoulders and chest, and his black trousers hugged his muscular legs.

If he hadn't had something to lean on, he'd probably fall on his face, the drunken moron.

The men were too busy gossiping and laughing to notice her approach until she was practically under their noses.

Then Lord Lovedon's dark gaze slanted her way.

"Ah, Miss Sharp," he said lazily. "Taken a wrong turn, have you? The duke's house is something of a labyrinth. All sorts of odd corners and not-so-secret floors between floors. Happily, you needn't fear his mad aunt's springing out of a concealed door. She's moved to Torquay."

Chloe stripped off one of her gloves and struck his cheek with it. She grabbed a glass of champagne from one of his startled companions and threw the contents in his face.

He didn't so much as flinch. The champagne dripped from his face onto his perfect neck cloth and down over his splendid silk waistcoat.

Over the room's sudden silence, the rain's hammering sounded like drumbeats. Her heart beat a harder and faster tempo.

"What is *wrong* with you?" she said. "How could you say such *hurtful* things? At a *wedding*, no less! How dare you make my sister cry on her wedding day, of all days? You *brute*."

"I say," someone said.

"What the devil?" someone else said.

She ignored them. "If I were a man," she said, "I'd draw

your cork for you. I'd— No. Why do I need to be a man? Be so good as to name your second, my lord."

She was aware of hurried footsteps behind her, and familiar voices. Her sister Sarah had come. And Amy Renfrew, Chloe's dearest friend after Althea.

"Oh, Lord, I knew it," Sarah said. "I saw that look. I know that look."

"Come away, Chloe," Amy said. "Whatever it is, let it be."

"Name your second, Lord Lovedon," Chloe said.

"Second?" Amy said.

Someone laughed.

"I believe Miss Sharp has challenged Lord Lovedon to a . . . duel?" one of the men said.

Chloe didn't know or care who spoke or who laughed. The world was a red fog of rage, and she could barely see. Except for him. His lordly hulk was all too clear, and she wanted to choke him, this spoiled lout who'd upset her sweet, gentle sister on what was supposed to be the happiest day of her life.

He stood, eyebrows aloft, still smiling his superior little smile. A drop of champagne clung to his thick black eyelashes. Another drop trickled down the hard angle of his jaw into his snow-white neck cloth.

"Oh, no," Sarah said. She grabbed Chloe's arm and tried to drag her away. "You can*not* make a scene, Chloe. Not here. Not *now*."

"A scene," Chloe said, her gaze locked with Lovedon's glittering black one. "I'll make a scene. By Jupiter, I'll—"

"Come away, Chloe," Amy said, taking hold of the other arm. "Whatever the trouble is, this is not the time."

"For God's sake, come away," Sarah said.

"I recommend you heed the ladies' advice, Miss Sharp," Lord Lovedon said. "Under no circumstances could I possibly agree to meet a young lady at thirty paces." He took out a large linen handkerchief, embroidered with an *L*, and calmly wiped his face. "I should be a deuced laughingstock."

"Yet it doesn't trouble you to make a laughingstock of one who has done you no injury," she said. "It's quite all right to demean someone you know nothing about—"

"Chloe, let it be," Amy whispered. "Come away before any of the others come looking for you."

Chloe wasn't done. She wanted to hurt him, the way he'd hurt Althea. But he was unreachable, the aloof, immovable aristocrat. He still wore the mocking little smile. He remained perfectly cool and collected even while he wiped his face.

Meanwhile her hands were shaking, and it took all the willpower she had to keep her voice at an even pitch.

"I shall expect to hear from your friends tomorrow morning," she said. "Or I shall evermore regard you as no gentleman—and a coward as well."

She shook off her sister and friend, turned on her heel, and walked away.

Lovedon watched her go.

The two girls fluttered anxiously about her. Miss Sharp didn't flutter. She didn't hurry away, either, which was generous of her. She had some fifty feet to travel to the door she must have irrupted from. This gave him ample time to appreciate the rear view.

For an inebriated female of negligible rank, she carried herself surprisingly well, tall and straight, without seeming stiff in the least. The only sign of unsteadiness was the slight undulation of her hips. The motion made her long, lacy scarf dance about her, and set the bows and ruffles of her pink dress atremble.

Until this moment, Miss Sharp had been no more to him than one of the numerous sisters and cousins and friends of the bride garbed in gorgeously extravagant dresses. He'd been introduced to them all, and his fearsome memory retained every name.

Beyond being able to put a name to her face—and catching Miss Sharp putting her gloved hand to her eye once or twice during the nuptials—he'd given her little thought. The girls were young and, for the most part, unsophisticated. The rites were lengthy and stupendously boring, and the fête thereafter, likewise in the tradition of the bridegroom's forbears, featured his country's quaint music. The music had driven Lovedon from the Gold Drawing Room to the picture gallery.

As one of the groom's attendants, he couldn't flee the house. His early departure would be taken a slight, and even he knew better than to offend one of the King's favorite cousins. Having no choice, Lovedon had remained, bored and irritated to within a hairsbreadth of insanity. He'd drunk enough champagne to float a flagship—possibly the entire Royal Navy—to no discernible effect.

Until a moment ago.

The last dose, the one Miss Sharp had administered externally, had brightened his mood amazingly. The eyes flashing at him had turned out be an interesting shade of green, with gold flecks. Her hair, which he'd previously dismissed as an insipid light brown, turned out to be the color of honey. Her skin was flawless, and the angry pink tingeing her cheeks had turned ordinary prettiness into something almost beautiful. Most important, she'd turned out to have a *personality*.

He watched until she'd turned into the doorway halfway down the gallery.

"Well, that was cool and refreshing," he said as he folded his handkerchief.

"What the devil was that about?" Hempton said.

"No idea," Lovedon said. He put the handkerchief away.

"Do you think she was foxed?" Crawford said.

Beyond a doubt. Though Lovedon hadn't thought he'd paid her any particular attention, his memory held images of Miss Sharp taking one after another glass of champagne from the many trays making their way through the crowd in the Gold Drawing Room.

Now he wondered what she was trying to drown.

Not boredom, surely, in her case. After all, It wasn't every day that a lawyer's daughter married a prince, and her sisters and friends enjoyed the privilege of mingling with the haut ton. Perhaps Miss Sharp had simply celebrated to excess her sister's matrimonial triumph. Or perhaps she wasn't used to superior champagne.

"I shouldn't venture to say," he said. "Women get emotional at weddings. She became overwrought."

"And abandoned the festivities, journeyed through two rooms and a passage where everybody takes a wrong turn and gets lost for days, then down half the length of the picture gallery—all to take it out on you?" Bates said.

"It's possible I said the wrong thing," Lovedon said.

"I should say that's more than likely," Bates said. "I'd better smooth the ruffled feathers before any Highnesses or Majesties get wind of it."

Lovedon abruptly recollected that the lady, being the bride's sister, was the Prince of Massbeck-Holveg's sister-in-law. A short time earlier, Lovedon had expressed certain less-than-sentimental views of the match. Prince Louis would not find those comments amusing.

If any unpleasantness resulted from Lovedon's little contretemps with Miss Sharp, he would receive a royal summons, a royal dressing-down (a skill at which the King, a former naval commander, excelled), and orders to make groveling apologies to about a thousand people, mostly foreigners.

"I ought to do that," Lovedon said. He started to push himself away from the wall.

Bates held up a hand. "You've done enough damage. I've never before seen you deal so clumsily with a woman. You'd do well to leave this to me."

Insisting that she needed to calm down before she returned to the company, Amy and Sarah steered Chloe into the sitting room where she'd revived her sister's spirits.

Sarah commenced by berating her.

That was so calming.

"A lord!" Sarah cried. "And *that* one, of all lords! What

on earth possessed you? He looked wet. You threw a drink at him, didn't you? Oh, Chloe, tell me you didn't."

"It seems she did," Amy said. "And challenged him to a duel as well."

"I thought of stabbing him with one of the carving knives," Chloe said, "but the servants had taken them all back to the kitchen."

"Oh, Chloe!" Sarah cried.

"What on earth did he do?" Amy said.

The blind rage was abating, and a conglomeration of feelings were sweeping in, including a sorrow Chloe was afraid would overwhelm her.

"I took exception to something he said," Chloe said. "Would you be so kind as to take Sarah back to the party? I need a moment's peace and quiet to collect myself, and I can't do that while she's taking fits."

"I am not taking fits! And you're a fine one to talk!"

Amy took Sarah's arm. "My dear, we're all agitated. What's a wedding without some hysteria? But Chloe's right. She needs time to compose herself, and our making a fuss isn't helpful."

She led Sarah away, but slowed once to look over her shoulder and mouth, "Later."

Chloe had hardly a minute's solitude before she heard footsteps, followed swiftly by a male voice. "Ah, there you are, Miss Sharp."

She didn't have to look that way to know it wasn't *his* voice.

She was on the brink of tears again—what a ninny she was, to regret her sister's happiness and fret about brainless aristocrats!—but she blinked hard and lifted her chin.

The gentleman—she couldn't remember his name—smiled as he approached. "Miss Sharp, I shall not waste words," he said. "I've come to beg your pardon for any offense Lord Lovedon has caused."

"Has he appointed you his second?" she said.

He gave a nervous laugh. "No, no, certainly not."

"Then why send a proxy?" she said. "Why not make his own apology?"

"He didn't send me," the gentleman said. "He's a bit . . ." He trailed off, frowning, apparently at a loss for the right word.

"A bit of an ass," she said.

"Bates thinks I'm half-seas over and not to be trusted with delicate diplomatic negotiations, Miss Sharp," came another, deeper voice, from the doorway.

No doubt whose drawling baritone that was.

Mr. Bates said something under his breath. Curses, Chloe supposed. She was tempted to utter several unladylike words herself. She wasn't nearly ready for another confrontation.

Though her heart beat so hard she thought she'd faint, she collected what remained of her dignity and made herself regard Lord Lovedon as coolly as he'd regarded her moments ago.

He didn't stagger into the room. He had too much self-control for that . . . even though they seemed to be upon a ship at sea.

The walls and floor ought not to be moving.

She'd been too furious before to notice but . . . maybe she oughtn't to have taken that last glass of champagne.

She forced herself to meet his mocking black gaze. "You

needn't be anxious, Lord Lovedon," she said. "I shan't create an international incident. I never tattle, and Althea is unforgivably forgiving. To calm her, I told her you were spouting nonsense because you were drunk as well as not very intelligent. By now, I daresay, she's not only forgiven you but has even made up a reason to think kindly of you. My sister—as Prince Louis had the *discernment* to recognize—is angelically beautiful not only outwardly but inwardly as well. She's incapable of thinking unkindly of anybody. She'd make excuses for Satan himself."

He drew nearer, blocking her view of his friend—and everything else. He loomed over her, all dark wool and blinding white linen and a gloriously embroidered—and now damp—blue silk waistcoat that must have cost as much as her dress.

"Am I to understand that you came and challenged me to a duel and made me quake in my boots—all for nothing?" he said.

"*She* has forgiven you," Chloe said. "I am not so saintly. I have not. You haven't apologized."

Nor would he, she supposed. Some men would rather be roasted on a spit and fed to wild boars than apologize, especially to a woman.

"It seems I must kill myself," he said. "It is impossible to continue in this world without Miss Sharp's approbation." He put the back of his hand to his forehead. "Farewell, all. I go to a better place."

"I think not," she said. "I think it will be rather worse than this one and a good deal hotter."

"But all my friends will join me there eventually," he said.

"I shall hope in time to see you there as well. You did say you weren't saintly."

"In that case," she said, "I wish you a very long, unceasingly unhappy life."

She gave him an exaggerated version of the simpering smile so many other women wasted on him, and dipped a little curtsey . . . and then kept sinking.

Lovedon lunged and caught her up in his arms before she toppled.

This wasn't the simplest feat. He wasn't as steady on his legs as he'd supposed, and she, with her great ballooning sleeves and billowing skirts, wasn't easy to capture securely.

Then, once he had her, he wasn't sure what to do with her. He thought of carrying her home and putting her to bed. He thought that might be fun.

Miss Renfrew hurried in. "Chloe, they're leav—"

She stopped short.

"Miss Sharp is not well," Bates said.

"Excess of . . . excitement," Lovedon said.

"We need to revive her," Bates said.

"She needs to go to bed . . . and sleep it off," Lovedon said. She was flushed, and under the miles of silk there seemed to be a splendidly rounded body, invitingly warm. His head dipped a little, and he inhaled a delicious blend of scents: soap and flowers and Woman.

She stirred in his arms. "Put me down."

"Probably not wise," he said, "considering you can't stand up."

"I need to say goodbye to the *happy* couple," she said. Her voice was slurred. "The madly-in-love-with-each-other couple."

"If you try to walk unaided, you'll fall on your face," Lovedon told her.

"If you keep trying to carry me, you'll fall on *your* face," she said. "I'll lean on Amy. Please put me down and go away. To the devil, preferably."

She was shapely and highly entertaining and she smelled delectable. Lovedon wanted to take her to a private corner—the house abounded in secret nooks and crannies—and set about winning her over. In her present condition, though, that would be unsporting. In any case, he preferred a woman to be fully conscious when he set about seducing her.

He let her down very carefully, so carefully that he felt every inch of her descent. For one heady moment, her breasts pressed against his chest. When her feet touched the floor, he cautiously released her. She started to turn away, swayed, and grabbed his lapels.

His arm went around her neat little waist.

"Oh, Lord," she said. "I do believe I'm actually drunk."

"You can't be drunk *now*," Miss Renfrew said. "It's time to take leave of the newlyweds."

"I . . . don't . . . know," Miss Sharp said. "I really need . . . to sit . . . lie . . . down." She slumped against Lovedon. "You smell like starch," she said. "And something else."

"Listen to me," he said. "You can do this, Miss Sharp. If you don't, your sister will wonder what's wrong. You don't want to worry her, I know."

"You were mean to her." She looked up at him, green-gold eyes wide and accusing and slightly crossed.

"Yes, I'm a brute," he said. "Ten minutes. That's all we'll need. I'll give you my arm and Miss Renfrew will support you discreetly on the other side. And Bates will bring up the rear. The crush will be so great that no one will notice we're propping you up. You'll wish the couple well and make your curtseys—"

"If I curtsey, I don't think I'll be able to get up again. I think I'd like to lie on the floor, please."

"Ten minutes," he said. "Pretend to be perfectly well for ten minutes, that's all. Then we'll get you safely away. If you'll do this, you and I shall have our duel."

She blinked up at him. "I get to shoot you?"

"Yes."

She smiled, and it was the genuine article this time. Her mouth softened and curved and her face took on the kind of blissful expression a man was accustomed to see—if he was skillful—in more intimate situations. His lower regions, which didn't understand the concept of proper time and place, became primed for action. And his mood soared so high so swiftly that his head spun, and the room whirled along with it.

The rain continued to beat at the windows, but in his world the sun had broken out, and life had blossomed into riotous colors.

"Very well," she said. "I accept your terms."

Getting Miss Sharp through those ten minutes wasn't the easiest thing Lovedon had ever done, though it might have been the most amusing. He suspected he'd damaged an internal organ, keeping a straight face throughout the proceedings.

But with Bates's and Miss Renfrew's help, he got her through the goodbyes. There followed several other interesting maneuvers, including flat-out lying to her parents while Miss Renfrew guarded her in an antechamber.

The crowd, the heat, fatigue, combined with strong emotion, had proved too much for Miss Sharp, Lovedon told them. To avoid disrupting the family's remaining commitments for the day, he offered to send her home in his carriage with her friend, Miss Renfrew.

Though initially alarmed, they did not, in fact, have much attention to spare their eldest unwed daughter. He knew they had other engagements this day, including a reception at Windsor, because he was expected to appear at the same events. After only a few mild protests about his lordship's taking so much trouble, they consented.

That done, Lovedon smuggled the drunken bridesmaid down the steep back staircase in the west wing to the ground floor. With him clasping her arm, she was able to get down the narrow stairs more or less unaided. As soon as they came out under the south front's arcade, though, the fresh air hit her—or rather she hit it, much in the way one runs abruptly into a wall.

She tottered backward. He caught hold of her, then wrapped one arm about her shoulder. "Now, *stay*," he said.

She heaved a great sigh and leaned against him. The top of her head came to his chin. They stood in the shelter of the great arcade, out of sight of anybody happening to look out of the windows. It was a fine opportunity to get up to no good . . . but she wasn't in proper condition. Not to mention that Bates stood only a few paces away, having a terse whispered dispute with Miss Renfrew.

Lovedon stood stoically with his armful of drunken deliciousness and gazed down the driveway, watching his carriage approach through the rain.

"Don't forget," came a slurred voice from the environs of his neck cloth.

He looked down.

She gazed somberly up at him.

"Believe me, I shall not forget this day," he said.

"Our duel," she said. "It was good of you to stop me from falling down, but . . ." She stared at him for a long moment.

"Think nothing of it, Miss Sharp," he said. "It's hardly the first time I've helped a drunken friend home."

She wagged a gloved finger under his chin. "Ah, but I'm not your friend."

"That's what you think," he said.

"I'll never be your friend," she said. "Though I will admit . . ." She bit her lower lip. A tiny crease appeared between her delicately arched eyebrows.

She was thinking, obviously.

He pictured thoughts staggering through her brain, trying to find their way.

The carriage neared, and Bates stepped out under one of the arcade's arches to signal the coachman where to stop. A footman leapt off the back, opened an umbrella, and hurried toward them.

After seeing Miss Renfrew stowed safely inside, the footman returned. Keeping a firm hold of Miss Sharp, Lovedon steered her toward the vehicle.

Getting her into it wanted ingenuity and quick reflexes. He could only hope that his broad back in combination with the large umbrella and the rain would prevent any onlookers in the house from observing the performance.

When he'd finally got her foot securely on the carriage step, she said, "I'll admit I might have made a small error of judgment."

"You made a fatal error," he said. "You attracted my attention. Now you'll have the devil of a time getting rid of me." He gave her a push. Miss Renfrew quickly reached out and pulled her friend, who landed on the seat in a flurry of swishing silk. She laughed. "Oh, you silly man."

The footman closed the door and Lovedon backed away from the carriage.

A moment later, the vehicle rolled away. He watched it go. As it reached the first curve of the driveway, the window went down and a white-gloved hand appeared and gave a jaunty wave.

Lovedon House
18th June, half-past eleven o'clock

Madam:

    I shall expect to meet you at dusk this day at Battersea Fields for the purpose of defending my honor against the charges of being a coward and no gentleman. I shall supply the weapons, and Bates will act as my friend, whether he likes it or not.

    A ticket porter has been engaged to loiter in the vicinity of your home. A written reply given into his keeping will make its way both discreetly and speedily to me.

 I have the honor to be,
 Madam,
 Your obedient servant,
  Lovedon

Portman Square
18th June, one o'clock

My Lord:

 I have the honor to acknowledge the receipt of your lordship's letter, which is thoroughly ridiculous. If your lordship thinks I propose to be hanged for killing a peer—and I ought to point out that I am an excellent shot—I recommend your lordship think again. Yesterday, as your lordship is well aware, I was deep in my cups—and it is perfectly beastly of your lordship to remind me of the fact.

 I have the honor to be,
 My Lord,
 Your lordship's obedient servant,
  Chloe Sharp

Lovedon House
18th June, half-past two o'clock

Madam:

 I have the honor to acknowledge the receipt of your letter of one o'clock. Does this mean you retract your words and apologize?

 I have the honor to be,

Madam,
Your obedient servant,
    Lovedon

Portman Square
18th June, three o'clock

My Lord:

I would rather hang than apologize to you. For anything.
Ever.
    I have the honor to be,
    My Lord,
    Your lordship's obedient servant,
        Chloe Sharp

Lovedon House
18th June, half-past three o'clock

Madam:

Your having declined to give the reparation which I
consider myself entitled to receive, I now call upon you to
give me that satisfaction for your conduct which a gentleman
has a right to require, and which a gentleman never refuses
to give. I shall expect to see you at Battersea Fields at seven
o'clock this evening.
    I have the honor to be,
    Madam,
    Your obedient servant,
        Lovedon

P.S. I dare you.

Portman Square
18th June, half-past four o'clock

My Lord:

The satisfaction which your lordship has demanded, it is of course impossible for me to decline.

I have the honor to be,
My Lord,
Your lordship's obedient servant,
   Chloe Sharp

Battersea Fields, half-past seven o'clock

Chloe stood by the cabriolet in which she and Amy had arrived. The setting sun cast a golden glow over the marshy wasteland, and she was pretending to be perfectly calm, enjoying the scenery, while Amy and Mr. Bates carried on their fussing about various dueling rules.

Lord Lovedon stood no great distance away, by his carriage—the one that had taken her home last night.

Her face didn't go up in flames at the recollection because it didn't need to. Her face had been burning since this morning, when the ferocious pounding behind her eyes had begun to abate enough to allow her memory to take over the job of tormenting her.

She had remembered, then, every single thing that had happened yesterday afternoon, down to the moment when she'd sent Lord Lovedon a saucy wave from his carriage window.

She'd discovered this morning what it meant to die of embarrassment.

A reasonable man of even minimal sensibility would have realized that she'd suffered enough for her extremely stupid and unladylike behavior.

A man of delicacy and understanding would have the tact to leave her to squirm with shame in the privacy of her home.

But no. He had to rub her face in it.

And now she had this idiot duel to fight, when they both knew that neither of them would do anything but fire into the air.

He probably thought it was amusing.

Everyone said he was whimsical.

Good grief, would Amy and Mr. Bates never cease bickering?

"They're making quite a project of this," came a deep, drawling voice from somewhere above her shoulder.

She gave a start and a mortifying little squeak of surprise.

"Was it absolutely necessary to sneak up on me?" she said.

"I'm over six feet tall in my bare feet," he said. "I'm wearing boots and a hat—and while I'll admit my clothes are uniformly dark, as is de rigueur for a duel, I should have thought I was hard to miss, Miss Sharp."

"I was not paying attention," she said. "I was . . . thinking."

"I observed that you were not paying attention to me," he said. "That's why I brought myself closer."

She remembered being swept up in his arms. She remembered the feel of his hand at the back of her waist, keeping her steady. She remembered his arm about her shoulders . . . the warmth and strength of his big body.

The sun was sinking but it seemed to be blazing down on her, on everything, and all the world seemed to be softening and melting.

She didn't want to melt. She didn't want to be one of the scores of women waiting for the exclusive attention he was probably incapable of giving.

Still, she remembered what he'd said yesterday and the way he'd charmed her by degrees without her quite realizing. She recalled the series of witty, provoking notes he'd sent this day . . . and how she'd wished he'd come in person to annoy her, so that she could throw something at him—and at the same time she'd laughed, too, at his absurd messages. And she had very greatly enjoyed composing her answers.

"Amy has never acted as a second before, and she spent two hours studying Papa's copy of *The British Code of the Duel*," she said. "It's her fault we weren't exactly on time—because she insisted that we couldn't proceed without a surgeon in attendance. I told her that was silly. If I kill you, no surgeon can do you any good. If I only wound you, naturally I shall leave you to bleed to death."

"I'm sure that goes without saying," he said in a stifled voice.

She looked up sharply. His expression was far too innocent.

"I know you think this is a hilarious joke, taunting me to come out to this place," she said.

"I wasn't sure how else to get you alone," he said.

"We are not alone," she said.

He glanced toward Amy and Mr. Bates, who seemed to having a controversy about the weapons. "This will do. For the moment."

"Since we are somewhat alone," she said, "I ought to warn you: I've actually decided not to kill you, no matter how great the temptation. I shall fire into the air."

"I beg you will not," he said. "You might harm an innocent bird."

"I most certainly will not fire at you."

"It would only be fair," he said. "Because I most certainly mean to fire at you."

"No, you don't," she said.

"I do—and I urge you to shoot straight at me," he said. "I promise you'll feel better afterward. *Trust me.*"

Amy stomped toward them. "This is most irregular," she said. "The combatants are not supposed to be enjoying a tête-à-tête."

"Lord Lovedon was bored," Chloe said. "He came to amuse himself at my expense, because you and Mr. Bates are taking an eternity."

"What seems to be the difficulty?" Lord Lovedon said.

"The dueling ground," Amy said.

"Ah, yes," Lord Lovedon said. "According to *The British Code of the Duel*, as Miss Renfrew is now aware, the seconds must 'choose out a snug sequestered spot, where the ground is level, and no natural, terrestrial, or celestial line presenting itself to assist either party in his views of sending his opponent into eternity.'"

Chloe stared at him.

"I have a terrifying memory," Lord Lovedon said.

"Well, we've settled it," Amy said. "Lord Lovedon, would you be so good as to accompany Mr. Bates. Chloe, you're to come with me."

The seconds chose the place where the Duke of Wellington and the Earl of Winchilsea had fought their duel a few years ago. It was the site Lovedon had suggested to Bates—fitting, Lovedon thought, today being the twentieth anniversary of Waterloo. Though Miss Renfrew evidently required persuading, she had to see it was a suitable spot, a stretch of flat ground near the river, not easily visible to passersby.

One had to cross a drainage ditch to get there. Lovedon offered to carry Miss Sharp over it.

"That won't be necessary," she told him. "Today I'm painfully sober."

He watched her make the small leap. For a second, her skirts lifted, and he had a glimpse of purple half-boots. He smiled.

It was the one bright element in her attire. She'd worn what he guessed was an archery dress: The dark blue garment's sleeves were not the vast, ballooning ones fashion dictated, but fitted tight, especially along the lower arms. Instead of an immense bonnet festooned with feathers and ribbons and lace, she wore a tiny black hat.

The costume made her a narrower target.

He supposed she'd done it on purpose to mock him. That was more or less why he'd donned dueling dress: uniformly dark clothing, including his neck cloth, which was black. He was mocking himself, as well he ought.

Thanks to boredom and drink, he'd been a stupendous lout yesterday. Yet if he'd behaved well, he wouldn't have discovered her. He wouldn't have had the fun of writing incendiary notes and picturing her gleefully composing her replies.

He watched the seconds gravely mark out the field. Then Miss Renfrew guided Miss Sharp to her place. Bates, wearing a look of exasperation, approached and said, "You'll stand here—and you had better pray that nobody gets wind of this."

"My lips are sealed," Lovedon said.

"How I wish that were ever true," Bates said.

He then proceeded to the halfway point between the duelists and asked if there was any possibility of reconciliation.

Miss Sharp shook her head.

Bates looked to Lovedon.

He shook his head.

The lowering sun gilded the fields. A gentle breeze caressed his face.

What a splendid evening for a duel, he thought.

Trust me.

Amy put the pistol in Chloe's hand. It was quite small and oddly shaped, double-barreled, and stunningly ornate: gold, with exquisite enameling, and set with pearls and diamonds. She stared at it.

"It's French," Amy said. "You cock it with this." She indicated a part. "Then it works the same as any other pistol, Mr. Bates said. But it has a very short range. I suspect it's easier to injure somebody by hitting them in the head with the grip. In any event, we need to shorten the dueling distance. Do you mind? I pointed out to Mr. Bates that the minimum distance is no less than three yards. I do wish I knew what was in Lord Lovedon's mind."

"He's whimsical," Chloe said.

"Yes, everyone says so. And it's mere form, of course. So many duels are, you know. One goes through the motions—"

"Yes, yes," Chloe broke in impatiently. "But we must do it Lord Lovedon's way." She'd called him a coward and no gentleman. She'd refused to apologize. That, Amy had said, gave him the choice of weapons and terms. And the first shot. "If he wants to dirty his pretty French pistols by shooting them off, that's his choice."

Shoot straight at me . . . Trust me.

Though she knew—she was *positive*—she had nothing to be afraid of, her heart was pounding very hard. She cocked the weapon as Amy had instructed and held it down by her side.

She was aware of Lord Lovedon following the same procedure, but it was a distant awareness. So many wild thoughts raced through her mind that she couldn't keep up with them, let alone make sense of them. Her heart wouldn't slow. She knew nothing terrible would happen, yet she was panicking all the same.

She was aware of Lord Lovedon coming much closer.

This was too close.

They were very small pistols, but small ones tended to be highly inaccurate. She might hurt him by accident. But no, they couldn't be loaded. He wouldn't shoot her and he couldn't possibly want her to shoot him.

Could he?

This was absurd. He was doing it on purpose to aggravate her. Whimsical, indeed.

Mr. Bates said, "Miss Renfrew will ask if you are ready, then count to two, and give the word to fire. Is that clear?"

Lord Lovedon nodded.

Chloe nodded, though nothing was at all clear.

"Ready?" Amy called out.

No, I'm not even slightly ready.

"One."

Chloe sucked in air.

"Two."

She let it out.

"Fire."

Lord Lovedon raised his pistol and pointed it at her.

Trust me.

He fired.

A little blue and green bird sprang up from between the two barrels.

It twirled and fluttered its wings and sang, "Tweet tweet tweet tweet tweet."

Her face was a picture. Lovedon had all he could do to maintain his composure.

Then laughter spilled out of her, great gulps and whoops and funny little snorts.

"Your turn, Miss Sharp," he said.

She turned away, laughing, holding her pistol to her belly.

He stood watching her, marveling at the exuberance and joy of her. She laughed in the same way she'd defended her sister: with all her heart.

"Miss Sharp," he said.

She went off into whoops again. Then she wiped her

eyes on the sleeve of her dress and returned to her dueling stance—body sideways, her glowing face straight on, pistol at her side. She brought up the pistol and fired.

A little blue and green bird popped up between the barrels and fluttered its wings and turned its head this way and that, so wondrously like a real bird, and it tweeted in the cheerful, beckoning way of a bird seeking its mate.

For a time, their birds tweeted and flirted with each other.

She watched the birds. When they stilled, she looked at him.

"I see," she said in a trembling voice. "They're French."

"I would say excessively so."

She held out the singing bird pistol. He took it from her, letting his hand graze hers. He put the birds back into their respective hiding places in the devices, then stepped away to return them to the pistol case, which Bates had left on the ground nearby. When Lovedon rose, he saw the two seconds walking back to the carriages, leaving the duelists to sort themselves out.

He turned to her.

She stood watching him. Her expression had grown serious, and he couldn't read it.

He grew anxious. If he muddled this part, he was finished.

"I realize I made a very bad first impression," he said. "But I can't apologize. If I hadn't behaved ill, you wouldn't have behaved ill, and then where should we be?"

"Not in Battersea Fields, certainly," she said. "This . . . it . . ." Her lower lip trembled. Her eyes filled.

She covered her face and wept then, great, racking sobs, as uninhibited as her laughter.

Heart pounding, he closed the distance between them and wrapped his arms about her and held her.

The storm abated as suddenly as it had begun. After a moment, she tried to draw away. He didn't let go. "I only want to know I'm forgiven," he said.

"I forgive you," she said. "That was not what I . . ." She paused and swallowed. "My sister was going away, and I was so sure I couldn't be happy again, for a very long time."

"And now?"

She didn't answer, but she pushed, harder this time, and reluctantly he released her. She'd felt right in his arms. She'd felt right, he realized, from the moment she'd slapped him with her glove.

She started to turn away.

"You did the right thing," he said, "calling me to account."

She waved this away. "I was pot-valiant."

"You'd have done it even if you'd been fully sober," he said. "You might have done it differently, but you would have acted—out of love and loyalty and . . . all the right things."

She turned back to him, surprised.

"I want to make reparations," he said.

"You've done that," she said. Her expression grew wry. "What a horrid waking up I had today."

"I've had my share of those," he said.

"You said you'd seen drunken friends home before," she said. "I've never done anything like that before in my life."

"Perhaps I bring out something special in you," he said.

"I was *mortified*," she said. "I was positive it would be years before I could look myself in the eye, let alone you."

She looked up. "I begin to understand why men do it. A duel clears the air and settles everything."

"And one can be friends again," he said.

"We can't be friends again," she said. "We weren't friends *before*. Our worlds would never have overlapped if not for Althea's marrying Prince Louis."

"The world changes on that *if*," he said. "We met, we had words, we had a duel. And now that we've cleared the air, I should like to start over."

The color rising in her face told him she was beginning to understand what he was about.

"I beg that you won't judge me by my actions yesterday," he said.

She stared down at the toes of her purple boots. "They were not, all things considered, *consistently* bad actions," she said.

"I improve on acquaintance, people say," he said. "Well, Bates wouldn't say it, but one must bear in mind that he's lately had a severe disappointment in love, which makes him bitter and quarrelsome. However, Miss Renfrew seems well able to hold her own with him, and really, I don't care much about them. I only care whether you will do me the honor of allowing me to take you for a drive in Hyde Park tomorrow afternoon."

She stared at her boots for quite a long time. She bit her lip.

He waited, calm on the outside, while his heart attempted to break all previous speed records.

Finally she looked up. "Are you quite sure?" she said.

Speeches wanted to tumble out of him, wild declarations. But that was mad. They'd met only yesterday. He would take this one step at a time, if it killed him.

"Quite," he said.

Castle de Grey, four weeks later

Lovedon drew Chloe into the passage between the drawing room and the picture gallery.

"It was here, wasn't it?" Lovedon said. "This was where you heard me talking rot about Prince Louis and your sister."

"Yes," she said. "But this isn't an immense royal wedding, only a dinner party, and we'll be missed."

"Let them miss us," he said.

He'd arranged the dinner party with his cousin the Duchess of Marchmont. She would have a very good idea why Lovedon had slipped out of the drawing room with Miss Sharp. Being far from conventional, Her Grace would cover up for them.

He wrapped his arms about Chloe and kissed her, firmly, so that there would be no question about it, and lingeringly, so that she wouldn't forget it in a hurry. And yes, certainly, he did it because he needed to and had needed to for what felt like eternity.

"There," he said, when he was sure he'd done the job properly. She started to pull away, but she stumbled, and he caught her about the waist. Her perfect waist, that went with the rest of her perfect body.

"I am not drunk," she said.

"I know that," he said. "I shouldn't have sneaked you in here if you were. You need to be completely in your senses."

"That's impossible, after what you just did," she said.

Her voice was a little husky, and even in the passage's dim light, he saw the soft glow in her eyes.

"Somewhat in your senses will be sufficient," he said. "But not dead drunk. That wouldn't be fair. And I need you to answer more or less rationally." He went on in a rush, "I meant to take this in slow stages, but I'm so stupidly in love with you that slow and steady is only going to drive me mad."

"In love," she said softly.

"Yes, of course. How could I not be? I meant to be romantic, but this was the best I could do on short notice. That is, I didn't mean it to be short notice. I meant to wait until at least Tuesday next, but preferably until September. But there you were, sitting across the dinner table, and I was thinking how agreeable it would be if we could go upstairs to the same bedroom, instead of separate houses, and you could sit in my lap instead of all the way across the table on a chair. And then . . ." He trailed off because his brain was conjuring images that activated his breeding organs while deadening his powers of speech and clear thinking.

He sounded, in short, like a complete nitwit.

"I'm trying to decide," she said, "whether this is meant to be an offer of carte blanche or a proposal of marriage."

"I adore you," he said.

"That declaration could take things either way," she said.

"My dear Chloe, if you don't marry me, I'll do something rash."

"By which you mean, I presume, hitting yourself in the

head repeatedly with the singing bird pistols until you lose consciousness and I take pity on you and say yes."

"I will certainly do that if necessary."

"Oh, you're the most ridiculous man. Of course I'll say yes. I was saying yes, very likely, at the same moment I threw champagne in your face. And I think it's the most romantic thing in the world, your proposing in this passage, instead of properly, on your knees in, say, our drawing room."

"I hoped you'd think that."

"You knew I'd think that," she said. "It's a tragic thing, but our minds are strangely alike."

"Yes, but I love you anyway," he said. He pulled her close again. "And I challenge you to put up with me until death us do part."

She reached up and caught him about the neck. "My lord," she said, "the satisfaction which your lordship has demanded, it is of course impossible for me to decline."

Despite Lord Lovedon's impatience, the marriage had to wait for the bride's dress and the bridesmaids' dresses, and these things take time if they're to be done properly. Since every item issuing from Maison Noirot was always done properly, it was nearly September before Chloe Sharp became Lady Lovedon.

They were married, naturally, in the Gold Drawing Room of Castle de Grey, and the laughing way they looked at each other at the end—so obviously sharing a private joke—told all the world that yes, undoubtedly, they'd married for love.

Not only are the singing bird pistols based on historical fact, but they still exist. To watch these wondrous mechanical devices in action, please go to:

http://www.christies.com/singing
-bird-pistols-en-1422-3.aspx

Keep reading for
an excerpt from
Loretta Chase's
next historical romance

SCANDAL WEARS SATIN

Available July 2012

CHAPTER ONE

For the last week, the whole of the fashionable world has been in a state of ferment, on account of the elopement of Sir Colquhoun Grant's daughter with Mr. Brinsley Sheridan ... On Friday afternoon, about five o'clock, the young couple borrowed the carriage of a friend; and ... set off full speed for the North.

—*The Court Journal*, Saturday 23 May 1835

London
Thursday 21 May 1835

Waving a copy of *Foxe's Morning Spectacle*, Sophy Noirot burst in upon the Duke and Duchess of Clevedon while they were breakfasting in, appropriately enough, the breakfast room of Clevedon House.

"Have you seen this?" she said, throwing down the paper on the table between her sister and new brother-in-law. "The ton is in a frenzy—and isn't it hilarious? They're blaming Sheridan's three sisters. Three sisters plotting wicked plots—

and it isn't *us!* Oh, my love, when I saw this, I thought I'd die laughing."

Certain members of Society had more than once in recent days compared the three proprietresses of Maison Noirot—which Sophy would make London's foremost dressmaking establishment if it killed her—to the three witches in *Macbeth.* Had they not bewitched the Duke of Clevedon, rumor said, he would never have married a *shopkeeper.*

Their Graces' dark heads bent over the barely dry newspaper.

Rumors about the Sheridan-Grant elopement were already traveling the beau monde grapevine, but the *Spectacle,* as usual, was the first to put confirmation in print.

Marcelline looked up. "They say Miss Grant's papa will bring a suit against Sheridan in Chancery," she said. "Exciting stuff, indeed."

At that moment, a footman entered. "Lord Longmore, Your Grace," he said.

Not now, dammit, Sophy thought. Her sister had the beau monde in an uproar, she'd made a deadly enemy of one of its most powerful women—who happened to be Longmore's mother—customers were deserting in droves, and Sophy had no idea how to repair the damage.

Now *him.*

The Earl of Longmore strolled into the breakfast room, a newspaper under his arm.

Sophy's pulse rate accelerated. It couldn't help itself.

Black hair and glittering black eyes . . . the noble nose that ought to have been broken a dozen times yet remained stubbornly straight and arrogant . . . the hard, cynical mouth . . . the six-foot-plus frame.

All that manly beauty.

If only he had a brain.

No, better not. In the first place, brains in a man were inconvenient. In the second, and far more important, she didn't have time for him or any man. She had a shop to rescue from Impending Doom.

"I brought you the latest *Spectacle*," he said to the pair at the table. "But I wasn't quick enough off the mark, I see."

"Sophy brought it," said Marcelline.

Longmore's dark gaze came to Sophy. She gave him a cool nod and sauntered to the sideboard. She looked into the chafing dishes and concentrated on filling her plate.

"Miss Noirot," he said. "Up and about early, I see. You weren't at Almack's last night."

"Certainly not," Sophy said. "The Spanish Inquisition couldn't make the patronesses give me a voucher."

"Since when do you wait for permission? I was so disappointed. I was on pins and needles to see what disguise you'd adopt. My favorite so far is the Lancashire maidservant."

That was Sophy's favorite, too.

However, her intrusions at fashionable events to collect gossip for Foxe were supposed to be a deep, dark secret. No one noticed servant girls, and she was a Noirot, as skilled at making herself invisible as she was at getting attention.

But *he* noticed.

He must have developed unusually keen powers of hearing and vision to make up for his very small brain.

She carried her plate to the table and sat next to her sister. "I'm devastated to have spoiled your fun," she said.

"That's all right," he said. "I found something to do later."

"So it seems," Clevedon said, looking him over. "It must have been quite a party. Since you're never up and about this early, I can only conclude you stopped here on your way home."

Like most of his kind, Lord Longmore rarely rose before noon. His rumpled black hair, limp neckcloth, and wrinkled coat, waistcoat, and trousers told Sophy he hadn't yet been to bed—not his own, at any rate.

Her imagination promptly set about picturing his big body naked among tangled sheets. She had never seen him naked, and had better not; but along with owning a superior imagination, she'd seen statues, pictures, and—years ago—certain boastful Parisian boys' personal possessions.

She firmly wiped her mind clean.

One day, she'd marry a respectable man who would not get in the way of her work.

Not only was Longmore far from respectable, but he was a great thickhead who constantly got in one's way—and who happened to be the eldest son of a woman who wanted the Noirot sisters wiped off the face of the earth.

Only a self-destructive moron would get involved with him.

Sophy directed her attention to his clothes. As far as tailoring went, his attire was flawless, the snug fit outlining every muscled inch from his big shoulders and broad chest and his lean waist and narrow hips down, down, down his long, powerful legs . . .

She scrubbed her mind again, reminded herself that clothing was her life, and regarded his attire objectively, as one professional considering the work of another.

She knew that he usually started an evening elegantly turned out. His valet, Olney, saw to it. But Longmore did not always behave elegantly, and what happened after he left the house Olney could not control.

By the looks of him, a great deal had happened after Olney released his master yesterday.

"You always were the intellectual giant of the family," Longmore said to the duke. "You've deduced correctly. I stopped at Crockford's. And elsewhere. I needed something to drive out the memory of those dreary hours at Almack's."

"You loathe those assemblies," Clevedon said. "One can only assume that a woman lured you there."

"My sister," Longmore said. "She's an idiot about men. My parents complain about it endlessly. Even I noticed what a sorry lot they are, her beaux. A pack of lechers and bankrupts. To discourage them, I hang about Clara and look threatening."

Sophy could easily picture it. No one could loom as menacingly as he; gazing down on the world through half-closed eyes like a great, dark bird of prey.

"How unusually brotherly of you," said Clevedon.

"That numskull Adderley was trying to press his suit with her." Longmore helped himself to coffee and sat down next to Clevedon, opposite Marcelline. "She thinks he's charming. I think he's charmed by her dowry."

"Rumor says he's traveling up the River Tick on a fast current," Clevedon said.

"I don't like his smirk," Longmore said. "And I don't think he even likes Clara much. My parents loathe him on a dozen counts." He waved his coffee cup at the newspaper. "They won't find this coup of Sheridan's reassuring. Still, it's deuced convenient for you, I daresay. An excellent way to divert attention from your exciting nuptials."

His dark gaze moved lazily to Sophy. "The timing couldn't have been better. I don't suppose you had anything to do with this, Miss Noirot?"

"If I had, I should be demanding a bottle of the duke's best champagne and a toast to myself," said Sophy. "I only wish I could have managed something so *perfect*."

Though the three Noirot sisters were equally talented dressmakers, each had special skills. Dark-haired Marcelline, the eldest, was a gifted artist and designer. Redheaded Leonie, the youngest, was the financial genius. Sophy, the blonde, was the saleswoman. She could soften stony hearts and pry large sums from tight fists. She could make people believe black was white. Her sisters often said that Sophy could sell sand to Bedouins.

Had she been able to manufacture a scandal that would get Society's shallow little mind off Marcelline and onto somebody else, Sophy would have done it. As much as she loved Marcelline and was happy she'd married a man who adored her, Sophy was still reeling from the disruption to their world, which always revolved around their little family and their business. She wasn't sure Marcelline and Clevedon truly understood the difficulties their recent marriage had created for Maison Noirot, or how much danger the shop was in.

But then, they were newlyweds, and love seemed to

muddle the mind even worse than lust did. At present, Sophy couldn't bear to mar their happiness by sharing her and Leonie's anxieties.

The newlyweds exchanged looks. "What do you think?" Clevedon said. "Do you want to take advantage of the diversion and go back to work?"

"I must go back to work, diversion or not," Marcelline said. She looked at Sophy. "Do let's make a speedy departure, *ma chère sœur*. The aunts will be down to breakfast in the next hour or so."

"The aunts," Longmore said. "Still here?"

Clevedon House was large enough to accommodate several families comfortably. When the duke's aunts came to Town on visits too short to warrant opening their own townhouses, they didn't stay in hotels, but in the north wing.

Most recently they'd come to stop the marriage.

Originally, Marcelline and Clevedon had planned to wed the day after he'd talked—or seduced—her into marrying him. But Sophy and Leonie's cooler heads had prevailed.

The wedding, they'd pointed out, was going to cause a spectacular uproar, very possibly fatal to business. But if some of Clevedon's relatives were to attend the ceremony, signaling acceptance of the bride, it would subdue, to some extent, the outrage.

And so Clevedon had invited his aunts, who'd descended en masse to prevent the shocking misalliance. But no great lady, not even the Queen, was a match for three Noirot sisters and their secret weapon, Marcelline's six-year-old daughter, Lucie Cordelia. The aunts had surrendered in a matter of hours.

Now they were trying to find a way to make Marcelline respectable. They actually believed they could present her to the Queen.

Sophy wasn't at all sure that would do Maison Noirot any good. On the contrary, she suspected it would only fan the flames of Lady Warford's hatred.

"Still here," Clevedon said. "They can't seem to tear themselves away."

Marcelline rose, and the others did, too. "I'd better go before they come down," she said. "They're not at all reconciled to my continuing to work."

"Meaning there's a good deal more jawing than you like," Longmore said. "How well I understand." He gave her a wry smile, and bowed.

He was a man who could fill a doorway, and seemed to take over a room. He was disheveled, and disreputable besides, but he bowed with the easy grace of a dandy.

It was annoying of him to be so completely and gracefully at ease in that big brawler's body of his. It was really annoying of him to ooze virility.

Sophy was a Noirot, a breed keenly tuned to animal excitement—and not possessing much in the way of moral principles.

If he ever found out how weak she was in this regard, she was doomed.

She sketched a curtsey and took her sister's arm. "Yes, well, we'd better not dawdle, in any event. I promised Leonie I wouldn't stay above half an hour."

She hurried her sister out of the room.

Longmore watched them go. Actually, he watched Sophy go, a fetching bundle of energy and guile.

"The shop," he said when they were out of earshot. "Meaning no disrespect to your duchess, but—are they insane?"

"That depends on one's point of view," Clevedon said.

"Apparently, I'm not unbalanced enough in the upper storey to understand it," Longmore said. "They might close it and live here. It isn't as though you're short of room. Or money. Why should they want to go on bowing and scraping to women?"

"Passion," Clevedon said. "Their work is their passion."

Longmore wasn't sure what, exactly, passion was. He was reasonably certain he'd never experienced it.

He hadn't even had an infatuation since he was eighteen.

Since Clevedon, his nearest friend, would know this, Longmore said nothing. He only shook his head, and moved to the sideboard. He heaped his plate with eggs, great slabs of bacon and bread, and a thick glob of butter to make it all slide down smoothly. He carried it to the table and began to eat.

He'd always regarded Clevedon's home as his own, and had been told he was to continue regarding it in the same way. The duchess seemed to like him well enough. Her blonde sister, on the other hand would just as soon shoot him, he knew—which made her much more interesting and entertaining.

That was why he'd waited and watched for her. That was why he'd followed her from Maison Noirot to Charing Cross. He'd spotted the newspaper in her hand, and deduced what it was.

By some feat of printing legerdemain—a pact with the
devil, most likely—*Foxe's Morning Spectacle* usually slunk
onto the streets of London and into the newspaper sellers'
grubby hands not only well in advance of its competitors, but
containing fresher scandal. Though many of the beau monde's
entertainments didn't start until eleven at night or end before
dawn, Foxe contrived to stuff the pages of his titillating rag
with details of what everyone had done mere hours earlier.

This was no small achievement, even bearing in mind that
"morning," especially among the upper classes, was a flexible
unit of time, extending well beyond noonday.

Curious about what was taking her to Clevedon House at
this early hour, he'd bought a copy from the urchin hawking
it on the next corner, and had dawdled for a time to look it
over. By now familiar with Sophy's writing, Longmore knew
it wasn't the sort of thing to take on an empty stomach. He'd
persevered nonetheless. Though he couldn't see how she could
have had a hand in the Sheridan scandal, that was nothing
new. She did a great deal he found intriguing—starting with
the way she walked: She carried herself like a lady, like the
women of his class, yet the sway of her hips promised something tantalizingly unladylike.

"I married Marcelline knowing she'd never give up her
work," Clevedon was saying. "If she did, she'd be like everyone
else. She wouldn't be the woman I fell in love with."

"Love," Longmore said. "Bad idea."

Clevedon smiled. "One day Love will come along and
knock you on your arse," he said. "And I'll laugh myself sick,
watching."

"Love will have its work cut out for it," Longmore said. "I'm not like you. I'm not *sensitive*. If Love wants to take hold of me, not only will it have to knock me on my arse, it'll have to tie me down and beat to a pulp what some optimistically call my brains."

"Very possibly," Clevedon said. "Which will make it all the more amusing."

"You'll have a wait," Longmore said. "For the moment, Clara's love life is the problem."

"I daresay matters at home haven't been pleasant for either of you, since the wedding," Clevedon said.

Clevedon would know better than most. Lord Warford had been his guardian. Clevedon and Longmore had grown up together. They were more like brothers than friends. And Clevedon had doted on Clara since she was a small child. It had always been assumed they'd marry. Then the duke had met his dressmaker—and Clara had reacted with "Good riddance"—much to the shock of her parents, brothers, and sisters—not to mention the entire beau monde.

"My father has resigned himself," Longmore said. "My mother hasn't."

A profound understatement, that.

His mother was beside herself. The slightest reference to the duke or his new wife set her screaming. She quarreled with Clara incessantly. She was driving Clara to distraction, and they constantly dragged Longmore into it. Every day or so a message arrived from his sister, begging him to come and Do Something.

Longmore and Clara had both attended Clevedon's

wedding—in effect, giving their blessing to the union. This fact, which had been promptly reported in the *Spectacle*, had turned Warford House into a battlefield.

"I could well understand Clara rejecting me," Clevedon said.

"Don't see how you could fail to understand," Longmore said. "She explained it in detail, in ringing tones, in front of half the ton."

"What I don't understand is why she doesn't send Adderley about his business," Clevedon said.

"Tall, fair, poetic-looking," Longmore said. "He knows what to say to women. Men see him for what he is. Women don't."

"I've no idea what's in Clara's mind," Clevedon said. "My wife and her sisters will want to get to the bottom of it, though. It's their business to understand their clients, and Clara's special. She's their best customer, and she shows Marcelline's designs to stunning advantage. They won't want her to marry a man with pockets to let."

"Are they in the matchmaking line as well, then?" Longmore said. "If so, I wish they'd find her someone suitable, and spare me these dreary nights at Almack's."

"Leave it to Sophy," Clevedon said. "She's the one who goes to the parties. She'll see what's going on, better than anybody."

"Including a great deal that people would rather she didn't see," Longmore said.

"Hers is an exceptionally keen eye for detail," Clevedon said.

"And an exceptionally busy pen," Longmore said. "It's

easy to recognize her work in the *Spectacle*. Streams of words about ribbons and bows and lace and pleats here and gathers there. No thread goes unmentioned."

"She notices gestures and looks as well," Clevedon said. "She listens. No one's stories are like hers."

"No question about that," Longmore said. "She's never met an adjective or adverb she didn't like."

Clevedon smiled. "That's what brings in the customers: the combination of gossip and the intricate detail about the dresses, all related as drama. It has the same effect on women, I'm told, as looking at naked women has on men." He tapped a finger on the *Spectacle*. "I'll ask her to keep an eye on Clara. With two of you on watch, you ought to be able to keep her out of trouble."

Longmore had no objections to any activity involving Sophy Noirot.

On the contrary, he had a number of activities in mind, and joining her in keeping an eye on his sister would give him a fine excuse to be underfoot—and with any luck, under other parts as well.

"Can't think of a better woman for the job," Longmore said. "Miss Noirot misses nothing."

In his mind she was *Sophy*. But she'd never invited him to call her by the name all her family used. And so, even with Clevedon, good manners dictated that Longmore use the correct form of address for the senior unmarried lady of a family.

"With you and Sophy standing guard, the lechers and bankrupts won't stand a chance," Clevedon said. "Argus himself couldn't do better."

Longmore racked his brain. "The dog, you mean?"

"The giant with extra eyes," Clevedon said. "'And set a watcher upon her, great and strong Argus, who with four eyes looks every way,'" he quoted from somewhere. "'And the goddess stirred in him unwearying strength: sleep never fell upon his eyes; but he kept sure watch always.'"

"That strikes me as excessive," Longmore said. "But then, you always were romantic."

A week later

"Warford, how *could* you?"

"My dear, you know I cannot command his majesty—"

"It is not to be borne! That *creature* he married—presented at *Court!*—at the King's Birthday Drawing Room!—as though she were visiting royalty!"

Longmore was trapped in a carriage with his mother, father, and Clara, departing St. James's Palace. Though court events bored him witless, he'd attended the Drawing Room, hoping to spot a certain uninvited attendee. But he'd seen only Sophy's sister—the "creature" his mother was in a snit about. Then he'd debated whether to sneak out or to hunt for an equally bored wife or widow. The palace was well supplied with dark corners conducive to a quick bout of fun.

No luck with the females. The sea of plumes and diamonds held an overabundance of sanctimonious matrons and virgins. Virgins were what one married. They weren't candidates for fun under a staircase.

"Odd, I agree," Lord Warford said carefully. Though he'd

given up being outraged about Clevedon's marriage, he'd also long ago given up trying to reason with his wife.

"Didn't seem odd to me," Longmore said.

"Not odd!" his mother cried. "Not odd! *No one* is presented at the King's Birthday Drawing Room."

"No one but foreign dignitaries," Lord Warford said.

"It was a shocking breach of etiquette even to request an exception," Lady Warford said, conveniently forgetting that she'd told her husband to commit a shocking breach of etiquette by telling the King not to recognize the Duchess of Clevedon.

But it was up to the husband, not the son, to point this out, and years of marriage had taught Lord Warford cowardice.

"I could not believe Her Majesty would do such a thing, even for Lady Adelaide," Mother went on. "But it seems I'm obliged to believe it," she added bitterly. "The Queen dotes on Clevedon's youngest aunt." She glared at her daughter. "Lady Adelaide Ludley might have used her influence on your and your family's behalf. But no, you must be the most ungrateful, undutiful daughter who ever lived. You must jilt the Duke of Clevedon!"

"I didn't jilt him, Mama," Clara said. "One cannot jilt someone to whom one is not engaged."

Longmore had heard this argument too many times to want to be boxed in a closed carriage, hearing it again, his mother's voice going higher and higher, and Clara's climbing along with it. Normally, he would call the carriage to a halt and get out, and leave everybody fuming behind him.

Clara could defend herself, he knew. The trouble was, that would only lead to more quarreling and screaming and messages for him to come to Warford House before she committed matricide.

He thought very hard and very fast and said, "It was clear as clear to me that they did it behind the scenes, so to speak, to spare your feelings, ma'am."

There followed the kind of furiously intense silence that typically ensued when his parents were deciding whether he might, against all reason and evidence, have said something worth listening to.

"What with the aunts and all, the Queen would be in a fix," he went on. "She could hardly snub Clevedon's whole family—which is what she'd be doing, since the aunts had accepted his bride."

"His bride," his mother said bitterly. "His *bride*." She threw Clara the sort of look Caesar must have given Brutus when the knife went in.

"This way at least, the deed was done behind the scenes," Longmore went on, "not in front of the whole blasted ton."

While his mother stirred this idea around in her seething mind, the carriage reached the front of Warford House. The footmen opened the carriage door, and the family emerged, the ladies shaking out their skirts as they stepped out onto the pavement.

Longmore said nothing and Clara said nothing but she shot him a grateful look before she hurried inside after their mother.

His father, however, lingered at the front step with Longmore. "Not coming in?"

"I think not," Longmore said. "Did my best. Tried to pour oil and all that."

"It won't end," his father said in a low voice. "Not for your mother. Shattered dreams and wounded pride and outraged sensibilities and whatnot. You see how it is. We can expect no peace in this family until Clara finds a suitable replacement for Clevedon. That's not going to happen while she keeps encouraging that pack of loose screws." He made a dismissive gesture. "Make them go away, will you, dammit?"

Countess of Igby's ball
Saturday 30 May 1835
One o'clock in the morning

Longmore had been looking for Lord Adderley for some time. The fellow having proven too thick to take a hint, Longmore had decided that the simplest approach was to hit him until he understood that he was to keep off Clara.

The trouble was, Sophy Noirot was at Lady Igby's party, too, and Longmore, unlike Argus, owned only the usual number of eyes.

He'd become distracted, watching Sophy flit hither and yon, no one paying her the slightest heed—except for the usual assortment of dolts who thought maidservants existed for their sport. Since he'd marked her as *his* sport, Longmore had started to move in, more than once, only to find that she didn't need any help with would-be swains.

She'd "accidentally" spilled hot tea on the waistcoat of one gentleman who'd ventured too close. Another had followed her into an antechamber and tripped over something, landing on his face. A third had followed her down a passage and into a room. He'd come out limping a moment later.

Preoccupied with her adventures, Longmore not only failed to locate Adderley, but lost track of the sister he was supposed to be guarding from lechers and bankrupts. This would have been less of a problem had Sophy been watching her more closely. But Sophy had her own lechers to fend off.

Longmore wasn't thinking about this. Thinking wasn't his favorite thing to do, and thinking about more than one thing at a time upset his equilibrium. At the moment, his mind was on the men trespassing on what he'd decided was his property. Unfortunately, this meant he wasn't aware of his mother losing sight of Clara at the same time. This happened because Lady Warford was carrying on a politely poisonous conversation with her best friend and worst enemy Lady Bartham.

In short, nobody who should have been paying attention was paying attention while Lord Adderley was steering Clara, as they waltzed, toward the other end of the ballroom, toward the doors leading to the terrace. None of those who should have been keeping a sharp eye out saw the wink Adderley sent his friends or the accompanying smirk.

It was the crowd's movement that brought Longmore back to his surroundings and his main reason for being here.

The movement wasn't obvious. It wasn't meant to be. Men like Longmore were attuned to it, though. He had no trouble recognizing the sense of something in the air, the shift in the attention in some parts of the room, and the drifting toward a common destination. It was the change in the atmosphere one felt when a fight was about to happen.

The current was sweeping toward the terrace.

His gut told him something was amiss. It didn't say what, but the warning was vehement, and he was a man who acted on instinct. He moved, and quickly.

He didn't have to push his way through the crowd. Those who knew him knew they'd better get out of the way or be thrust out of the way.

He stormed out onto the terrace. A small audience had gathered. They got out of his way, too.

Nothing and nobody obstructed his view.

#1 *New York Times* bestselling author **STEPHANIE LAURENS** began writing as an escape from the dry world of professional science, a hobby that quickly became a career. Her novels set in Regency England have captivated readers around the globe, making her one of the romance world's most beloved and popular authors. All of her previous works remain in print and readily available. Readers can contact Stephanie via e-mail at slaurens@vicnet.net.au. Readers can join Stephanie's Private E-mail Newsletter List via her web site at www.stephanielaurens.com. For information on all of Stephanie's books, including updates on novels yet to come, visit her web site at www.stephanielaurens.com.

GAELEN FOLEY is the *New York Times* bestselling author of seventeen rich, bold historical romances set in the glittering world of Regency England and the Napoleonic Wars. Her books are available in fifteen languages around the world and have won numerous awards, including the Golden Leaf (three times), the Booksellers' Best (twice), the National Readers'

Choice Award, the Holt Medallion, the CRW Award of Excellence, the Beacon, the *Romantic Times* Reviewers' Choice Award for Best Historical Adventure, and more. She lives in Pennsylvania with her hero-husband and a mischievous bichon frise. To learn more about Gaelen, her novels, and the romantic Regency period in which her books are set, please visit www.gaelenfoley.com.

LORETTA CHASE holds a B.A. from Clark University, where she majored in English and minored unofficially in visual art. Her past lives include clerical, administrative, and part-time teaching at Clark and a Dickensian six-month experience as a meter maid. In the course of moonlighting as a corporate video scriptwriter, she fell under the spell of a producer, who lured her into writing novels . . . and marrying him. The union has resulted in more than a dozen books and a number of awards, including the Romance Writers of America's RITA® Award. You can talk to Loretta via her e-mail address Author@LorettaChase.com, visit her website at www.LorettaChase.com, and blog with her and six other authors at WordWenches.com.

Give in to your impulses . . .
Read on for a sneak peek at four brand-new
e-book original tales of romance
from Avon Books.
Available now wherever e-books are sold.

CIRCLE OF DANGER
By Carla Swafford

HEAT RISES
By Alice Gaines

SOMEBODY LIKE YOU
By Candis Terry

A MOST NAKED SOLUTION
By Anna Randol

An Excerpt from

CIRCLE OF DANGER
by Carla Swafford

The top-secret assassins of The Circle are back and on the hunt for a dangerous drug lord capable of bringing women to the brink of pleasure . . . and devastation.

Marie Beltane, a lowly data-entry specialist intent on proving she's worthy of being a full operative, has just been injected with the drug responsible for the death of four local women . . . a drug that puts her sex drive into overdrive.

Arthur Ryker wants nothing more than to protect Marie, even if it means fulfilling her drug-induced . . . needs. But now a new evil has reared its ugly head—how far is Arthur willing to go to find an antidote and save the woman he always loved?

AN AVON RED NOVEL

CHAPTER ONE

Arthur Ryker sprang out of bed and immediately stood at attention, feet apart, his scarred hands in the "ready" position at waist level. One hand cupped by the other, restrained but prepared to kill. He shook his head and sighed. Just once he wanted to leave his bed like a regular person and not like a trained monkey.

"A bad dream?" a deep voice asked from the bedroom entrance. With one pierced black eyebrow lifted, Jack Drago leaned against the doorjamb.

Ignoring the question, Ryker walked naked into the bathroom. When he returned to grab some clothes out of the closet, Jack hadn't moved, but his gaze had most likely inspected every inch of the room. There wasn't much to see. A king-sized bed sat in a corner while a mirrorless dresser was centered against one wall—no pictures or the usual brica-a-brac to give away the occupant's personality. Then again, maybe it did. Rather stark for a man who owned enough properties and businesses to keep his organization in the best covert weapons money could buy. He didn't care what Jack thought about his bedroom. Except for a few hours of sleep and a shower and shave, Ryker rarely spent time in the room.

"What do you want?" he asked, glaring at his second-in-command.

With cold blue eyes, Jack studied him, then his gaze shifted away.

Ryker grunted. Not many people could deal with looking at the thick scars down the side of his body, but it was his blind eye that bothered most. White from the scar tissue damaged in a fire so many years ago, it was normally hidden beneath a patch. But Ryker'd be damned before he slept with one on. So if Jack decided to make a habit of waking him in the morning, he could fucking well get use to the sight. Considering the man had four visible piercings—and who knew how many hidden—along with tattoos covering one arm, Jack shouldn't have a problem with his scars. The man understood pain.

With sure, quick movements, he thrust his legs into jeans and yanked on a black T-shirt. After tugging on his boots, he strapped a small pistol at his ankle. With his patch in place, using his fingers he combed hair over the strap securing its position. Hell, he needed a haircut again. Maybe he'd shave his head like Jack. A simple enough solution. If only the rest of his problems could be so easily solved.

"She's in trouble," Jack said in an even tone as if his voice could defuse a bad situation.

Ryker's stomach and chest tightened as if he'd been hit. He knew who Jack referred to without adding a name. She happened to be part of why his life was so complicated.

"Did you hear me?" Jack straightened his stance.

"Yeah." Desire to break someone's neck raced through his body. "Where is she? What happened?"

With a sharp snap, he inserted a snub-nose into the shoulder holster hanging at his side and jerked on his leather jacket. He gritted his teeth for a few seconds to regain his composure. Then he took a deep breath, squared his shoulders, and exhaled.

"Last time Bryan heard from her, she'd entered the target's house in Chattanooga and was downloading information off a laptop. He lost communication with her." Jack quickly stepped out of the way for Ryker to move into the dark hallway. "They believe she's still in the house. If the Wizard sticks to his MO, we'll have about three hours before he takes her away or kills her."

Ryker wasted no time in reaching a massive room with mirrors from ceiling to floor. When the mansion was built in the eighteen hundreds, the room was used as a ballroom. It was empty now, except for a Steinway covered with a white sheet, and the high-sheen hardwood floor sounded hollow as he tramped across it. He used the room for one purpose only—to reach the stairwell hidden behind one of the mirrors.

"Took you long enough to spit it out." Ryker glanced at his second-in-command.

Jack remained quiet, staring straight ahead. Ryker didn't really expect an excuse. The man knew how he felt about that. No excuse for failure, especially when it came to protecting Marie.

Four months earlier, Ryker had moved The Circle compound from the suburbs of Atlanta to an area near the Smoky

Mountains. The mansion was situated in the middle of almost ten thousand acres, which included a large mountain filled with a network of tunnels and bunkers perfect to house the facility he needed. Last year, the final phase of the project was completed and now they were training new recruits in the underground Sector. The nearly fifteen square miles provided the privacy he needed. In a world filled with evil people, his covert organization of assassins came in handy.

Their footsteps echoed in the long, well-lit tunnel. A semi could pass through the passageway without scraping the side mirrors or the tips of muffler stacks.

"Who was her backup?" Ryker asked.

When a few seconds passed without an answer, Ryker stopped and faced Jack.

"They're handling it."

Ryker continued to stare.

His second-in-command sighed. "She went in without a backup."

Jaw clenched, Ryker strode to the iris scan next to a large metal door. A buzz sounded and he slammed the door against the inner wall.

The gripping pain in his belly grew and reminded him of the fear he had lived with for years before he took over control of The Circle. She could not keep doing this to him. He refused to allow anything more to happen to her. She knew this and still didn't listen.

The noise level in the basketball court-sized room almost broke the sound barrier with printers running and people shouting or talking to those sitting next to them—or to others on the Internet or satellite phones—along with the clicking of keyboards. Each wall covered with large screens captured a different scene of people living their lives in various parts of the world. In the center of the room, faces bleached white by the monitors in front of them, the supervisors and handlers communicated with their operatives.

Ryker stopped in the middle of the bullpen, searching for his prey.

The balding, whipcord-thin Bryan Tilton stood over a handler shouting instructions and pointing at the screen. Maybe a sixth sense alerted Bryan. He looked up and his eyes widened.

Ryker charged toward him, ignoring the people ducking for cover behind partitions and beneath desks.

"You son of a bitch!"

His fist clipped Bryan on the chin, sending the man sliding across the floor. Desire to flatten the asshole's pointy nose almost overrode all of Ryker's control. Good thing Bryan remained sprawled out on the linoleum.

Standing over the man, Ryker opened and closed his fists. The temptation to punish him further for his stupidity warred with the fear of jabbing the cartilage of the idiot's nose into his brain.

"I swear, sir, I told her to wait until I could get backup in place, but she wouldn't listen." Bryan cupped his jaw and shifted it from side to side. "Two of our operatives are held up in a traffic accident about twenty-five miles from her last location."

"Last location?" Ryker gritted his teeth.

"The target's house, off Riverview Road." Bryan scooted back when Ryker took a step. The man's head bobbled on his skinny neck. "As soon as Phil and Harry reach it, they'll extract her."

Afraid he would crack the man's chicken neck, Ryker turned away and pointed at the nearest handler. "You! Sal?"

Mohawk trembling, the pale man nodded.

Ryker said, "Tell Phil and Harry to call me on my cell as soon as they reach the house. Do not go inside! Jack and I will be there in twenty minutes. Have them wait for us. AHH" He turned back to Bryan. "Have the Spirit ready in five minutes." His helicopter could cover the miles quickly and land almost anywhere.

Marie Beltane struggled against the chains restraining her on a cot that reeked of sex and urine. She stifled a groan. No, no, no. Nausea traveled up her throat.

All the beams and pipes overhead felt like they were squeezing the air out of the room. Basements were never among her favorite rooms. The dampness and creepy-crawly things always gave her the willies.

She still couldn't believe she'd been caught. Bryan had sworn it would be an easy gig. Prior surveillance had revealed the man worked each evening at a massive bank of computers. Go in and download a flash drive load of info and get out. The target always left his house at nine in the morning and didn't return until nine that evening. Breaking into the house when most people ate dinner in the surrounding homes had sounded so easy. Few would look out their windows as they settled down in front of their plates or televisions or both.

Hours would pass before he returned home. But he came back early.

Oh, God, she'd screwed up big time!

He looked like a fourteen-year-old with his cartoon-themed T-shirt and his mop of hair, but she knew from his file he was between twenty-six and twenty-eight. During their surveillance, they never got a clear photograph of him. Whenever he entered or exited his house, he did so through his garage. His SUV had tinted windows, preventing anyone from seeing inside.

The man standing with his back to her had outmaneuvered every defensive tactic she'd been taught. He didn't fight like a kid. Jack was right. She needed to work harder on her moves. If she had, she wouldn't be in this predicament. The nerd had surprised her, taking her down with unexpected ease.

She refused to cry even though she couldn't stop the trembling in her body. Every inch ached from his battery of hits and kicks. For a scrawny man, he'd moved fast and hit hard.

Her head hurt from holding back tears. She'd hoped never to be in this position again, to be under someone's control. No matter how many times she reminded herself this was different from before, the horror of repeating history pushed her to keep her eyes open. Staying aware of her enemy helped to keep her calm.

"You're not very smart. I'm efficient in seven different types of martial arts." His stiff words failed to impress her. He moved, revealing what he held in his hand. The huge syringe with a shiny green substance in the barrel had a needle longer than her forefinger. "Just because I'm a geek doesn't mean I'm unacquainted with ways to defend myself."

Marie stared at the needle. The duct tape covering her mouth muffled her scream. Ever since he jumped her, she'd tried to see a way to escape, while keeping calm.

She tried to be brave. She kept telling herself that screaming would only be a waste of energy. Stifling the panic engulfing her would keep her alive.

"Wait until this stuff hits your bloodstream. I'm told the sensation is similar to that last second before reaching an orgasm. In other words, you'll do anything to get off." He chuckled and lifted her shirt. He tugged at the waistband of her jeans.

She flinched when the needle slid into the soft skin near her hip.

"Perfect for where I'm sending you." He jerked on the jeans until the tips of his fingers brushed her pubic hair. "White American women—especially petite, natural blondes like you—are quite popular in parts of the Middle East and Asia. Virgins are preferred but rare here unless we go much younger." He shrugged. "Then you get into Amber Alerts and they're too much trouble. Anyway, bitches like you are plentiful and disposable."

He pulled harder at her jeans, taking her panties down.

She froze. Her stomached churned with the thought of what he might do next. Then he pushed the needle deeper. The liquid burned, becoming hotter as he eased the plunger down. The pain took her mind off her fear for only a second. When she tried to move away, the rattling chains reminded her she wasn't going anywhere. Tears pooled at the corner of her eyes and she turned her head, refusing to let him see her cry.

"A formula created by . . . a fucking genius! Especially created to use on sneaky sluts like you. The Wizard is a god!" He laughed. The back of his hand grazed her cheek. "I know it stings, baby. Sorry . . . no. I'm not sorry. You have the look of an ice princess. I love seeing an uptight cunt like you suffer. You have no idea what you've gotten yourself into. This wonder drug is highly addictive and from what I'm told, it has long-lasting effects. You'll grow to love it."

The grin on his smooth face terrified her more than anything else he'd done. Her vision blurred. The man leaned over her, his brown eyes dark and merciless. She whimpered. Every cell of her body tingled.

"Do you feel it? It takes a little while to set in. The Wizard said it tingles all over and next, for a small time, you'll feel like you're floating on water. Then you'll get sleepy and then—*bam!*—you'll be like a bitch in heat." He cackled and thrust his groin several times against her leg and the side of the cot. He punched the air with his fist and did a little dance. When he turned his back, he reached for something on a table nearby. "Now let's see what all of you looks like."

Light glinted off the scalpel. He swiped at the air above her as if he wielded a sword. No matter how brave she tried to be earlier, she couldn't stop her limbs from shaking harder and her stomach from twisting. She squealed behind the tape.

The sound of slicing material had her arching away from his touch. *Please don't cut me. Oh, please, God, help.* In seconds, he peeled away her clothes. He rubbed his groin and a lascivious grin marred his youthful face.

"Not bad, though I find the scars a shame, yet rather interesting. It looks like someone used a belt or whip on you.

Have you been a bad girl?" He slid his hand down her bare thigh and over a long, thin white scar. "There are clients who would love to add to them."

She turned her head. Swallowing several times to keep from choking on vomit, she concentrated on the number of blocks in the basement wall. She could get through this. It wouldn't be the first time her body had been used. Eventually, she'd find a way out.

Just as she heard his zipper go down, a loud blast shook the walls. Dust sprinkled onto her face. She blinked her eyes. The room looked smoky, choked with plaster powder.

"What the hell?" The man ran toward the stairs as he struggled to pull up his pants. One foot on the bottom step, he stopped, staring at the door.

A smaller blast was followed by shouting and heavy footsteps running across the floor above. Whoever had come a-knocking were making their way through the house.

"Well, babe, you're on your own. I hope they appreciate the gift I'm leaving them." He laughed and disappeared beneath the stairs into a black void.

Her eyelids felt so heavy. Tingling traveling across her torso rushed down her legs and arms, and then a feeling of lightness and floating followed. A strong breeze brushed her naked body. Someone had found the basement. A wave of dizziness pushed her under and she closed her eyes, unable to lift them even when she felt someone fighting with the chains holding her down.

"Damn it, Marie. You'd better be alive," a deep voice growled.

She smiled. Deep inside, she knew he'd come for her.

An Excerpt from

HEAT RISES

by Alice Gaines

Welcome to Alice Gaines's "Cabin Fever" series: Who knows what naughty games you'll play when you've got nowhere else to go? Laura Barber gets to put her imagination to the test when she finds herself snowbound in a cabin with Ethan Gould, a man she's dreamt of doing unspeakably delicious things to for years. Find out what happens when . . . *Heat Rises.*

AN AVON RED NOVELLA

CHAPTER ONE

So much for making it to her job interview. Laura Barber might as well have been looking at a moonscape rather than a deserted mountain highway. Still shivering, she gazed out the window of the country store as the falling snow covered the pavement and filled in the road completely. The storm had started only half an hour ago. What would this place look like by morning?

"You're a mighty lucky young lady," said the shopkeeper, handing her a Styrofoam cup with steam coming out the top. "If you'd gone off the road any farther from here, you'd still be out in that."

She took a sip of the coffee and did her best not to grimace at the bitter taste. The man may be right about her luck, but she'd probably ruined her shoes on the trek here. The low-heeled pumps had cost a bundle, and she'd worn them just enough that her feet felt comfortable when she dressed for business.

"Yep," the man said as he gazed out at the accumulating snow. "Nobody'll be moving around in these parts for days."

"Mister—"

"Beaumont," he said, offering his gnarled hand.

"Mr. Beaumont," she said, studying him as they shook hands. The twinkle in his blue eyes suggested more youth than the fringe of white hair did. If you called central casting for a country store owner, they'd probably send someone like this man.

"You'd be in a heap of trouble if you'd broken down farther away," he said.

"Can someone come out and put me back on the road before things get worse?" she asked.

"You don't understand storms in these mountains, Miss."

"Ms.," she said. "Ms. Laura Barber."

"Well, Ms. Barber, won't nobody get out of here until the plows come through."

"When will that be?"

"Days," he answered. "Probably not a week, though."

"A week?" Darn it all. She was supposed to be at the bottom of this mountain by evening and at an interview in the morning. She'd planned carefully to get ahead of this storm, but her plane had landed late. Still, she ought to have been able to make her destination. She'd grown up in Connecticut and had driven in winter weather before. Snow was snow, wasn't it? Apparently not.

"What am I going to do?" she asked. "I can't stay here for days."

"That you can't. I'll be closing up and heading home in a few minutes."

"Is there a motel nearby?" she asked.

"Nope. We'll have to find a family to put you up."

"I can't impose on strangers for days."

He shrugged. "Don't see that you have much choice."

Wonderful. Not only would she not make it to her interview but she'd also have to spend days with people she didn't know. She managed well enough in business situations where procedures and rules of engagement were clearly laid out. In someone's home, she'd have to interact. She probably couldn't disappear behind her laptop without appearing rude.

"Unless . . ." Mr. Beaumont said. "Your solution might be pulling up right now."

Headlights shone in from outside—bright enough to blind her for a moment—a huge SUV or pickup, with its engine at a low roar. The motor shut off, and the lights went dim. A man climbed out and headed into the store. A blast of cold air whooshed in through the front as he entered. "Hey, Phil."

Mr. Beaumont shuffled off. "Hey, you young pup. What are you doing out in weather like this?"

"Business down in the city. Thought I could outrun the storm."

The voice tugged at her memory. Low and dark. She knew it. Even though she hadn't heard it recently enough to place it in her brain, something about the tone registered in her body.

She glanced over at the counter where he stood, his back to her. Tall and broad-shouldered, he commanded the space around him. She had a physical memory of that too, enough to warm her skin. Whoever this was, she'd do best to avoid him. But how?

"Good thing you're here," Mr. Beaumont said, gesturing toward her. "This lady is going to need a ride somewhere."

The man turned and all the memory nudges turned into one huge sucker punch. Ethan Gould.

Good Lord, not him. It had to be five years . . . no, six. That night at the party. After three years of fantasies about the handsome guy who always sat at the front of the class, she'd decided to at least try to find out if the attraction was mutual. Tequila fortification, too much, had led to a night of humiliation. Oh God, all the things she'd said to him. Her stomach sank remembering them after all this time.

Other than that, they'd almost never interacted all through business school. He'd have forgotten her by now. Women probably came on to him all the time—women more remarkable than herself. He wouldn't remember. Please God, don't let him remember.

Sure enough, he smiled at her as he would at any stranger. A genial expression he used so easily. The famed Gould charm would come next. So potent it worked even on men. On women . . . well, forget trying to resist it.

After a moment, his brows knitted together. "Do we know each other?"

"No . . . I don't think . . . haven't met," she said. Damn it all, how could he force this reaction from her after so much time? She'd actually lie about her identity if she could get away with it. She'd avoided him successfully since that horrible night. She'd actually followed his career so that she'd know where he was. He couldn't have just happened on her on a snowy mountain, and yet here he stood, as tempting and as terrifying as he'd been at that party.

"This is Ms. Laura Barber," Mr. Beaumont said. "You two know each other?"

"Right." Recognition dawned in his amber eyes, followed by a slight tension to his jaw. Remembering, no doubt. Her skin went from warm to burning. By now, her face would be a bright pink.

He recovered quickly, with a big smile. He still had perfect teeth, of course, and perfect skin. Only his too-large ears kept him from total perfection, but the flaw made him all the more attractive.

"It's been a while," he said. "Good to see you again."

"Hi." A stupid reply but innocent enough, she thought.

"Seeing as you two know each other, won't you mind taking Ms. Barber to where she wants to go?" Mr. Beaumont asked.

He rested a hand on a nearby rack of magazines and struck a casual pose. A light of cunning in his eyes belied his apparent ease. "Where are you headed?"

"The city," she said. "I'm already late."

"How'd you get this far?"

"Rental car"—she gestured toward the outside as if she could point at the thing—"I ran off the road."

"Can't say I'm surprised," he said, his gaze never leaving her face. She did her best to look straight back at him, but she'd never win a staring contest with this man. Eventually, she gave up and studied his shoes, instead. Boots, rather—the sort ranchers wore. His had a broken-in appearance, as did the faded jeans that covered his legs up to the hem of his shearling jacket.

"We won't be getting to the city tonight," he said. "But we can make it to my friend's cabin."

"Cabin?" she repeated. "In the middle of a blizzard?"

"My friend's an engineer. The place is self-sufficient with a generator and solar panels."

"The sun's not out now," she said. In fact, with the heavy snow, it was already dark.

"And storage batteries," he said. "We'll be fine."

"I haven't agreed to go with you."

"What choice do you have?" he asked, as he straightened and pulled a slip of paper from his jacket. "I'll need a few things, Phil."

"Coming right up." Mr. Beaumont took the list from him and retreated to the back of the store.

"Look, this is really nice of you—"

Before she could get the "but" out, he took a step toward her. " 'Nice' isn't exactly the word I was thinking of."

She made herself stand her ground, even though everything in her wanted to back away. "I don't want to impose."

"Don't be silly. No one around here would put someone out on a night like this."

"Mr. Beaumont said he'd find a family here to take me in."

He crossed his arms over his chest. "So, you're a social butterfly now? Happy to move in with strangers for several days?"

Damn him, he knew she wasn't. He had to remember from graduate school that she kept to herself, quietly getting top grades from her place in the back of the class.

"I . . . I . . ." Damn it. He actually had her stuttering. She took a breath. "I can't go with you."

"Why not?" he asked, as he studied her, his gaze assessing and not without a light of admiration. Her heartbeat responded, speeding up. The feeling might be pleasant with another man—one who hadn't heard about her sexual fantasies after she'd had too many margaritas. She'd told him about how her mind had wandered during boring lectures, imagining how his hands would feel on her breasts. About how she played images of him in her mind when she used her vibrator. She'd even asked if his sex was as big as she'd imagined it, and then giggled when she'd fumbled against his pants and discovered it was even larger. Oh God, humiliation. Utter and total humiliation.

"Maybe you're afraid to be alone with me," he said. He might have read her mind.

"Ridiculous." Okay, that was a lie, but she wouldn't cower before him. She'd gone on from that night to establish a good career. As a grown woman with more experience since graduate school, she shouldn't have to fear men any longer, even this one. Even if she did, she wouldn't let him know he frightened her.

"Laura, you have a choice of crowding in with a family you don't know or sharing a cabin with me. I won't even speak to you if you don't want."

"I don't think that will be necessary." Great. She'd agreed to go with him. No matter. A few days together, and she'd get away again.

"Good." He smiled yet again, the blasted man. "The cabin it is."

You could have knocked Ethan Gould over with a feather. First, to run into Laura Barber at Phil Beaumont's store, way out here in the middle of no place. At least there was a logical explanation for that. She was probably up for the same job at Henderson that he was. A bit odd, as their talents—skill sets, she would have called them—lay in very different areas. But they were both übercompetent, as any headhunter would have to know. Still, what were the chances that she'd end up at that country store, needing a ride in one of the mountains' worst storms of the season just as he pulled in? Fate was trying to tell them something, and he, for one, was listening.

The fact that she'd end up staying with him in an isolated cabin fell into a different category of unlikelihood. Impossibility, more like. And yet, there she sat in the bucket seat next to his, staring out at the snow as if it held some message.

Laura Barber, the shy thing who'd turned into a wild woman one night, nearly dragging him into an empty bedroom at the end-of-semester party. The woman who'd promised sex so uninhibitedly she'd singed the edges of his imagination. The woman who never spoke up in class but who'd whispered filthy words in his ear while she'd unfastened his belt and started in on the zipper of his slacks. Unfortunately, she'd given off enough clues of her intoxicated state to keep him from following through, just barely managing to stop things before they'd gone too far.

Laura Barber . . . the one who got away. Hell, the one he'd let get away. Damn his conscience all to hell.

"Do you own this truck?" she asked after several minutes of silence.

"Rented."

"Do you always drive something so big?"

Right. The queen of green. "What were you driving?"

"A hybrid."

"If you'd had one of these, you wouldn't have gone off the road."

"Touché." She looked him in the eyes for probably the first time since she'd climbed aboard. "Truce?"

"Sure." Although, how he'd manage that would take some mental gymnastics. She wore the same scent she had all through business school. Nothing exotic, just kind of clean and sweet. She'd wrapped the scent around him that night. It still went straight to his gut, and now he had the mother of all hard-ons. Truce, indeed.

He stared out the windshield. "That your hybrid up ahead?"

She squinted, peering forward. "It is."

He pulled up beside the car, set the brake, and pushed the gear lever to park. "Leave the engine running for heat. Give me your keys."

"I can get my bag myself."

He held out his hand. "I thought we had a truce."

After fishing in her purse, she produced a key on rental company chain and handed it over. Now, he could get away from her perfume for a few seconds. Maybe the cold would do something to ease his boner too.

He climbed out of the truck and shut the door behind him. His boots sinking into snow halfway to his knees, he trudged the few feet to the hybrid and used the key to open the trunk. She traveled light—just one carry-on and a suit bag. If he looked inside, which he wouldn't, he'd no doubt find a formless skirt and jacket combination. She could almost, but not quite, hide her plush figure under all the layers of clothing she wore.

After closing the trunk, he scrambled back to the truck and stowed her things in the back. Then he took his seat in front and set the gear to low to take them down the frosted highway.

"You seem to know your way around," she said.

"I grew up near here."

"You look the part. All you need is a Stetson." She actually smiled. Not much but enough to curve that tempting lower lip. No matter how hard she tried to blend into the woodwork, that mouth and her enormous brown eyes kept her from pulling it off. Great, now he was thinking about her mouth.

"What are you doing in these parts?" he asked, even though he had a pretty good idea of the answer.

"Job interview," she answered.

"Henderson?"

"How did you know?"

"My interview is day after tomorrow," he said. "Doesn't look as if either of us is going to make it."

She groaned. "Oh no."

"Don't worry. You still have a chance."

"Why wouldn't I?" she said. "They'll understand about the storm."

"I didn't mean that. I meant the competition."

"What . . . oh." She glared at him. "You don't think I can beat you for the job."

He didn't answer but only smiled.

"Competitive to the end, eh?" she said.

"Pot . . . kettle."

"Is this your idea of a truce?"

"Sorry. Force of habit." He turned the truck off the main highway onto the narrow road that led to Jeff's cabin. Here, even the four-wheel drive wouldn't help them if he made a bad move. He'd have to concentrate on something besides the chaos in his jeans. The heavy vehicle inched along while the wipers slap-slapped against the windshield and the wind howled outside, swirling the snow around them. Laura sat huddled in the corner, her arms wrapped around her ribs.

"Frightened?" he asked.

She bit her lower lip. Even a short glimpse of that out of the corner of his eye put his mind in places where it didn't belong.

"A little," she said after a moment.

"I'll take care of you." Boy, howdy, would he. *Stop it, damn it. Now.*

Normally, she'd have bristled at any suggestion that she needed help with anything. She must have been really scared not to say a word but just sit there, making herself small. If he wasn't careful, she'd start tugging at his protective instincts. But then, when had he ever been careful where a woman was concerned? Well, maybe once . . . with this woman.

"Is it much farther?" she asked.

"A few more yards." Of course, in a storm in the mountains, a few more yards could stretch on forever. How had the pioneers ever managed?

The cabin came up on him unexpectedly. He must have misjudged how far they'd come because the outline of the building appeared directly ahead of them before he'd realized they'd arrived. He let a breath out slowly, and his shoulders relaxed. Though he'd never admit it to Laura, navigating under these conditions was a bit of a crapshoot, and he hadn't felt all that comfortable himself.

He steered the truck into the carport and cut the engine. When he turned off the headlights, they fell into darkness for a moment. All the better for him to sense the woman next to him. Her scent and the sound of her breathing filled the space around him. It was going to be an interesting few days.

If the cabin had appeared rustic from the outside, the interior somehow managed romantic and high-tech at the same time. Laura left her ruined shoes in the enclosed entryway, what Ethan referred to as a "mini mudroom," and followed him into the main living area. When he hit the switch, lights came on around the baseboards, producing enough illumination to suggest the interior of an elegant restaurant.

"Solar power?" she asked as she tipped up her carry-on and draped the suit bag over it.

"From batteries beneath the house," he said. "The system gives off heat as well as light."

"And the heat rises to fill the room."

"Once I get the woodstove and a fire going, we'll be toasty."

"Nice." They'd been bandying that word around a lot. This time, it didn't carry extra meaning.

Ethan put the bag of groceries on the counter in the kitchenette. "Settle in."

She glanced around. "Are there other rooms?"

"Bathroom."

"Then, where would you like me to settle in?"

He paused in the act of stowing a carton of eggs in the refrigerator. After a moment, he straightened, placed his elbow on the door and assumed his too-casual pose again. "You take the sleeping loft. I'll camp out on the couch."

She checked the piece of furniture in question. "Is it big enough for you?"

"I'll fold into it."

"Because, I don't really have to—"

"Take the loft. As you observed, heat rises. You'll be comfortable up there."

The baseboard heating was having an effect on the temperature, but not enough for her to remove her coat.

"I'll lay a fire," she said.

"You know how to do that?"

"It's not rocket science."

"Be my guest."

While he continued putting away groceries, she went to the huge stone fireplace and knelt to check out the supplies. Plenty of wood and kindling. Starting with crumpled newspaper, she built what should soon be a good blaze. She found matches, lit the paper, and sat back on her heels to watch the fuel catch.

Out of nowhere, a male hand appeared in front of her, holding a glass of red wine. She took it and glanced up at the towering figure of Ethan Gould. "Thanks."

"I didn't know for sure if you'd want anything to drink."

"I'm good with wine. It's tequila I need to stay away from." Damn it, why had she said that? She shouldn't have mentioned anything that could remind him of that night. Or remind herself, for that matter. She sipped some of her drink and stared into the fire.

Of course, he didn't do the easy thing and go back to the kitchenette and leave her alone with the memory. Oh no, he had to sit down beside her in front of the fire.

"Want to talk about the two-ton elephant in the room?" he asked.

"No."

"I do."

"Fine," she said. "You talk. I'll listen."

"Doesn't work that way."

"Look, Ethan." She took a fortifying sip of her wine and let it roll around on her tongue. He had good taste, she'd give him that. Eventually, she had to face him. When she did, she somehow ended up lost in the reflection of the fire in his eyes.

"Laura . . ." he prompted.

"I wasn't myself that night." Lord, how embarrassing. If he wanted to talk about this, why didn't he say something or do something? Why was he putting it all on her? "I behaved inappropriately toward you."

He gave her a lopsided smile. "Is that what they're calling it now?"

"Please. You'll make me blush."

"So what?" he said. "No one's ever died of blushing."

She could. Her heart fluttered in her chest, and her stomach felt full of cold lead. When her hands trembled, she set her glass on the hearth rather than spill red wine on the carpet.

"Hey, hey." He put his glass next to hers and took her hands in his. "It's not that serious."

When she couldn't take any more gazing into his eyes, she

switched to staring at the fire. "You could probably have sued me for harassment."

"Harassment?" he repeated. "How do you figure that?"

"You obviously didn't welcome . . . um, feel the same . . ."

"Because I didn't follow through?"

She clenched her teeth together and sat in utter, silent shame.

"You'd had too much to drink, Laura," he said. "Only a bastard takes advantage like that."

"Well," she pulled her hands from his and took a steadying breath. "It was a long time ago. I'm glad we settled it."

"I don't call that settled," he said.

She stared into the fire again. If she didn't look at him, maybe he'd go away. "I do."

"Damn it, Laura, you're going to deal with this." Taking her chin in his hand, he turned her head until she had to look at him. "Do you know how exciting you were that night?"

"I was drunk and disorderly." Drunk enough for him to have rejected her but not enough for her to have forgotten all the things she'd said to him. No one on earth had ever heard of her fantasies, but after that encounter, this man had.

"You turned me on like crazy," he said. "I went nuts trying to figure out how to get you to make the same invitation sober."

"It was a long time ago, Ethan."

"I would have called you, but I figured that would have embarrassed you."

"I'm glad you didn't."

"I kept putting myself in places where I'd bump into you

by accident, but you disappeared"—he gestured with both hands—"poof."

"I don't want to talk about this," she said. "You promised."

He studied her for a long moment before picking up his wine again. "Yeah, I guess I did."

"Thanks for understanding." This time, when she lifted her glass, it didn't wobble.

"You'll at least eat dinner with me, I hope."

"Of course," she said. "This is excellent wine, by the way."

"It should go with the steaks. How do you like yours?"

"Rare."

"Rare it is." With the knuckle of his free hand, he tapped the end of her nose before rising and sauntering back to the stove.

She took a deep breath—the first truly relaxing one she'd had since he strolled into the country store—and watched him rinse vegetables for salad in the sink. She ought to help him, but he seemed to know what he was about. Besides, the world was a safer place with distance between them.

So, he'd refused her that night out of gallantry. Or so he said. That made things marginally less humiliating. Sort of.

As he worked on their dinner, his movement fluid as he went from counter to refrigerator to cabinet and back, she couldn't erase the memory of that lean body against hers. The kisses . . . sweeter and more potent than the margaritas that had caused her to lose control. And the misery, the soul-crushing disappointment, when he'd pushed her away.

Now that they'd discussed the two-ton elephant, the whole incident was closed. Over and dealt with. Finito. Somehow, that only made her stomach sink even lower.

An Excerpt from

SOMEBODY LIKE YOU
by Candis Terry

Welcome Back to the Sugar Shack

Straitlaced . . . Chicago prosecutor Kelly Silverthorne has a perfect record in the courtroom and a big fat zero in the bedroom. When she loses her first case ever, she returns home to Deer Lick, Montana, to regain her confidence and shake off the "Sister Serious" moniker she's been strapped with since childhood. Only a few hours into her repentance, karma thrusts her face-to-face with yet another of her major fiascos—a one-night stand with the hottest cop in the county.

Rebel with a Cause . . . Deputy James Harley has always played with fire. When smart and sexy Kelly pops back into his life, he doesn't mind going for a full burn. And that might be exactly what happens when his past threatens to catch up with his future.

A Match Made in . . . Heaven only knows what Kelly's dearly departed mom has planned from the *other side*—especially since she's already meddled in Kelly's siblings' love lives. But even heaven knows that when love comes knocking, there's no stopping the good things to come.

CHAPTER ONE

Kelly Silverthorne despised killers.

Especially the type who possessed the charm of a movie star that belied the icy heart of the snake that beat in their chest.

"I think it's dead."

Jarred from the dark images in her head, Kelly looked up at her fellow Chicago prosecutor, Daniel Bluhm. A streak of sunlight shot through the window of the deli and glimmered in his golden hair. While they awaited word that the jury had reached a verdict in the Colson murder case, lunch had seemed a good idea. The nerves coiled in her stomach said otherwise. "Excuse me?"

"Your potato salad." Daniel pointed to her plate. "Or maybe I should call it lumpy soup."

Kelly glanced down at the fork in her hand and the mess she'd made of what had once been a tasty side dish. She dropped the utensil to her plate and glanced around the old-fashioned restaurant and the retro decorations that adorned the walls. "Sorry."

A smile crossed his mouth before he stuffed in the last bite of his patty melt. "Nervous?"

She nodded.

"You did a hell of a job with closing arguments."

"Daniel?" Kelly sipped her diet Pepsi and wiped her mouth with the paper napkin. "I don't know if I mentioned this or not, but this murder case we've been working on for more than a year? The case in which I pushed for an arrest and prosecution against the state attorney's better judgment? The case I swore we had enough evidence to get a conviction?"

"You mean the case that's been plastered all over the real *and* entertainment news networks?"

"Yes!" Her eyes widened in feigned surprise and she pointed at him with the straw in her soda. "*That* one. In case I forgot to tell you, it involves a popular movie-starlike senator and a glamorous cast member of "Real Housewives of Chicago." By the time I wrapped up, the jury looked at me like I'd kicked their dog."

"Don't be so hard on yourself." Her partner chuckled. "We went in prepared. We had forensics, motive, and—"

"No body." She shrugged. "Bottom line, Bluhm. No. Body." Kelly grabbed a French fry off his plate and shoved it into her mouth.

"Hey. No fair eating my food because you trashed your own."

"Partners share."

He reached across the table and covered her hand with his. "Some partners would like to share even more."

Kelly playfully poked his hand with her fork. "Not gonna happen, Romeo."

"You're killing me, Silverthorne." He leaned back in his chair. His sharp blue eyes focused on her face, much the same way they focused on a defendant he intended to break. "I've been asking you out for two years. When are you going to cut me some slack and let me take you on a date? I promise dinner, a movie, the whole shebang. I'll even be a gentleman even though it might kill me."

She laughed at the exaggerated whine in his tone. "Daniel. You are a really nice—"

"*No.*" Comically he covered his face with both hands. "Do *not* give me the *friends* speech."

His reaction sent her into a fit of laughter which helped to ease the tension churning the tuna salad sandwich in her stomach. Her phone chimed. She and Daniel looked at each other before she picked it up and checked the text message. "Jury's in."

One golden brow lifted. "Two hours to deliberate?"

Kelly nodded.

"Shit."

"Yeah." She tossed her napkin on the table and grabbed the check. "Let's go."

It took another two hours for the media to be notified and for everyone to reassemble in the courtroom. Kelly had stood outside in the warm June sunshine until the last possible moment. Praying. Searching for a lucky penny on the ground or a stray rabbit's foot. Heck, if it would mean a conviction she'd haul a whole danged bunny into the courtroom.

Her high heels clicked on the marble floor as she passed

through security, headed toward the elevator, and pressed the button. She reviewed the trial in her head while the floor numbers lit up like Christmas lights. With the exception of admitting two questionable exhibits into evidence, she'd done everything possible to nail Andrew Colson for the murder of his wife, Alicia. Over the past year Kelly had given meticulous consideration to the evidence. She'd role played. She'd spent hours and hours at the law library looking up comparable cases. She'd interviewed dozens of character witnesses. By the time she and Daniel had the case packaged and ready to present, she'd been confident they'd get a conviction.

Two hours to deliberate.

An icy chill shot up her back as the elevator doors slid open.

She wished she felt that confident now.

Inside the courtroom she set down her expandable briefcase and returned the anxious regard Daniel gave her when their gazes met. She sat down and busied herself with collecting her notes and her thoughts. Minutes later the defendant in his Armani suit and expensive haircut strolled in with his high-powered attorneys. He cast an arrogant glance toward the already seated jury then sat down and leaned back as though he were in a bar waiting for his scotch.

Geez, couldn't the guy even pretend to be human? After all, this was a trial for the murder of his wife. A woman he had pledged to honor and cherish all the days of their lives. His two children were now motherless and, if Kelly had done her job, they would be fatherless too. In a moment of sheer compassion, she felt bad about that. Not for the defendant, but for the children who would grow up forever wondering what had really happened to the woman who poured their cereal every day, taxied them to soccer practice, and tucked them into bed at night.

Kelly slid her gaze across the courtroom to where Alicia Colson's family sat together, holding hands like linked chains. They would be there for the kids. Thank God for that.

Judge Reginald Dawson entered and the courtroom stood until he was seated. Kelly gripped her pen in her hand and mentally began her customary chant.

He is guilty. He will pay. He is guilty. He will pay.

"Has the jury reached a verdict?" Judge Dawson's deep voice boomed through the packed room.

The jury foreman stood and sweat broke out on the back of Kelly's neck.

"Yes, Your Honor."

"Has the jury signed the appropriate verdict form? If so, please provide them to Deputy Southwick who will then present them to me."

As Judge Dawson opened the envelope and silently reviewed the documents, Kelly crossed her ankles and squeezed them together. Her heart pounded.

The judge passed the papers to the court clerk who then began to read. "We, the jury in the above titled action, find the defendant . . ."

CHAPTER TWO

Defendant not guilty.

They were only three words. But for Kelly they were three words that had taken all the wonderful things she believed about life and made them hideous.

Surrounded by the scent of caramel, and chocolate, and cinnamon raisin bread warm from the oven, Kelly propped her head up with one hand and shoveled another bite of chocolate chip cheesecake into her mouth with the other. When the golden retriever at her feet begged for a taste, Kelly guarded her plate like security at Fort Knox.

"Dream on, pooch."

The smooth dessert melted in her mouth while she studied the small office in which she'd sequestered herself a little over an hour ago. A calendar on the wall denoted "Sweet Sale" days at the Sugar Shack, the bakery established by her parents, now run by her kid sister, Kate. On the dinged-up desk sat a faded photo of her parent's wedding thirty-six years ago, and a photo of Kate's wedding to Deer Lick's new sheriff, taken just seven short months ago. Ceiling to floor shelves lined the back wall where a rainbow of sugar sprinkles, edible sparkles, and candy crunches lined up cap-to-cap next to an array of both PG and X-rated cake pans. Enormous differences existed between the Silverthorne women. While her mother had once created basic cakes with buttercream icing, her sister Kate's creations reflected her imaginative and often racy specialty cakes. Kelly, though she had a talent for making kickass fudge, couldn't fashion a buttercream rose to save her life.

She glanced back up to her parents' wedding photo and studied the faded print of her mother who'd died suddenly last fall. Mixed emotions rumbled around inside her heart as she thought of the last time she'd spoken to the woman who'd given her life. Well, the last time she'd heard her mother's voice. Kelly had placed her scheduled weekly call expecting their conversation would go as usual. Fluff calls, she'd come to name them because they'd become little more than generalities.

On that last call her mother had been too busy to talk. Several days later she'd returned the call but Kelly had been in court and unable to talk. It seemed like that had become the pattern of their relationship. Mom was always too busy, and when she'd find time Kelly would be unable to connect.

Kelly shoveled in another bite of cheesecake, closed her eyes, and swallowed her guilt. She'd worked in this bakery beside her family from the time she'd been old enough to hold a mixing spoon in her hand until the day she'd left for Northwestern University. Today, the place felt foreign and isolation echoed in her soul.

Her fault.

Like the inexorable loss of her mother, the events of the past month slammed through her head as if she still stood on that courtroom floor fighting for a justice that would be denied. Fighting for the rights of a woman whose life had been ripped away by a monster. A fiend now able to roam free because *she* hadn't convinced the jury of his crime.

Her fault.

She'd pushed for that arrest. Pushed for an indictment with the grand jury. Pushed for a homicide case without a corpse.

Nausea and half a mountainous slice of cheesecake roiled through her stomach as she visualized the disbelief on the faces of the victim's family when the verdict had come down. The family she'd promised that she'd get a conviction.

In her mind she could still hear the collective gasp echo across the chamber walls. She heard the grief and torment in the family's voices when they'd pointed their fingers at her and her fellow prosecutor and accused them of incompetence. Of failure.

She'd been so sure.

But she'd been wrong.

She'd never been wrong before. Never lost a case. Never led so many innocent people into such a clusterfuck of bad judgment, poor execution, and weak evidence. Not once since she'd been an intern with the state attorney's office had she ever been doubted. Until that verdict had come in. The eyes that followed her out of that courtroom and back down the hall to her office had been teeming with accusation and disappointment.

She'd failed each and every one of them.

Horribly.

She'd lost her touch. Lost her confidence. And she had no idea where to go from here.

Her sister's monstrous golden retriever pup curled around Kelly's feet and groaned as though he could read her thoughts.

"Nice try, Happy."

The pup looked up at her with big understanding brown eyes, but no one could imagine the agony and guilt that spun a toxic web around her heart. Not even the man who'd stood beside her in that courtroom for months. When the verdict came down, he'd shrugged as if it didn't matter. For him, maybe it hadn't. She'd been the one who'd had to face the family, the media, the critics. She'd been the lead on the case.

Her fault.

The office door opened and her sister with her shiny auburn hair and clashing pink apron barged into the office. The dog got up to greet her and his long furry tail swept the floor in a happy wag.

"When you said you needed to hide out, I didn't think you meant literally." Kate used her foot to scoot a chair out from the wall and she plopped down. She leaned her forearms on her knees and she studied Kelly for a good long moment. "You look like hell, big sister."

"I imagine that's an understatement." Kelly leaned back against the rickety chair in which her mother had sat to order flour and sugar for over three decades. "I haven't slept much since the verdict came in."

"You did your best, Kel."

"Did I?" The pressure between Kelly's eyes intensified.

"Yes," Kate insisted. "You used every bit of evidence you

had. Your arguments were clear and concise. You led the jury down a path where they could visualize the timeline and the crime. It's hard to win a murder case without a corpse." Kate leaned forward and wrapped her arms around Kelly's shoulders. "What more could you have done?"

"That's what I keep asking myself."

Kate gave her a squeeze then leaned back. "Well, you're home now. And if anybody in the press shows up to harass you I will personally kick their ass." Kate's brows lifted. "It wouldn't be the first time."

"It feels good to be home."

"You say that now, but wait until you're tucked into that lumpy twin bed tonight and you hear dad snoring from down the hall."

Kelly smiled for the first time in weeks. "Icing on the cake."

"Speaking of . . . I hate to impose but would you mind giving me a hand out front? I've got a few orders I need to box up and I still have to ice two dozen cupcakes for Mary Clancy's baby shower. Dad's busy with a batch of dinner rolls."

"You *don't* hate to impose, but I'd be happy to help anyway." Kelly shoveled the last bit of cheesecake into her mouth, stood, and grabbed an apron off the hook on the wall.

"Good thing you came home wearing jeans and a T-shirt instead of your usual lawyer regalia."

Kelly draped the apron over her head and nodded. She didn't think now was the right time to tell her sister she had doubts she'd ever wear another Brooks Brothers suit. Her colossal failure had led to a murderer's freedom—and there was no doubt in her mind that Andrew Colson had murdered his wife. She couldn't afford to screw up again.

Someone's life may depend on it.

She followed Kate out of the small office tying an apron around her waist and preparing herself to dive back into life in Deer Lick. She'd taken a leave of absence to attend her brother's wedding. But she'd also come home to hide. To lick her wounds. To overcome her guilt. If that was even possible. She hadn't quite planned to shovel cookies and cupcakes into white boxes, but that's exactly what she was about to do.

As she passed him in the kitchen she gave her dad a quick kiss on the cheek then headed toward the front counter. A glance over the top of the glass display case indicated a number of patrons reading the menu or pointing out sugary delights they intended to take home. Kelly's gaze skipped over the fresh Neapolitan ice cream colors of the shop, the vintage photo of her mom and dad on the Sugar Shack's opening day, and came to a sliding stop near the door. Back turned toward her, a wide set of khaki-clad shoulders blocked the summer's glare off the patrol car parked outside.

She sucked back a groan.

Apparently karma wasn't done playing *gotcha*.

Her hands stilled on the apron ties. Her heart knocked against her ribs. The knot in her stomach pulled tight. On the other side of the lunch counter stood another of her monumental screw-ups.

As if she'd called his name, he turned his sandy blonde head. His brown eyes brightened and a smile tipped the corners of lips that were sinfully delicious. She knew. She'd tasted them.

She took a wobbly step backward.

In her thirty-two years she'd been struck with accusatory

scowls from a judgmental mother and murderous glares from convicted felons, but nothing had ever hit her below the belt like a smile bursting with sexual promise from one of Deer Lick's finest.

Deputy James Harley.

His intense gaze perused her body like he was on the cruise of a lifetime and enjoying the trip. He'd looked at her that same way just a few months ago—braced above her on arms thick with muscle while the rest of his hot, hard body did the talking.

A tingle ignited from her head, sizzled like a fuse down the front of her shirt, and detonated beneath the zipper on her jeans. Her skin turned hot and a flush crept up her chest. All thanks to the memory of one night in James Harley's bed.

As a deputy sheriff he'd sworn to serve and protect. During the hours she'd spent rolling in his sheets, he'd done both. At least from what she remembered.

The night of Kate's wedding reception, Kelly knew she should have stayed focused on carrying out her maid-of-honor duties. But one too many glasses of exceptional champagne had dislodged a few of her bolts and screws and she'd completely given herself over to whim and mind-bending orgasms. Afterward, she'd made a promise to herself to get a serious handle on the sometimes uncontainable urges that never ceased to embarrass the hell out of her. Even if they did provide a real jolt of excitement.

She blinked away the sweaty memory of the hot, sexy man on the opposite side of the counter, sucked in a breath, and stepped up beside Kate. "What do you need me to do?"

"Could you box up that chocolate cake and then fill James's lunch order?"

Crap. "Sure." *Kill me now. Please.*

Her hands uncharacteristically trembled as she opened a pastry box and lifted Dr. Robinson's double chocolate birthday cake from the display case. She didn't know why her stomach was so keyed up. She'd spent the last seven years in the heat of the spotlight, prosecuting some of the dirtiest criminals in the state of Illinois, and she'd never once been nervous.

So why did taking a lunch order seem so damned intimidating?

With a smile she handed the pastry box over the counter to Dr. Robinson's nurse and rang up the bill on the register. She closed the cash drawer and wiped her hands down the front of her apron, leaving a streak of chocolate. When she looked up *hot cop* was standing at the lunch counter. Muscled arms expanded from beneath his short uniform sleeves while the fitted shirt hugged his wide chest and slim waist. Kelly knew that beneath all that khaki fabric was a talented body of pure strength and muscle. A *very* talented body.

God, her thoughts were a train wreck.

She grabbed the pencil and order pad. "Can I help you?"

A smile crinkled the corners of his brown eyes and a slow blink swept long, dark lashes across his cheeks. "You're back."

"Apparently."

He chuckled. "And you're not happy to see me."

"I'm not *not* happy to see you."

"Okay then. I'll take that for starters."

Oh, no. His days of taking from her were over. She was on a *save your soul and sanity* mission. No boys allowed. "And what would you like to eat?"

The spark in his eyes guaranteed she wouldn't need a Geiger counter to detect what he was thinking. "Sandwich, Deputy Harley. What kind would you like?"

"I'd like two tuna subs. No tomato. Two iced teas." He settled a lean hip against the counter. "And your phone number."

A laugh escaped before she could stop it. "That will be nine fifty-six."

"Is that a no?" He reached into his back pocket, withdrew a worn leather wallet, and handed her a twenty.

Her fingers curled around the money. "I'm sure you have all the numbers you can handle."

James held on to the cash, just to be able to touch her for half a second. "I'd be willing to throw all those numbers away in exchange."

Since she was a pro and could read a lie a mile away she probably thought he was bullshitting her. But he'd never been more serious.

One night with Kelly Silverthorne hadn't been nearly enough. Once she'd hightailed it out of town he'd tried to discount the hours he'd spent with her in his arms but it had been impossible. Now here she was again. And everything inside of him was buzzing with awareness.

As expected she looked up and studied his face like he'd been named a prime suspect. He knew that look. On the job he'd used it himself once or twice.

"Without all those phone numbers what would you do on a rainy day, Deputy?" Her head tilted just slightly and her ivory hair fanned like silk across her shoulder. "I'd hate to be the cause of your ultimate frustration."

"Nice jab, Counselor." James steadied his breath as he watched her delicate fingers punch the amount into the register and slide the cash into the drawer. Kelly Silverthorne was the most beautiful woman he'd ever laid eyes on. And he'd seen plenty. From the second grade he'd watched her, admired her, and had probably had a crush on her even though the only glances she'd ever returned had been rife with warnings to keep his distance.

The night she'd ended up in his bed? No one could have been more surprised. Oh, he wasn't about to complain. No way. The counselor was hot. And sweet. And way out of his league. Though he knew he'd had his one and only shot with her, he craved her like a decadent dessert or a fine wine. One taste was just not enough to satisfy.

He watched as she grabbed the sandwich rolls, cautiously sliced through them, and spread a thin layer of mayonnaise across the surface. She topped the bread with perfectly rounded scoops of tuna salad and carefully placed leaves of crunchy lettuce on top. Every movement was smooth and calculated as if she'd be judged on her placement and presentation.

In an attempt to gain control over his body and all the odd stirrings around his heart, he looked away. A quick glance at the two sisters revealed the vast differences. Kate, his best friend's new wife, was a bit taller and looked as if in a scrap she could hold her own. Her straight auburn hair displayed a meager reflection of her fiery personality. Whereas Kelly, a few inches shorter, teetered on the more delicate side. She looked like a woman a man would jump to protect. Her long ivory hair had a soft curl that made her glow like sunshine.

He smiled.

At least she'd lit up his world. For a night.

"So what made you leave the windy city and come all the way back to our little town?" he asked as she wrapped each sandwich in white paper as carefully as if she'd been swaddling a newborn.

"Just needed a break." She slid the packaged sandwich into a crisp white bag.

"Most people who need a break hit a tropical beach. Not some dusty back road to nowhere."

"Maybe *nowhere* is exactly where I want to be." She shoved the second sandwich into the bag a little less carefully.

Whoa. Was it his imagination or was he detecting some underlying aggression?

"Well, I'm sure your family will be happy to have you around for a little while," he said, watching her graceful fingers fold down the top of the bag.

She gave him no response as she set the bag on the counter, grabbed two paper cups, and began to fill them with iced tea.

"So . . . exactly how long of a little while will that be?" he asked.

The glass pitcher thunked on the counter and tea sloshed up the sides. "The length of my stay is really no concern of yours, Deputy Harley."

"True. But I'm more than willing to change that if you are."

A smile tilted her soft, full lips. "You really are incorrigible."

He mirrored her expression. "It's a cross I bear."

She set the cups of tea down in front of him and pushed plastic caps over the rims. "I hope you enjoy your lunch, Deputy Harley. Please do come again soon."

"Is that an invitation?" *Say yes, Angelface.*

Her delicate brows pulled together over sea green eyes. "Are you serious?"

"As a tortoise trying to cross the road."

"I'm sorry, Deputy—"

"I think we know each other well enough to be on a first name basis, don't you?" Her slight hesitation gave him hope.

"Like I said, I'm sorry, *Deputy*, I'm not here to engage in anything other than some rest and relaxation. I need a break. Not an opportunity to . . . lose control," she whispered.

James smiled. He knew exactly how loudly Kelly lost control. And exactly what made her lose it. Then again, he was more than willing to invent new techniques to make that happen too. Even if it took all night. *Please, God, let it take all night.*

If Princess Prosecutor imagined him as a man who gave up easily she'd be very wrong.

"You know . . ." He leaned closer and spoke low for her ears only. "If you give me your number you might just have a little fun losing a little control for the little while you're here." He lifted the bag and cups from the counter, stepped back, and gave her a good long appreciative once over. "Or is that what you're afraid of?"

An Excerpt from

A MOST NAKED SOLUTION

by Anna Randol

Lady Sophia Harding: beautiful, blonde, and . . . capable of murder? That's what Lord Camden Grey intends to find out.

Sophia knows that to keep her family's secrets she must avoid any entanglements with the powerful and brutally handsome man. But the pull of their mutual desire is all-consuming. Can Sophia trust Camden with the truth when she knows it might kill the love that grows between them?

CHAPTER ONE

Weltford, England, 1816

Sir Camden Grey glared at the ink-spotted paper in front of him. Damnation. Was that a six or an eight? Perhaps a three? He placed his quill back in the ink and pressed the heels of his hands against his bleary eyes.

He should have stopped working on the equation hours ago, but the solution had seemed so close this time. If he'd worked only a little harder or faster, perhaps he'd have been able to—

A knock again sounded on his door, reminding him of what had startled him into splashing ink everywhere in the first place.

"Yes?" He knew his tone was harsher than it should have been, but he hadn't slept in—he checked the clock—twenty hours, and his servants knew better than to disturb him. If that fool Ipswith found an answer first, Camden would never again be able to set foot in the Royal Mathematical Society. The chairman, his father, would see to it. Just as he had seen to convincing Ipswith to research the exact same theorem to put Camden in his place.

The door opened and Rafferty entered, his stoic butler façade remaining in place despite the crumpled papers littering the carpet at his feet. "There is a . . . man to see you, sir." There was a significant distaste in his pronunciation of the word *man*.

Camden raised his brow. What was he then, a goat? Really, it was no wonder he found conversing such a waste. It was an imprecise medium. "What is his business?"

"He wishes to speak to the Justice of the Peace."

Camden glanced at the clock. "At three in the morning? Has there been a death?"

Rafferty cleared his throat and didn't make eye contact. "It is three in the afternoon, sir."

Camden swiveled to stare at the drawn curtains behind him. Indeed. Amend that—he'd been awake for thirty-two hours instead of twenty. Suddenly exhaustion hit him like a blow to the side of his head. He scrubbed at the grit in his eyes. "Did he say if it was urgent?"

As impressive as the title of Justice of the Peace sounded, it usually only amounted to settling squabbles about sheep and stolen chamber pots. He wouldn't have accepted the appointment to the position at all if there had been any other men who met the requirements in Weltford save drunk-off-his-arse Stanfield.

"The fellow claims to have information on the Harding death, sir."

Camden straightened in his chair. That would be worth delaying sleep. "Where did you put him?"

"In the library, sir."

Camden stood, twisting side to side briefly to loosen the knots in his back, then strode past his butler and down the stairs.

He smelled his guest before he saw him. The air in the corridor stank of stale onions and spoiled ale. And he wasn't even in the same room yet.

Camden stepped into the library, then silently groaned when he saw his guest. "Mr. Spat?" Lloyd Spat, less than affectionately known about the village as Tubs, sat in the center of the room, his enormous girth filling the settee from arm to arm.

"Ah, Sir Camden! A pleasure to see to see you. A real pleasure." He tried to struggle to his feet but gave up after a single attempt. "There was a reward for information on the death of Lord Harding? A sizable one?"

"If your information proves to be of use." But he had offered the money over three months ago at the death of Viscount Harding. While he still found it difficult to believe the death was a result of a poacher's misplaced bullet, he found it more difficult to believe that Tubs wouldn't have come forward if he had real information. The man would do anything for his next pint. "Why wait to come forward?"

"Well, I feared for my life. Near trembled at the thought of what would happen to me if they found out I spoke."

"If who found out?" Camden focused on breathing through his mouth only.

"The men."

He was too tired for this. His only hope was a strict linear line of questioning. Camden spun the standing globe next to him absently, tapping every third line of longitude. He returned to the original question. "Why tell me now?"

"Well you might ask, sir. Mr. Haws, that greedy old bastard, has decided that my word is no longer good enough for him. He says if I'm wanting another drop of ale from his tavern, he needs to be seeing some of the coin he's owed. Now I'm rightly offended at such rudeness and I have a mind to take my business to another tavern, but my health's no longer what it was. And I need to be close to my lodgings and my dear Mrs. Spat."

So he'd decided that his next drink was worth more than information that might cost him his life. That logic would have been too much to follow on a day when fully awake; Camden stood no chance of sorting it out now.

Tubs rubbed his hands together, then glanced nervously about the room. "No one will find out the news came from me, right?"

"Not unless you tell them."

Tubs nodded, his chin disappearing into the rippling folds at his neck. "Well, then. The day after the murder I was at the tavern."

Camden had never seen him anywhere but at the tavern.

"I was sitting at my table in the corner when I heard voices behind me. It was two blokes discussing getting paid. Now I normally keep to my own business but one of the gents says, 'The deed is done?' Now I know that when men are talking about deeds, that's not something that I need to be hearing, but I was right there so I couldn't not hear them."

Camden stopped spinning the globe, his hand coming to rest somewhere in Russia. Tubs finally had his full attention.

It wasn't Camden's responsibility as Justice of the Peace to investigate crimes, only to rule on small squabbles, or for more serious matters, to decide if there was enough evidence for a criminal to be sent on to the formal court. While he gave the cases he heard his full attention, he'd never been tempted to become involved past his limited role. It was the responsibility of the victim or his family to prosecute the crime. But something about the Harding case had seemed suspicious. Camden had finally ruled with the coroner's jury because he'd had no evidence to contradict the theory of the poacher's bullet, but it had always seemed too convenient. As if someone had decided three plus three equaled five because they didn't want to be bothered to count to six.

Then the widow's powerful family had swooped in to ensure the whole matter stayed quiet. Her father and her brothers stayed at her side, keeping her distant from everyone. Lady Harding's father, the Earl of Riverton, himself, had visited Camden to ask for discretion when dealing with the case.

Camden had agreed because he knew better than to deny a powerful man like the earl without cause. He also knew the earl's oldest son, Darton, personally, and he trusted him.

To a point.

But the whole situation had made him wary. More alert. He'd asked a few questions about town but had come up empty.

Tubs cracked his knuckles, the popping interspersing his words. "Then the other fellow says, 'He fell like a sack of turnips. Easiest job I've ever done.' Then he laughed. Now I hadn't heard about the good viscount's death yet, but something in his voice made my skin fair crawl off my body."

"Did you get a good look at either of the men?"

Tubs's eyes bulged. "There's no way I was going to let them know I'd heard them. What with them being hired killers."

Camden could hear his own teeth grinding. "Then what information do you have that you think will earn you the reward?"

"Well, then they started talking about returning to London." He looked hopeful at this bit of information, then sighed when Camden didn't react. "Then one of the fellows said, 'Did you collect the rest of the blunt from her?'"

Camden stepped away from the globe. "Her?" Why had an image of Lady Harding suddenly appeared in his mind?

"That's what he said as clear as day."

"Did they give a name? Anything more specific?" Camden tried to think of what he knew of Lady Harding, but could come up with little. Oh, he could picture her clearly enough, the pretty young woman who'd lingered outside her brother's mathematics lessons when Camden had gone to tutor him almost seven years ago. The slender delicate grace of her body and the almost elfin point of her chin. He'd liked knowing that she hid in the corridor to hear his lessons.

But he knew nothing of the woman she'd become. The Hardings had been at their house in Weltford only rarely. He couldn't remember if he'd ever been invited to an event at Harding House. He'd paid little attention to the social engagements in the area. Besides, his knighthood was recent and that left him below the notice of the oldest of the blue-bloods like the Hardings.

And if he was completely honest with himself, he'd had

no desire to see the girl who'd written him the only letter he'd received while in the army—a love letter—with another man.

Tubs grunted and tugged on his ear. "No. They left right quick after that."

Camden had little reason to think Lady Harding the woman that the killers referred to. Except, why hadn't she or her family done more to find the shooter? Why had she been content with the coroner's ruling? Why had her family been so intent on keeping him away from her? They'd claimed her prostrate with grief. All his questions had gone through her father.

"Do I get the money?" Tubs asked.

"Only if your information proves to be correct." Despite his own suspicions, he had no proof that Tubs's story was true.

"But I took time away from my dear wife to come to help with your investigation."

Frowning, Camden tossed him a guinea. "For your trouble. But you get no more unless your information leads to an arrest."

The money disappeared into Tubs's pocket. "It will, sir. Everything I told you is as true as my name."

Tubs lumbered to his feet and Rafferty escorted him out.

Camden had planned to pay his respects to Lady Harding at some point, perhaps see what manner of woman she'd matured into. Now it appeared he had no choice.

She may have grown up to be a murderer.

"You want me to give away all of the books in the library?" Lady Sophia Harding's housekeeper stared at her in shock. "But, my lady, the books must be worth hundreds of pounds."

Eight hundred and sixty-three pounds, to be precise. Sophia knew. She'd purchased every one of them when they had renovated the house last year.

But now the gilded leather spines sickened her.

She took a deep breath. "Yes, every one of them."

"What will you put in here instead, my lady?" Mrs. Gilray asked.

Sophia smiled. She had absolutely no idea. She would pick what she liked. She didn't even know what that would be. Perhaps piles of penny dreadful or scandalous novels. More books on mathematics.

All she knew was that no one would have a say in it but her.

She wouldn't fret over her choices, thinking and rethinking each one. Trying to pick those Richard would approve of while knowing she'd never be able to guess correctly.

Richard was dead.

And now she intended to reclaim the library from his influence. Sophia traced a finger down the edge of one of the books. If only it was as easy to reclaim herself. "Send them to St. Wilfred's orphanage."

"Very good, my lady." Mrs. Gilray was too new to dare question her.

Sophia turned at the sound of heavy boots in the corridor. Her eyes widened at the sight of her head gardener.

Mud caked Wicken's boots and his white hair jutted out

from his head in awkward clumps. "There's an urgent matter I must discuss with you regarding the *rose gardens*."

Sophia tried to smile as if urgent meetings about greenery were a normal occurrence, but her mind was racing. "That will be all, Mrs. Gilray."

Mrs. Gilray's fascinated gaze swung back and forth between the other two occupants of the room, but she bobbed a curtsey and glided from the library.

Wicken closed the door behind her with a click, the kindly lines on his face deep with worry. "Sorry, my lady. I know this is most unusual. But I thought it important that you know."

Sophia swallowed against sudden unease. "Is something amiss?"

"My daughter just sent word from the village. The Justice of the Peace has been asking questions about your husband's death."

"What questions?"

He rubbed his right arm, the arm her husband had broken when Wicken refused to tell Richard where she was hiding.

Sophia fought not to stare, not to choke on the guilt that burned in her chest at the stiff way the arm hung at his side.

"What enemies Harding might have had. Same as he did right after the death."

"Has anyone said anything?"

"Not as far as I know, but it's only a matter of time before one of the villagers lets something slip."

Sophia's hands clenched into fists at her sides. Sir Camden wouldn't find anything. She wouldn't allow it. Not when that slip might lead him directly to her husband's killer—her father.